EVELYN E. SMITH RESURRECTED

Selected Stories of Evelyn E. Smith

By Evelyn E. Smith
Edited by Greg Fowlkes

Includes the Special Bonus Story
AND NOW A MESSAGE...
By Greg Fowlkes

EVELYN E. SMITH RESURRECTED

© 2010 Resurrected Press
www.ResurrectedPress.com

Published by Intrepid Ink, LLC

Intrepid Ink, LLC provides full publishing services to authors of fiction and non-fiction books, eBooks and websites. From editing to formatting, to publishing, to marketing, Intrepid Ink gets your creative works into the hands of the people who want to read them.
Find out more at www.IntrepidInk.com.

ISBN 13: 978-1-935774-41-9

Printed in the United States of America

FOREWORD

During an era when women authors rarely appeared in science fiction magazines, Evelyn E. Smith featured regularly in the pages of magazines such as Galaxy and Fantastic Universe. This was certainly not an accident. She was a talented writer who could be humorous and sardonic at the same time. I suspect it was the humor that persuaded editors to accept her stories rather than a search for the 'feminine touch.'".

I first came across Evelyn E. Smith in the early 60's with the story "The Vilbar Party" in the collection *The Third Galaxy Reader*. That story has stayed with me when the memories of many others have faded from my mind. That story of how a visiting professor from Saturn becomes a "party animal" is typical of much of her writing, turning the conventions of alien-human encounters on their heads.

It is evident from her writing that she spent some time in the halls of academe. She seems to have formed a rather jaundiced view of some of its denizens. Fortunately, this provided her with a wealth of material, and many of her stories skewer academics and students alike with caricatures that one suspects are all too accurate.

Her aliens didn't conform to the stereotypes of the time. They were more likely to take the form of teddy bears or sentient vines than bug eyed monsters, not that their motives might not be as malevolent as the creatures of her peers. The humans in her stories flouted conventions, too. No strong he-men against the universe. They were much more likely to be vane, self-centered, and not to bright no matter what their academic credentials might say.

Smith's career didn't end with the 50's. She published a number of novels in the 60's and 70's and then in the 80's she began a series which featured a middle-aged woman who turns to a career as an assassin when her life falls apart. They were written with the same wit that her earlier works exhibited.

Resurrected Press is proud to issue this volume of her stories. Evelyn E. Smith is too important a writer to be forgotten. We hope that you will find them as engaging as we have.

About The Author

Evelyn E. Smith (January 1, 1927-January 1, 2000) was an American author of Science Fiction. During the 50's her works appeared regularly in magazines such as Galaxy and Fantastic Universe. In the 80's she wrote a number of novels featuring the character Miss Melville about a middle-aged assassin. She also wrote as Delphine C. Lyons and Christopher Grimm.

Greg Fowlkes
Editor-In-Chief
Resurrected Press
www.ResurrectedPress.com

TABLE OF CONTENTS

COLLECTOR'S ITEM

ORIGINALLY PUBLISHED IN *GALAXY SCIENCE FICTION*
DECEMBER 1954

ILLUSTRATED BY ILLUSTRATED BY ED EMSHWILLER

Being trapped in the steaming hell of Venus is no excuse for forgetting one's manners–but anyone abducted, marooned, tricked, kept from tea might well crack under the strain!

COLLECTOR'S ITEM

"What I should like to know," Professor Bernardi said, gazing pensively after the lizard-man as he bore the shrieking form of Miss Anspacher off in his scaly arms, "is whether he is planning to eat her or make love to her. Because, in the latter instance, I'm not sure we should interfere. It may be her only chance."

"Carl!" his wife cried indignantly. "That's a horrid thing to say! You must rescue her at once!"

"Oh, I suppose so," he said, then gave his wife a nasty little grin that he knew would irritate her. "It isn't that she's unattractive, my dear, in case you hadn't noticed, though she's pretty well past the bloom of youth–"

"*Will* you stop making leering noises and go save her or *not*?"

"I was coming to that. It's just that she persists in using her Ph.D. as a club to beat men into respectful pulps. Men don't like being beaten into respectful pulps, whether by a man or a woman. Now if she'd only learned that other people have feelings–"

"If you don't stop lecturing and go, I will!" his wife threatened.

"All right, all right," he said wearily. "Come on, Mortland."

*   *   *   *   *

The two scientists slogged through the steamy, odorous jungle of Venus and soon reached the lizard-man, who, weighed down by his captive, had not been able to travel as fast.

"You blast him," the professor told Mortland. "Try not to hit Miss Anspacher, if you can manage it."

"Er–I've never fired one of these things before," Mortland said. "Can't stand having my eardrums blasted. However, here goes." He pointed his weapon at the lizardlike creature in a gingerly manner. "Ah–hands up," he ordered. "Only fair to give the–well, blighter a sporting chance," he explained to Professor Bernardi.

To their amazement, the lizard-man promptly dropped Miss Anspacher into the lavender-colored mud and put up his hands. Miss Anspacher gave an indignant yelp.

"Seems intelligent in spite of the kidnaping," Mortland commented. "But how does he happen to understand English? We're the only expedition ever to have reached Venus ... that I know of, anyway." He and the professor stared at each other in consternation. "There may have been a secret expedition previously and perhaps they left a—a base or something, which would explain why—"

"If you two oafs would stop speculating, you might help me out of here!" Miss Anspacher remarked in her customary snappish tone. Professor Bernardi leaped forward to obey. "You don't have to pull quite so hard! I haven't taken root yet!" She came out of the mud with a sound like two whales kissing. She brushed hopelessly at her once-white blouse and shorts. "Oh, dear, I look a mess!"

Professor Bernardi did not comment, being engaged in slapping at a small winged creature—about the size of a bluejay, but looking like a cross between a bat and a mosquito—that seemed interested in taking a bite out of him. It escaped his flapping hand and flew to the top of Mortland's sun helmet, where it glared at the professor.

"Since you seem to understand English," Miss Anspacher said to the lizard-man through a mouthful of hairpins, "perhaps you will be so kind as to explain the meaning of this outrage?"

"I was smitten," the alien replied suavely. "Passion made me forget myself."

Professor Bernardi looked thoughtfully at him. "A prior expedition isn't the answer. It wouldn't have troubled to educate you so thoroughly. Therefore, the explanation is that you pick up English by reading our minds. Correct?"

The lizard-man turned an embarrassed olive. "Yes."

*   *   *   *   *

Now that he was able to give the creature a more thorough inspection, Bernardi saw that he really didn't look too much like a lizard. He definitely appeared to be wearing clothes of some kind, which, in the Venusian heat, indicated a particularly refined degree of civilization–unless, of course, the squamous skin protected him from the heat as well as the humidity.

More than that, though, he was humanoid in almost a Hollywood way. He had a particularly fine profile and an athletic physique, which, oddly, his scales seemed to enhance, much like a movie idol dressed in fine-meshed Medieval armor. Naturally, he had a tail, but it was as well proportioned as a kangaroo's, though shorter and more graceful, and it struck Professor Bernardi as a particularly handsome and useful gadget.

For one thing, the people from Earth were standing uncomfortably in the slippery mud, while the lizard-man was using his tail much in the fashion of a spectator stool, leaning back against it almost in a sitting position, with his armor-shod feet supporting him comfortably. For another, the tail undoubtedly served for balance and the added push of a walking stick and perhaps for swift attack or getaway. Very practical and attractive, the professor concluded–too bad Man had relinquished his tail when climbing down from the trees.

"Thank you," the saurian said with uneasy modesty, looking at him. "Good of you to think so. You are a fairly intelligent species, aren't you?"

"Fairly," the professor acknowledged, preoccupied with a clever idea. Perhaps existence on Venus wasn't going to be as unpleasant as he had anticipated. "From reading my mind, you know what this blaster can do, don't you?"

"I'm afraid so."

"Then you know what I expect of you?"

"Yes, sahib. I'se comin', massa. To hear is to obey, effendi." The creature turned and went briskly back toward the camp, leaving the others to stumble after him.

Mrs. Bernardi gave a shriek as his handsome scaled form emerged from the greenish-white underbrush, haloed in luminous yellow mist. Algol, the ship's cat, prudently took sanctuary behind her, then peered out to see what was going on and whether there was likely to be anything in it for him.

"This is our native bearer," Professor Bernardi explained as the three scientists burst out of the jungle.

"My name is Jrann-Pttt." The creature bowed low. "At your service, madame."

"Oh, Carl!" Mrs. Bernardi clapped her hands. "He's just perfect! So thoughtful of you to find one that speaks English! I do hope you can cook, Pitt?"

"I will do my best, madame."

*   *   *   *   *

Algol daintily picked his way through the mud toward the saurian, sniffed him with judicial deliberation; then, deciding that anyone who smelled so much like the better class of fish must be All Right, rubbed against his legs.

"Well," remarked Miss Anspacher, using the side of the spaceship as a mirror by which to redden her somewhat prissy lips, "that makes it practically unanimous, doesn't it?"

"All except Professor Bernardi," said Jrann-Pttt, looking at the scientist with what might have been a smile. "He doesn't like me."

"I see that your telepathic powers are not quite accurate," the professor returned. "I do not dislike you; I distrust you."

"The fact that the two terms are not entirely synonymous in your language would argue a certain degree of incipient civilization," the lizard-man observed.

"You know, Carl," Mrs. Bernardi whispered, "he has an awfully funny way of talking, for a native."

"Frankly I don't like this at all, Professor," Captain Greenfield said, mopping his brow with a limp handkerchief. "If I hadn't been off looking for a better berth for the ship—all this mud worries me—this'd never have happened."

"You mean you would have let the lizard get away with Miss Anspacher?"

The big man's face flushed crimson. "I don't think that's funny, Professor."

Bernardi quickly changed the subject, for he realized that the captain, being by far the most muscular of the party, was not a man to trifle with. "Tell me, Greenfield, did you succeed in finding a better spot for the ship? I must admit I'm worried about that mud myself."

"Only remotely dry spot around is an outcropping 'bout two kilometers away," Greenfield said grudgingly. He shifted his camp stool in a futile search for shade. Even though the sun never penetrated the thick layer of clouds, the yellow light diffused through them was blinding. "Might be big enough, but it's not level. Could blast it smooth, but that'd take at least a week–Earth time."

Bernardi pulled his damp shirt away from his body. "Well, I daresay we'll be all right where we are, if we're not assailed by any violent forces of nature. On Earth, this might be a monsoon climate."

"If you ask me, that monster is more of a danger than any monsoon."

Bernardi sighed. Although by far the most competent officer available for the job of spaceship captain, Greenfield was not quite the man he would have chosen to be his associate for months on end. Still, beggars–as Miss Anspacher might have eloquently put it–could not be choosers. "What makes you say that?" he asked, trying to set an example of tolerance.

"Don't like the idea of him cooking for us," the captain said stubbornly. "Might poison us all in our beds."

"Well, don't eat in your bed," suggested Mortland, strolling out of the airlock in the company of the cat. Algol, however, finding that the spot beside the captain's camp stool was as dry as anything could be on Venus, decided to turn back.

* * * * *

"The difficulty is easily overcome, Captain," the professor said, still holding on to his patience. "You can continue to cook your own meals from the tinned and packaged foods on board ship. The rest of us will eat fresh native foods prepared by Jrann-Pttt."

"But why," Miss Anspacher interrupted as she emerged from the airlock with a large cast-iron skillet, "should you think Jrann-Pttt wants to poison us?"

Both men rose from their stools. "Stands to reason he'd consider us his enemies, Miss Anspacher," the captain said. "After all, we—as a group, that is—captured him."

"Hired him," Professor Bernardi contradicted. "I've telepathically arranged to pay him an adequate salary. In goods, of course; I don't suppose our money would be of much use to him. And I think he's rather glad of the chance to hang around and observe us conveniently."

"Observe us!" Greenfield exclaimed. "You mean he's spying out the land for an attack? Let's prepare our defenses at once!"

"I doubt if that's what he has in mind," Professor Bernardi said judiciously.

"He may be staying because he wants to be near me," Miss Anspacher blurted. Overcome by this unmaidenly admission, she reddened and rushed from them, calling, "Yoo-hoo, Jrann-Pttt! Here is the frying pan!" Algol woke up instantly and followed her. "Frying" was one of the more important words in his vocabulary.

Captain Greenfield stared across the clearing after them, then turned back to Bernardi with a frown. "I don't like to see one of our girls mixed up with a lizard—and a foreign lizard at that." But his face too clearly betrayed a personal resentment.

"Don't tell me you have a—a fondness for Miss Anspacher, Captain," Professor Bernardi exclaimed, genuinely surprised. Undeniably Miss Anspacher—

although no longer in her first youth—was a handsome woman, but he would not have expected her somewhat cerebral type to appeal to the captain. On the other hand, she was the only unattached woman in the party and they were a long way from home.

Greenfield picked a fleck of dried violet mud from the side of the ship and avoided Bernardi's eye. "One of the reasons I came along," he said almost bashfully. "Thought I'd have the chance to be alone with her now and again and impress her with, with...."

"Your sterling qualities?" Bernardi suggested.

The captain flashed him a glance of mingled gratitude and resentment. "And now this damned lizard has to come along!"

"Cheer up, Captain," said the professor. "I'll back you against a lizard any time."

*   *   *   *   *

Although the long twilight of Venus had deepened into night and it could never really be cool there by terrestrial standards, the temperature was almost comfortable. Everything was quite black, except for the pallid purple campfire glowing through the darkness; the clouds that perpetually covered the surface of the planet prevented even the light of the stars from reaching it.

"Tell me more about the cross-versus the parallel-cousin relationships in your culture, Jrann-Pttt," Miss Anspacher breathed, wriggling her camp stool closer to the saurian's. "Anthropology is a great hobby of mine, you know. How do your people feel about exogamy?"

"I'm afraid I'm rather exhausted, dear lady," he said, using one arm to mask a yawn, and one to surreptitiously wave away the saurian head that was peering out of the underbrush. "I shouldn't like to give a scientist like yourself any misinformation that might become a matter of record."

"Of course not," she murmured. "You're so considerate."

*   *   *   *   *

A pale face appeared in the firelight like some weird creature of darkness. Terrestrial and extraterrestrial both started. "Miss Anspacher," the captain growled, "I'd like to lock up the ship, so if you wouldn't mind turning in—"

Miss Anspacher pouted. "You've interrupted such an interesting conversation. And I don't see why you have to lock up the ship. After all, the night is three hundred and eighty-five hours long. We don't sleep all that time and it would be a shame to be cooped up."

"I'm going to try to rig up some floodlights," Greenfield explained stiffly, "so we won't be caught like this again. Nobody bothered to tell me the day equals thirty-two of ours, so that half of it would be night."

"Then I won't see you for almost two weeks of our time, Jrann-Pttt? Are you sure you wouldn't like to spend the rest of the night in our ship? Plenty of room, you know."

"No, thank you, dear lady. The jungle is my natural habitat. I should feel stultified by walls and a ceiling. Don't worry—I shan't run away."

"Oh, I'm not worried," Miss Anspacher said coyly, throwing a stick of wood on the fire.

"Small riddance if he does."

"Captain Greenfield!"

That part of the captain's face not concealed by his piratical black beard turned red. "Well, if he can read our minds, he knows damn well what I'm thinking, anyway, so why be hypocritical about it?"

"That's right—he is a telepath, isn't he?" Miss Anspacher's face grew even redder than the captain's. "I forgot he.... It *is* getting late. I really must go. Good night, Jrann-Pttt."

"Good night, dear lady." The saurian bowed low over her hand.

Leaning on the captain's brawny arm, Miss Anspacher ploughed through the mud to the ship, followed by the mosquito-bat and Algol, who had been toasting themselves more or less companionably at the fire. The door to the airlock clanged behind all four of them.

*   *   *   *   *

The other saurian's head appeared again from the bush. *Jrann-Pttt*, the insistent thought came, *shall I rescue you now?*

Why, Dfar-Lll? I am not a prisoner. I'm quite free to come and go as I please. But let's get away from the strangers' ship while we communicate. They do have a certain amount of low-grade perception and might be able to sense the presence of another personality. At any rate, they might look out of a port and see you.

Keeping the illuminator on low beam, Dfar-Lll led the way through the bushes. *Seems to me you're going to an awful lot of trouble just to get zoo specimens*, the youngster protested, disentangling its arms from the embrace of an amorous vine. *There's really no reason for carrying on the work since Lieutenant Merglyt-Ruuu ... passed on.*

Jrann-Pttt sat down on a fallen log and, tucking up his graceful tail, signaled his junior to join him. *In the event that we do decide to return to base, some handsome specimens might serve to offset the lieutenant's demise.*

Return to base? But I thought we were....

We haven't found swamp life pleasant, have we? After all, there's no real reason why we shouldn't go back. Is it our fault that Merglyt-Ruuu happened to meet with a fatal accident?

We-ell ... but will the commandant see it that way?

On the other hand, if we don't go back, wouldn't it be a good idea to attach ourselves to an expedition that, no matter how alien, is better equipped for survival than we? And carrying out our original purpose seemed the best way of getting to meet these strangers informally, as it were.

They are unquestionably intelligent life-forms then?

After a fashion. Jrann-Pttt yawned and rose. *But why are we sitting here? Let's start back to our camp. We will be able to converse more comfortably.*

They made their way through the jungle—now walking, now wading where the mud became water. Small creatures with hardly any thoughts scurried before them as they went.

The commandant may have already made contact with their rulers, Dfar-Lll suggested, springing forward to illuminate the way. *In that case, we couldn't hope to remain undiscovered for long.*

Oh, these creatures are not Venusians. There's no intelligent life here. They hail from the third planet of this system and, according to their thoughts, this is the only vessel that was capable of traversing interplanetary space. So we needn't worry about extradition treaties or any other official annoyances.

If they're friendly, why didn't you spend the night in their ship? It certainly looks more comfortable than our collapsible moslak—which, by the way, collapsed while you were gone. I hope we'll be able to put it up again ourselves. I must say this for the lieutenant—he was good at that sort of thing.

Jrann-Pttt made a gesture of distaste. *He was unfortunately good at other things, too. But let's not discuss him. I'm not staying with the strangers because I want to pick up one or two little things—mostly some of our food to serve them. I used up all the supplies in my pack and I want them to think we're living off the land. They believe me to be a primitive and it's best that they should until I decide just how I'm going to make most efficient use of them. Besides, I didn't want to leave you alone.*

The younger saurian sniffed skeptically.

*   *   *   *   *

"Honestly, Pitt," Mrs. Bernardi said, keeping to leeward of the tablecloth the lizard-man was efficiently shaking out of the airlock, "I've never had a–an employee as competent as you." But the word she had in mind, of course, was "servant." "I do wish you'd come back to Earth with us."

"Perhaps you would compel me to come?" he suggested, as Algol and the mosquito-bat entered into hot competition to catch the crumbs before they sank into the purple ooze.

"Oh, no! We'd want you to come as our guest—our friend." *Naturally,* her thoughts ran, *a house guest would be expected to help with the washing up and lend a hand with the cooking–and, of course, we wouldn't have to pay him. Though my husband, I suppose, would requisition him as a specimen.*

I fully intend to go to Earth with them, Jrann-Pttt mused, *but certainly not in that capacity. Nor would I care to be a specimen. I must formulate some concrete plan.*

The captain was crawling on top of the spaceship, scraping off the dried mud, brushing away the leaves and dust that marred its shining purity. The hot, humid haze that poured down from the yellow clouds made the metal surface a little hell. Yet it was hardly less warm on the other side of the clearing, where Miss Anspacher tried desperately to write up her notes on a table that kept sinking into the spongy ground, and hindered by the thick wind that had arisen half an hour before and which kept blowing her papers off. The sweet odor of the flowers tucked in the open neck of her already grimy white blouse suddenly sickened her and she flung them into the mud.

"We won't be going back to Earth for a long time!" she called. Gathering up the purple-stained papers, she came toward the others, little puffs of mist rising at each step. "We like it here. Lovely country."

How could she think to please even the savage she fancied him to be by such an inanity, Jrann-Pttt wondered. No one could possibly like that fetid swamp. Or was it not so much that she was trying to please him as convince herself? Was there some reason the terrestrials had for needing to like Venus. It hovered on the edge of the women's minds. If only it would emerge completely, he could pick it up, but it lurked in the shadows of their subconscious, tantalizing him.

"I'd like to know when we're going to start putting up the shelters," Mrs. Bernardi said, pushing a streak of fog-yellow hair out of her eyes. "I can't stand being cooped up for another night on that ship."

"You're planning to put up shelters—to live outside of the ship?" This would seem to confirm his darkest suspicions. Even a temporary settlement would leave them too open to visitation from the commandant. What his attitude toward the aliens might be, Jrann-Pttt didn't know. He might consider them as specimens, as enemies or as potential allies. What his attitude toward Jrann-Pttt and his companion would be, however, the saurian knew only too well. Had they reported the lieutenant's demise immediately, it was possible the commandant might have been brought to believe it was an accident. Now he would unquestionably think Jrann-Pttt had killed Merglyt-Ruuu on purpose—which was not true; how was Jrann-Pttt to know that the mud into which he'd knocked the lieutenant was quicksand?

"Anything against putting up shelters?" Captain Greenfield growled from his perch.

"Monster!" the mosquito-bat shrieked at the cat. "Monster! Monster!"

* * * * *

There was a painfully embarrassed silence.

"The creature is not intelligent," Jrann-Pttt explained, smiling. "It merely has vocal apparatus that can reproduce a frequently heard word, like—you have a bird, I believe, a—" he searched their minds for the word—"a parrot."

"Monster!" the mosquito-bat continued. "Monster! Monster!"

"Shut up or I'll wring your neck!" the captain snarled. The mosquito-bat obeyed sullenly, apparently recognizing the threat in his tone.

But the concept of "monster" hung heavily in the air between the terrestrials and the lizard-man. *They should not feel so bad about it,* he thought, *for they are the monsters themselves. But that would never occur to them and I can hardly reassure them by saying....*

"Don't worry," Professor Bernardi said smoothly. "To him, it's we who are the monsters."

A sudden gust of wind nearly whipped the tablecloth out of Jrann-Pttt's hands. He fought with it for a moment, glad of something tangible to contend with. "About the shelters," he said. "They might not stand up against a storm."

"So this is monsoon country," Bernardi observed thoughtfully. "Do you know when the storms usually come, Jrann-Pttt?" The other shook his head. "Peculiar. There usually is a season for that sort of thing."

"I ... come from another part of the planet."

"Storms here are bad, eh?" the captain commented, swinging himself down easily. "Frankly, that worries me. Ship's resting on mud as far as I can see, and if there's one thing I do know something about, it's mud. If it got any wetter, the ship might sink."

"Maybe we should leave," Mrs. Bernardi suggested. "Go to another part of the planet where it's drier, or—" she tried not to show the sudden surge of hope—"leave for home and come back after the rainy season."

There was a sudden silence, and Jrann-Pttt found himself able to pick up the answers to some of his questions from the alien minds. His worst fears were confirmed. Plan A was out. But something could still be done with these creatures.

"Doesn't she know?" the captain demanded accusingly. "You brought her here without telling her?"

Bernardi spread his hands wide in a futile gesture. "She should know; I've told her repeatedly. She just doesn't understand ... or doesn't want to."

"I know they'll forgive us," Mrs. Bernardi said stubbornly. "We—you—haven't done anything really wrong, so how could they do anything terrible to us? After all, didn't they refuse you the funds because they said you couldn't—"

"Shhh, Louisa," her husband commanded.

Jrann-Pttt smiled to himself.

—"do it," she went on. "And you did. So they were wrong and they'll have to forgive us."

"Tcha!" Miss Anspacher said. "Since when was there any fairness in justice?"

"On the other hand," Mrs. Bernardi continued, "we have no idea of how dangerous the storms here could be."

"Very dangerous," Jrann-Pttt said.

"For you, perhaps," the captain retorted. "Maybe not for us."

"Now that's silly," Miss Anspacher said. "You can see that Jrann-Pttt is much more—" she blushed—"sturdily built than we are."

"I don't mean that we could face it without protection," the captain replied angrily. "Naturally I mean that our superior technology could cope with the effects of any storm."

"Well, Captain, we'll have to put that superior technology to use at once," the professor told him. "You'd better start blasting that rock."

Laden with equipment and malevolent thoughts, the captain trudged off into the murky jungle. The others would not even offer to help. Confounded scientists; they certainly took his status as captain seriously. He wished, for a disloyal moment, that he had stayed on Earth. The quiet routine of a test pilot had prepared him for nothing like this. Were Miss Anspacher and adventure worth it? At the moment, he thought not. But he was on Venus and it was too late to change his mind.

Jrann-Pttt followed him into the jungle, keeping some distance behind, for he had good reason to suspect that Greenfield would take his warm interest in terrestrial technology for plain spying. Or, worse yet, he might try to press the lizard-man into service; Jrann-Pttt felt he had demeaned himself quite enough already.

"Have you noticed," Miss Anspacher asked, pushing the mass of damp brown hair off her neck as she came alongside him, "how the–the smell–" *a scientist does not mince words–*"of the swamp has grown stronger?"

Jrann-Pttt halted. He had a good idea of what the captain's reactions to the sight of himself and Miss Anspacher arriving hand-in-hand would be. "Yes, it is getting rather overpowering. Perhaps, for a lady of your delicate sensibilities, it would be best to–"

"I can stand a bad smell just as well as a male–any male!"

"Perhaps even better," Jrann-Pttt said, "for I was on the verge of turning back myself."

"Oh," she said, appeased. "Well, in that case, I'll go back with you ... how quiet everything is!"

He had not noticed. For him, it would never be quiet because of the stream of jangled thoughts constantly pouring into the back of his mind from everything sentient that surrounded him.

For a moment, he wondered what it would be like to be non-telepathic like the terrestrials, to have peace from the clamor of confused impressions, emotions and ideas that persistently beat at his mind. But that would be wondering how it was to be deaf to avoid discord, or blind to shut out ugliness.

"The lull before the storm, I suppose," she said brightly. *Now is his opportunity to kiss me—only perhaps they don't have kissing in his society. His mouth does seem to be the wrong shape. And if I kissed him, it might violate a taboo.*

During their short absence, the citrine clouds that closed off the sky had changed to a sinister umber. It was now almost as dusky in the clearing as in the jungle itself, when Jrann-Pttt and Miss Anspacher returned and joined the others.

Professor Bernardi stood looking up with sharp gray eyes at a sky he could not see. "I hope Greenfield can finish the blasting more quickly than he estimated," he muttered.

"Will we hear the noise way out here, Carl?" his wife worried nervously.

"Only two kilometers away? Of course we'll hear it. I do wish you wouldn't always be asking such stupid questions."

She shivered. "Well, I hope they get it over with right away. If we just have to sit here waiting and waiting and waiting, I'll go mad. I know I will."

"You should try to keep your nerves in check, Louisa," Miss Anspacher snapped. *Silly little fool.*

"At least I can control my glands!" Mrs. Bernardi flared back. *Sex-starved spinster.*

"I shall make some tea, ladies," Jrann-Pttt interposed. "I'm sure we will all feel the better for it."

Mrs. Bernardi smiled at him feebly. "You're such a comfort, Pitt. I don't know why you of all creatures should be the one to remind me of home."

"Home," remarked Mortland, emerging from the airlock, "is where the heart is. Did I hear someone say 'tea'?"

*   *   *   *   *

As Jrann-Pttt hung the kettle over the fire, suddenly the air erupted in stunning violence of sound. The ground undulated under their feet and water slopped out of the kettle, almost putting out the fire that rose high to claw at it. Rivulets of thick, muddy liquid welled out of the ground and drabbled their feet. The women turned pale. Algol gave a faint cry and hid under Mrs. Bernardi's skirts, trembling, while the mosquito-bat tried to lift Mortland's toupee and hide in his hair. The ship itself quivered and seemed to jump slightly in the air, then returned to its resting place.

All was quiet again, quieter than it had been before. Mortland anxiously gnawed his light mustache. "Better hurry with that tea, there's a good fellow. I'm violently allergic to loud noises."

"They'll probably continue all day," the professor said with almost malevolent cheerfulness, "so you might as well get used to them." *Who is he to have nerves? I am easily the most sensitive person here, but I manage to control myself.*

"I don't know how I'm going to stand it!" Mrs. Bernardi shrieked. "I just know something terrible is going to happen."

"Please try to restrain yourself, Louisa," her husband ordered. "After it's over, you'll find we'll be much more comfortable and secure with the ship resting on rock."

"If you ask me, that blast made it sink a little," Mortland said. "I wonder whether—"

He was interrupted by a thrashing in the bushes. Dfar-Lll burst forth, shedding scales. *Do not despair, Jrann-Pttt. I am here, ready to save you or die at your side.*

The women clutched each other, Miss Anspacher praying silently and fervently to Juno, Lakshmi, Freya, Isis and a host of other esoteric female deities she had picked up in the course of her avocational researches.

"He seems to be one of Jrann-Pttt's people," Bernardi observed, "so there should be nothing to fear."

Dfar-Lll, you fool! Jrann-Pttt ideated angrily. *Nothing's wrong. They're just blasting out a better berth for their vessel. And now you've spoiled my plans.*

"What did you think at that poor little creature!" Mrs. Bernardi blazed. "He's crying!" And, sure enough, amethyst tears were oozing out of the young saurian's large, liquid eyes.

I du-didn't mean any harm.

"Monster!" Mrs. Bernardi accused Jrann-Pttt. "All men are monsters, whether they're aliens or not."

"You're so right, Louisa!" Miss Anspacher exclaimed, regarding the younger creature in an almost kindly manner.

I'm sorry, r-Lll, Jrann-Pttt apologized. *I was upset by that noise, too. How could you possibly know what it was? Come, let me introduce you to the creatures.*

Dfar-Lll stepped forward diffidently. Jrann-Pttt put a hand on the moss-green shoulder. "Allow me to introduce my companion, Dfar-Lll," he said aloud.

The youngster looked at him.

Mrs. Bernardi thrust out her hand. "I'm very glad to meet you, Lil."

Agitate it with one of yours. It's a courtesy. Don't let her see how repulsive she is to you. Remember, you're just as repulsive to her.

Dfar-Lll offered a shy, seven-fingered hand. "Pleased ... to meet you ... ma'am," the young lizard squeaked.

"Why, he's just a baby, isn't he?" Mrs. Bernardi asked.

I am not a baby! Dfar-Lll thought indignantly. *At the end of this year, I shall celebrate my pre-maturity feast, or I would have. And furthermore–*

There was another thunderous blast of sound. After the ground had stopped trembling, the six found themselves ankle-deep in muddy water. Algol, who was in considerably deeper than his ankles, mewed fretfully.

Mrs. Bernardi picked him up and comforted him.

"Perhaps blasting wasn't such a good idea," the professor muttered. "Maybe I should tell Greenfield to call a halt and we'll take our chances with the storm. As a matter of fa—"

"The ship!" Mortland cried. "It *is* sinking!"

And the big metal ball slowly but visibly was indeed subsiding into the mud.

"Stop it, somebody!" Miss Anspacher snapped in her customary schoolroom manner.

The professor was pale, but he held on to his calm. "What can we do? Even if we could get the captain back in time, there's no way we can stop it. It's too heavy to pull out manually, and the engines, of course, are inside."

As they watched in horror, the ship sank deeper and deeper, picking up momentum as more of it went under. With a loud, sucking sound, it vanished into the ooze. Muddy water gurgled over it and, where the ship had been, there was now a small lake.

"This could be the beginning of a legend," Miss Anspacher murmured. "Or the end."

There was another vibrant detonation. "Someone ought to go tell the captain there's no use blasting any more," Bernardi said wearily. "We have nothing to put on the rock when he smooths it off." He began to laugh. "I suppose you could call this poetic justice." And he went on laughing, losing a bit of his former self-control.

There goes Plan B, Jrann-Pttt thought.

A star of intensely bright green lightning split the clouds and widened to cover the visible expanse of sky. There was a planet-shaking clap of thunder that made Greenfield's puny efforts sound like the snapping of twigs in comparison and it began to rain hard and fast.

*   *   *   *   *

"If only I hadn't gone and blasted that damn rock," the captain grumbled, squeezing water out of his shirt-tails, "we'd have been all right. Probably the storm wouldn't have done a thing to the ship except get it wet. If you can even call it a storm."

"I can and I do," Jrann-Pttt replied, haughtily squeegeeing his wet scales. "All I said was that a storm might be coming up and it might be dangerous. How was I to know it would last only half an hour?"

"Even the camp stools pulled through," Greenfield pointed out, "and you said shelters wouldn't stand up."

"I only said they might not. Can't you understand your own language?"

The fissure in the clouds had not quite closed yet and through it the enormous, blazing disk of the sun glared at them, twice as large as it appeared from Earth. It was a moot point as to whether they'd be dried out or steamed alive first.

"Might as well collect whatever gear we have left and get it to higher ground," Miss Anspacher said efficiently. "Two feet of water won't do anything any good—even those camp stools."

"It's my belief you wanted this to happen," Greenfield accused Jrann-Pttt. "You wanted to get rid of us."

"My dear fellow," Jrann-Pttt replied loftily, "the information I gave you was, to the best of my knowledge, accurate. However, I happen to be a professor of zoology and not a meteorologist. Apparently you people live out in the open like primitives," he continued, ignoring Dfar-Lll's admiring interjection, "and are accustomed to the vicissitudes of weather. I am a civilized creature; I live—" *or used to live*—"in an air-conditioned, light-conditioned, weather-conditioned city. It is only when I rough it on field trips like this to trackless parts of the—globe that I am forced to experience weather. Even then, I have never before been caught in a situation like this."

In fact, I was never before caught or I wouldn't be in this situation at all.

"Oh, Jrann-Pttt," sighed Miss Anspacher, "I knew you couldn't be just an ordinary native!"

"How did you get into this situation then?" Professor Bernardi asked. He had an unfortunate talent for going directly to the point.

"The third member of our expedition died," Jrann-Pttt explained. "He was our dirigational expert. Our guide."

"How did he happen to—"

"Are we just going to stand here chatting," Miss Anspacher demanded, "or are we going to do something about this?"

"What can we do?" Mrs. Bernardi asked weakly. "We might just as well lie down and—"

"Never say die, Louisa," Miss Anspacher admonished.

"I suggest we go to my camp to see what shape it's in," Jrann-Pttt said, furiously putting together Plan C. "Some of the supplies there might prove useful."

Captain Greenfield looked questioningly at Bernardi. The professor shrugged. "Might as well."

"All right," the captain growled. "Let's pick up whatever we can save."

*   *   *   *   *

Since there wasn't much that could be rescued, the little safari was soon on its way. Jrann-Pttt led, carrying Algol in his arms. Behind came Mortland, bearing a camp stool and the kettle into which he had tucked a tin of biscuits and into which the mosquito-bat had tucked itself, its orange eyes glaring out angrily from beneath the lid. Next came Mrs. Bernardi with her knitting, her camp stool and her sorrow.

Dfar-Lll followed with two stools and the plastic tea set. Close behind was Miss Anspacher, with the sugar bowl, the earthenware teapot and an immense bound volume of the *Proceedings of the Physical Society of Ameranglis* for 1993. Professor Bernardi bore a briefcase full of notes and the table. The rain had damaged the latter's mechanism, so that its legs kept unfolding from time to time, to the great inconvenience of Captain Greenfield, who brought up the rear with the blasting equipment. Behind them and sometimes alongside them came something—or someone—else.

"Surely your camp must have been closer to ours than this," Miss Anspacher finally remarked after they had been slogging through mud and water and pushing aside reluctant vegetation for over an Earth hour.

"I am very much afraid," Jrann-Pttt admitted, "that our camp has been lost—that is to say, inundated."

"What are we going to do now?" the captain asked of the company at large.

Professor Bernardi shrugged. "Our only course would seem to be making for one of the cities and throwing ourselves upon the na—Jrann-Pttt's people's hospitality. If Professor Jrann-Pttt has even the vaguest idea of the direction in which his home lies, we might as well head that way." *I wonder whether the natives could help us raise the ship.*

"I'm sure my people will be more than happy to welcome you," Jrann-Pttt said smoothly, "and to make you comfortable until your people send another ship to fetch you."

The terrestrials looked at one another. Dfar-Lll looked at Jrann-Pttt.

Professor Bernardi coughed. "That was the only spaceship we had," he admitted. "The first experimental model, you know." *We don't expect to stay on this awful planet forever. After all, as Louisa says, the government will have to forgive us. Public opinion and all that.*

"Oh," the saurian said. "Then we shall have the pleasure of your company until they build another?"

There was silence. "We have the only plans," the professor said, gripping his briefcase more tightly. "I am the inventor of the ship, so naturally I would have them." *If we brought back some specimens of Venusian life–of intelligent Venusian life–to prove we'd been here....*

"Matter of fact, old fellow," Mortland said, "we took all the plans with us so they couldn't build another ship and follow–"

"Mortland!" the professor exclaimed.

"But they're telepaths," Miss Anspacher said. "They must know already."

Everyone turned to look at the saurians.

"I have ... certain information," Jrann-Pttt admitted, "but I cannot understand it. You are in trouble with your rulers because they would not give you the funds, claiming space travel was impossible?"

"That's right," Bernardi said. *Not really specimens, you understand. Guests.*

"And you went ahead and appropriated the funds and materials from your government, since you were in a trusted position where you could do so?"

Bernardi nodded.

"Of course the question is now academic, for the ship is gone, but since you proved the possibility of space travel by coming here, wouldn't your government then dismiss the charges against you?"

"That's exactly what I keep telling him!" Mrs. Bernardi exclaimed.

But her husband shook his head. "The law is inflexible. We have broken it and must be punished, even if by breaking it we proved its fundamental error." *Why let him know our plans?*

Why, Jrann-Pttt, that sounds just like our own government, doesn't it?

Yes, it does. We should be able to establish a very satisfactory mode of living with these strangers.

"We'd hoped that after a year or so the whole thing would die down," Mortland explained frankly, "and we'd go back as heroes."

"Do you know the way to your home, Jrann-Pttt?" the professor asked anxiously.

"Since we were able to catch a glimpse of the sun, I think I can figure out roughly where we are. All we must do is walk some two hundred kilometers in that direction–" he waved an arm to indicate the way–"and we should be at the capital."

"Will your people accept us as refugees?" Miss Anspacher demanded bluntly, "or will we be captives?" *Which is what I'll bet the good professor is planning for you, if only he can figure some way to get you and, of course, ourselves back.*

"We should be proud to accept you as citizens and to receive the benefits of your splendid technology. Our laboratories will be placed at your disposal."

"Well, that's better than we hoped for," the professor said, brightening. "We had expected to have to carve our own laboratories out of the wilderness. Now we shall be able to carry on our researches in comfort." *No need to trouble the natives; we'll be able to raise the ship ourselves. Or build a new one. And I'll see to it personally that they have special quarters in the zoo with a considerable amount of privacy.*

"If I were you, I wouldn't trust him too far," the captain warned. "He's a foreigner."

"You ought to be ashamed of yourself, Captain!" Miss Anspacher said. "I, for one, trust Jrann-Pttt implicitly. Did you say this direction, Jrann-Pttt?" She stepped forward briskly. There was a loud splash and water closed over her head.

Captain Greenfield rushed forward to haul her out. "Well," she said, daintily coughing up mud, "I was wet to begin with, anyway."

"You're a brave little woman, Miss Anspacher," the captain told her admiringly.

"This sort of thing may present a problem," Professor Bernardi commented. "I hope that was only a pot-hole, that the water is not going to be consistently too deep for wading."

"There might be quicksand, too," Mrs. Bernardi said somberly. "In quicksand, one drowns slowly."

Dfar-Lll gave a start. *Surely you don't intend to lead them back to base?*

Precisely. The swamp is unfit for settlement.

But to return voluntarily to captivity?

Who mentioned anything about captivity? Assisted by our new friends, we have an excellent chance of taking over the ship and supplies by a surprise attack.

But why should these aliens assist us?

Jrann-Pttt smiled. *Oh, I think they will. Yes, I have every confidence in Plan C.*

"I suggest," the professor said, ignoring his wife's pessimism, "that each one of us pull a branch from a tree. We can test the ground before we step on it, to make sure that there is solid footing underneath."

"Good idea," the captain approved. He reached out the arm that was not occupied with Miss Anspacher and tugged at a tree limb.

And then he and the lady physicist were both floundering in the ooze.

"Well, really, Captain Greenfield!" she cried, refusing his aid in extricating herself. "I always thought you were at least a gentleman in spite of your illiteracy!"

"Wha—what happened?" he asked as he struggled out of the mud. "Something pushed me; I swear it."

Jrann-Pttt mentalized. "It seems the tree did not like your trying to remove a branch."

"The tree!" Greenfield's pale blue eyes bulged. "You're joking!"

"Not at all. As a matter of fact, I myself have been wondering why there were so many thought-streams and yet so few animals around here. It never occurred to me that the vegetation could be sentient and have such strong emotive defenses. In all my experience as a botanist, I–"

"I thought you were a zoologist," Bernardi interrupted.

"My people do not believe in excessive specialization," the saurian replied.

"Trees that think?" Mortland inquired incredulously.

"They're not very bright," Jrann-Pttt explained, "but they don't like having their limbs pulled off. I don't suppose you would, either, for that matter."

"I propose," Miss Anspacher said, shaking out her wet hair, "that we break up the camp stools and use the sticks instead of branches to help us along."

"Good idea," the captain said, trying to get back into her good graces. "I always knew women could put their brains to use if they tried."

She glared at him.

"I thought we'd use the furniture to make a fire later," Mortland complained. "For tea, you know."

"The ground's much too wet," Professor Bernardi replied.

"And besides," Miss Anspacher added, "I lost the teapot in that pot-hole."

"But you managed to save the *Proceedings of the Physical Society*," Mortland snarled. "Serve you right if I eat it. And I warn you, if hard-pressed, I shall."

"How will we cook our food, though?" Mrs. Bernardi demanded apprehensively. "It's a lucky thing, Mr. Pitt, that we have you with us to tell us which of the berries and things are edible, so at least we shan't starve."

The visible portion of Jrann-Pttt's well-knit form turned deeper green. "But I regret to say I don't know, Mrs. Bernardi. Those 'native' foods I served you were all synthetics from our personal stores. I never tasted natural foods before I met you."

"And if the trees don't like our taking their branches," Miss Anspacher put in, "I don't suppose the bushes would like our taking their berries. Louisa, don't do that!"

But Mrs. Bernardi, with her usual disregard for orders, had fainted into the mud. Pulling her out and reviving her caused so much confusion, it wasn't until then that they discovered Algol had disappeared.

*   *   *   *   *

The party had been trudging through mud and water and struggling with pale, malevolent vines and bushes and low-hanging branches for close to six Earth hours. All of them were tired and hungry, now that their meager supply of biscuits and chocolate was gone.

"Remember, Carl," Mrs. Bernardi told her husband, "I forgive you. And I know I'm being foolishly sentimental, but if you could manage to take my body back to Earth—"

"Don't be so pessimistic." Professor Bernardi absent-mindedly leaned against a tree, then recoiled as he remembered it might resent being treated like an inanimate object. "In any case, we'll most likely all die at the same time."

"I never did want to go to Venus, really," Mrs. Bernardi sniffled. "I only came, like Algol did, because I didn't have any choice. If you left me behind, I'd have had to bear the brunt of.... Where is Algol?" She stared at Jrann-Pttt. "You were carrying him. What have you done with him?"

The lizard-man looked at her in consternation. "He jumped out of my arms when you fainted and I turned back to help. I was certain one of the others had him."

"He's dead!" she wailed. "You let him fall into the water and drown—an innocent kitty that never hurt anybody, except in fun."

"Come, come, Louisa." Her husband took her arm. "He was only a cat. I'm sure Jrann-Pttt didn't mean for him to drown. He was just so upset by your fainting that he didn't think...."

"Not Jrann-Pttt's fault, of course," Miss Anspacher said.

"After all, we can't expect them to love animals as we do. But Algol was a very good sort of cat...."

"Keep quiet, all of you!" Jrann-Pttt shouted. "I have never known any species to use any method of communication so much in order to communicate so little. Don't you understand? I would not have assumed the cat was with one of you, if I had not subconsciously sensed his thought-stream all along. He must be nearby."

Everyone was still, while Jrann-Pttt probed the dense underbrush that blocked their view on both sides. "Over here," he announced, and led the way through the thick screen of interlaced bushes and vines on the left.

About ten meters farther on, the ground sloped up sharply to form a ridge rising a meter and a half above the rest of the terrain. The water had not reached its blunted top, and on this fairly level strip of ground, perhaps three meters wide, Algol had been paralleling their path in dry-pawed comfort.

"Scientists!" Louisa Bernardi almost spat. "Professors! We could have been walking on that, too. But did anybody think to look for dry ground? No! It was wet in one place, so it would be wet in another. Oh, Algol–" she reached over to embrace the cat–"you're smarter than any so-called intelligent life-forms."

He indignantly straightened a whisker she had crumpled.

$$*\qquad*\qquad*\qquad*\qquad*$$

"Look," Mortland exclaimed in delight as they attained the top of the ridge, "here are some dryish twigs! Don't suppose the trees want them, since they've let them fall. If I can get a fire going, we could boil some swamp water and make tea. Nasty thought, but it's better than no tea at all. And how long can one go on living without tea?"

"We'll need some food before long, too," Professor Bernardi observed, putting his briefcase down on a fallen log. "The usual procedure, I believe, would be for us to draw straws to see which gets eaten—although there isn't any hurry."

"I'm glad then that we'll be able to have a fire," Mortland said, busily collecting twigs. "I should hate to have to eat you raw, Carl."

Mr. Pitt and his little friend are delightful creatures, Mrs. Bernardi thought. *So intelligent and so well behaved. But eating them wouldn't really be cannibalism. They aren't people.*

That premise works both ways, dear lady, Jrann-Pttt ideated. *And I must say your species will prove far easier to peel for the cooking pot.*

"Monster! What are you doing?" Mortland dropped his twigs and pulled the mosquito-bat away from a bush. "Don't eat those berries, you silly ass; the bush won't like it!" The mosquito-bat piped wrathfully.

Jrann-Pttt probed with intentness. "You know, I rather think the bush wants its berries to be eaten. Something to do with—er—propagating itself. Of course it has a false impression as to what is going to be done with the berries, but the important fact is that it won't put up any resistance."

"All right, old fellow." Mortland released the mosquito-bat, which promptly flew back to the bush. "I'm not the custodian of your morals."

"I wonder whether we could eat those berries, too," Professor Bernardi remarked pensively.

"Carl!" Mrs. Bernardi's tear-stained face flushed pink. "Why—why, that's almost indecent!"

"We eat beans, don't we?" Mortland pointed out. "They're seeds."

"We also eat meat," Miss Anspacher added.

There was silence. "I imagine," Mrs. Bernardi murmured, "it's because we never get to meet the meat socially." She avoided the saurians' eyes.

"We'd better see how Monster makes out, though," Miss Anspacher observed, replenishing her lipstick, "before we try the berries ourselves. The fact that the bush is anxious to dispose of them doesn't mean they can't be poisonous."

"Why should Monster sacrifice himself for us?" Mortland retorted hotly, overlooking the fact that Monster's purpose in eating the berries was almost certainly not an altruistic one. "If we can risk his life, we can risk our own." He crammed a handful of berries into his mouth defiantly. "I say, they're good!"

Algol sniffed the bush with disgust, then turned away.

"See?" said Miss Anspacher. "They're undoubtedly poisonous. When he's really hungry, he isn't so fussy." She combed her hair.

"But is he really hungry?" Bernardi asked suspiciously. "Come here, Algol. Nice kitty." He bent down and sniffed the cat's breath. The cat sniffed his interestedly. Their whiskers touched. "I thought so. Fish!"

"You mean," Mrs. Bernardi shrieked, "that while we were struggling through that water, alternately starving and drowning by centimeters, that wretched cat has not only been walking along here dry as toast, but gorging himself on fish?"

"Now, now, Mrs. Bernardi," Jrann-Pttt said. "Being a dumb animal, he wouldn't think of informing you about matters of which he'd assume that you, as the superior beings, would be fully cognizant."

"You might have told us there were fish on this planet, Mr. Pitt."

"Dear lady, there is something I feel I should tell you. I am not—"

"They're here on the other side of the ridge," Greenfield called, bending over and peering through the foliage. "The fish, I mean."

"The pools look shallow," Bernardi said, also bending over. "The fish should be easy enough to catch. Might even be able to get them in our hands." He reached out to demonstrate, proving the error of both his theses, for the fish slipped right through his fingers and, as he grabbed for them, he lost his balance, toppled over the side of the ridge into the mud and water below and began to disappear, showing beyond a doubt that the pools were deeper than he had thought.

"Carl, what are you doing?" Mrs. Bernardi peered into the murky depths where her husband was threshing about. "Why don't you come out of that filthy mud?"

His voice, though muffled, was still acid. "It isn't mud, my dear. It's quicksand!"

"Rope!" the captain exclaimed, grabbing a coil.

"Hold on, chaps!" cried a squeaky voice. "I'm coming to the rescue!" A stout twelve-foot vine plunged out of the shadows and wrapped one end of itself around a tree— disregarding the latter's violent objections—and the other end around Professor Bernardi's thorax, which was just disappearing into the mud. "Now if one or two of you would haul away, we'll soon have him out all shipshape and proper. Heave ho! Don't be afraid of hurting me; my strength is as the strength of ten because my heart is pure."

"It's that vine!" Dfar-Lll exclaimed. "So that's what has been following us all along!"

*　　*　　*　　*　　*

"I can accept the idea of a vegetable thinking," Professor Bernardi gasped as he was pulled out of the quicksand, "although with the utmost reluctance." He shook himself like a dog. "But how can it be mobile?"

"You chaps can move around," the vine explained, "so I said to myself: 'Dammit, I'll have a shot at doing that, too.' Hard going at first, when you're using suckers, but I persevered and I made it. Look, I can talk, too. Never heard of a vine doing that before, did you? Fact is, I hadn't thought of it before, but then I never had anyone to communicate with. All those other vines are so stupid; you have absolutely no idea! Hope you don't mind my picking up your language, but it was the only one around–"

"We are honored," Professor Bernardi declared. "And I am deeply grateful to you, too, sir or madam, for saving my life."

"Think nothing of it," the vine said, arranging its leaves, which were of a pleasing celadon rather than the whitish-green favored by the rest of the local vegetation. "Now that I can move, I'll probably be doing heroic things like that all the time. Are you all going to the city? May I go with you? I've heard lots about the city," it went on, taking consent for granted, "but I never thought I'd get to see it. Everybody in the swamp is such an old stick-in-the-mud. I thought I was trapped, too, forced to spend the rest of my life in a provincial environment. Is it true that the streets are filled with chlorophyll? Do you think I can get a job in a botanical garden or something? Perhaps I can give little talks on horticulture to visitors?"

The mosquito-bat looked out of the tea kettle austerely. "Monster!" it piped shrilly.

"The very idea!" the vine snapped back indignantly. "Oh, well," it said, calming down, "you probably don't know any better. It's up to me as the intelligent life-form to forgive you, and I shall."

Jrann-Pttt and Dfar-Lll looked at each other in consternation. *Do you think there really are cities on this planet, sir? Can there be indigenous intelligent life? If so, it may have already got in touch with the commandant.*

Impossible, Jrann-Pttt replied. *The vine probably just heard us talking about a city. After all, it picked up the language that way; very likely it absorbed some terrestrial concepts along with it. If there are any real settlements at all, they must be quite primitive–nothing more than villages. No, it's we who will build the cities on Venus.*

*Combining our technology with the terrestrials', we could
develop a pretty little civilization here–after we've
disposed of the commandant, so he can't report our
disappearance. We don't want any publicity. So much
better to keep our little society exclusive.*

*   *   *   *   *

"Wonder what time it is," the captain remarked as he
rose and stretched in the dim yellow light of the long
Venusian day. "Must have slept for hours. My watch
seems to have stopped."

"Mine, too." Mortland unstrapped his from his wrist
and shook it futilely. "Waterproof, hah! If we ever get
back to Earth, I shall make the manufacturer eat his
guarantee."

"Oh, well, what does time matter to us now?"
Professor Bernardi pointed out as he rose from his leafy
couch with a loud creak. All of them–even the saurians–
had aches and pains in every joint and muscle as a result
of the unaccustomed exercise and the damp climate. "We
are out of its reach. It has no present meaning for us."

This depressed them all. Only the vine seemed in good
health and spirits. "I notice you're all wearing clothes
except for the short four-legged gentleman with the
home-grown fur coat," it chattered happily. "Do you think
I'll be socially acceptable without them? I wouldn't want
to make a bad impression at the very start–or would
leaves do?"

Everybody looked at Jrann-Pttt. "We are not a
narrow-minded species," he said hastily. "I'm sure your
leaves will be more than adequate."

After a breakfast of fish and berries stewed in tea–
which the vine declined with thanks–the various
members of the party gathered up their belongings and
resumed their journey. Encrusted with dried purple mud
and grime, their clothes deliberately torn by anti-social
shrubbery, their chins–of the males, that is–disfigured by

hirsute growths, the terrestrials made a sorry spectacle. It was hot, boiling hot, and more humid than ever.

"Well," said Miss Anspacher, letting the Swahili marching song with which she had been attempting to encourage the company peter out, "I do hope we'll reach your city soon, Jrann-Pttt. I must say I could use a hot bath." She added hastily, "Hot baths are a peculiar cultural trait of ours."

"I could use one myself," Jrann-Pttt said. He brushed his scales fastidiously.

"I'm looking forward so to meeting your relatives," she said, grabbing his left arm determinedly. "I'm not violating a taboo or anything, am I?" *It isn't really slimy; it just feels that way.*

"Not one of my people's. But I'm afraid you are violating a terrestrial taboo, judging from the thoughts I pick up from your captain's mind."

"Oh, him—he's a stupid fool!"

"Not at all. Rough, perhaps. Untutored, yes. But with a good deal of native intelligence, although fearfully primitive."

"Perhaps I was too harsh," Miss Anspacher observed thoughtfully. *The captain ... is good-looking in a brutal sort of way, although not nearly as handsome or even as spiritual in appearance as Jrann-Pttt. And sometimes I almost think he—*she blushed to herself—*shows a certain partiality for my company.*

She did not, however, let go of the saurian's arm when the captain bustled up, prepared to put a stop to this, but tactfully, if possible, for he had begun to realize that his rude ways did not endear him to her.

"Ah—we're making very good progress, aren't we, Pitt?" he interrupted, trying to insinuate himself between the two.

"Excellent."

"How soon do you think we'll be at your city at this rate?"

Jrann-Pttt shrugged. "Since I have no way of telling what our rate is or how far we have gone, how can I tell? As a matter of fact, you might as well learn now as later—I am not a Venusian. There is no intelligent life native to Venus."

"Oh, really!" the vine interposed indignantly. "Saying a thing like that right in front of me! What would you call me, then, pray tell?"

Jrann-Pttt kept his actual thoughts to himself. "A mutation," he said. "Probably you are the first intelligent life-form to appear upon this planet. Scholarly volumes will be written about you."

"Oh?" The vine seemed to be appeased. "I accept your apology. Perhaps I'll learn to write and do the books myself, because I'm the only one who can understand the real me."

"But how can you show us the way to your city if you're not native to Venus?" Bernardi demanded, whirling fretfully upon the saurian. "What is this, anyway? Each time you come up with a different story!"

"See?" said the captain. "Didn't I tell you he was up to no good?"

"I should like to lead you to our base," Jrann-Pttt replied with quiet dignity. "I am telling you the truth now since I feel I should have your consent before proceeding farther."

??????? Dfar-Lll projected.

"I hesitated before, because I wasn't sure I could trust you. You see, the spaceship in which we came to this planet is a prison ship, with a crew consisting of malefactors—thieves, murderers, defrauders—dispatched to the remote fastnesses of the Galaxy to fetch back zoological specimens. Our zoo, I must say, is the finest and most interesting in the Universe."

"Monster!" the mosquito-bat squeaked.

"Shhh," Mortland admonished. "Don't interrupt."

"I was in command of our ill-fated expedition...."

Oh, Dfar-Lll projected. *For a moment there, sir, you had me worried.*

"When we reached Venus, I was, I must admit, careless. I gave the crew a chance to mutiny and they did. Slew most of the officers. Dfar-Lll and I were lucky to escape with our lives."

"But you might have told us!" Mrs. Bernardi's voice held reproach.

"Until we knew what kind of beings you were, we couldn't let you know how helpless and unprotected we were."

The women seemed moved, but not the men.

"Leading us on a wild goose chase, were you?" the captain challenged.

Jrann-Pttt drew a deep breath. "It was my hope that all of you would consent to help us get our ship back from these criminals. Then we could fly to my planet—which is the fifth of the star you know as Alpha Centauri—where, I assure you, you would be hospitably received."

We aren't really going back home, Jrann-Pttt, are we? I'd sooner stay here in the swamp than go back to that jail.

Have confidence in me, r-Lll. As soon as we have disposed of the commandant and his officers, I can put our ship out of commission. The terrestrials won't be able to tell what's wrong. They know nothing about space travel. The fact that they got their crude vessel to operate was probably sheer luck.

But the younger was not to be diverted. *Will we kill them after we've disposed of our officers? I should hate to.*

Certainly not. We shall need servants and I don't trust the prisoners in the ship—all criminals of the lowest type! Aloud, he said to the bewildered terrestrials, "If you don't want to help us, I shall understand. No sense your interfering in another species' quarrels, particularly as we must seem like monsters to you."

"Monster!" the mosquito-bat agreed. "Monster, monster, monster!" No one tried to stop him. Jrann-Pttt sensed that somehow he had lost a good deal of his grip on the terrestrials. Finesse, he thought angrily, was wasted on these barbaric life-forms.

Bernardi sighed. "I suppose we'll have to help you." *No reason why his ship shouldn't stop off at Earth before it goes to Alpha Centauri. No reason why it should even go to Alpha Centauri at all, in fact.*

"If you ask me," the captain said, "he's one of the criminals himself."

"But nobody asked you," Miss Anspacher retorted, the more acidly because she had been wondering the same thing. "Shall we resume our journey?"

"Hold on," the vine said. "I don't want to intrude or anything, but it hasn't been made quite clear to me whether or not I'm included in the invitation to this Alpha Centauri place, and I wouldn't want to keep going only on the off-chance that you might ask me. I really think you should, because you led me astray with your fair promises of glittering cities."

"The cities of our planet do not glitter," Jrann-Pttt replied, wishing it would wither instantly, "but certainly you are invited. Glad to have you."

"Oh, that's awfully decent of you," the vine said emotionally. "I shan't forget it, I promise you."

*   *   *   *   *

They plodded onward, the vine chattering so incessantly that a faint gurgling which accompanied them went unnoticed. The gurgling grew louder and louder as they pushed on. Finally, "I keep hearing water," Mortland remarked. "We must be approaching a river of some kind."

A few minutes later, bursting through a screen of underbrush, they found themselves confronted by a river whose bubbling violet-blue waters extended for at least four kilometers from shadowy bank to bank, with the ridge tapering to a point almost in its exact center.

Apparently, while they had been trekking along the elevation, the surrounding terrain, concealed from them by the dense and evil-minded vegetation, had imperceptibly taken off, leaving the ridge to become a peninsula that jutted out into the river. They seemed to be stranded. All they could do was retrace their steps and, since they had no idea how far back the split became part of the mainland again, the return journey might last almost as long as it had taken them to get there.

"I know we're heading in the right direction," Jrann-Pttt defended himself. "I wasn't aware of the river because we must have come by an overland route." Although he was telling the truth, at least insofar as he knew it himself, no one, not even Dfar-Lll, believed him.

"But let's rest a bit before we turn back," Mortland proposed, flopping to the ground. "I'm utterly used up."

"Maybe we don't need to go back," the vine said. "Not all the way, anyhow." Everyone stared. It waved its leaves brightly at them. "I notice the captain thoughtfully brought along lots of rope and there were scads of fallen logs just a bit back. Couldn't you just lash the logs together with the rope and make a—a thing on which we could float the rest of the way? On the water, you know."

The others continued to look at it open-mouthed.

"Just a little idea I had," it said modestly. "May not amount to much, but then you can't tell until you've tried, can you?"

"It—he—means a raft, I think," Mrs. Bernardi said.

Jrann-Pttt probed the raft concept in her mind, for he found the vegetable's mental processes curiously obscure. "What an excellent idea!" he exclaimed.

"It does not seem infeasible," Professor Bernardi admitted tightly. By now, he was suspicious of everyone and everything. *If I had never broached the idea of space travel to those peasants*, he thought, *I would be on Earth in the dubious comfort of my own home. That's what comes of trying to help humanity.*

*   *   *   *   *

"Well," observed the captain as the heavy raft hit the water with a tremendous splash, "she seems to be riverworthy." He rubbed his hands in anticipation, much of his surliness gone, now that he was about to deal with something he understood. "Since she is, in a manner of speaking, a ship, I suppose I assume command again?" He waited for objections, glancing involuntarily in Jrann-Pttt's direction. There were none. "Right," he said, repressing any outward symptoms of relief.

He efficiently deployed the personnel to the positions on the raft where he felt they might be least useless, the gear being piled in the middle and surmounted by Algol, who naturally assumed possession of the softest and safest place by the divine right of cats.

The captain does have a commanding presence, Miss Anspacher thought, *and a sort of uncouth grace. Moreover, he cannot read my mind–in fact, he often cannot even understand me when I speak.*

"All right!" he bellowed. "Cast off!"

The vine unfastened the rope that it had insouciantly attached to a tree trunk, remarking to the others, "Don't let the trees intimidate you. Actually their bark is worse than their bite." Now it dropped lithely on board the raft, looking for a comfortable resting place.

"Please don't twine around me," Miss Anspacher said coldly. "If you insist upon coming with us, you will have to choose an inanimate object to cling to."

"All right, all right," it tried to soothe her. "No need to get yourself all worked up over such a mere triviality, is there? I'll just coil myself tidily around one of those spare logs. I must say you're warmer, though."

Yes, she is, isn't she? thought the captain, and squeezed her hand.

*   *   *   *   *

The raft drifted down the river. Since the current was flowing in the desired direction, there did not appear to be any need to use the poles, and everyone sat or reclined as comfortably as possible in the suffocating heat. The yellow haze had become so thick that they seemed to be at the bottom of a custard cup.

"I do hope we're heading the right way," Professor Bernardi said, *although who knows what is right and what is wrong any more?*

"Perhaps we aren't," Mrs. Bernardi mused, stroking Algol, who had crawled into her lap. "Perhaps we will go drifting along endlessly. Every sixteen days, it will get dark and every sixteen days it will get light, and meanwhile we will continue floating along, never going anywhere, never getting anywhere, never seeing anything but haze and raft and river and each other." Algol wheezed in his sleep.

"Nonsense!" Jrann-Pttt said rudely. "I have a compass. I know the direction perfectly well."

"And yet you let us think we were wandering about blindly." Miss Anspacher gave him a contemptuous look. The captain pressed her hand.

"Since you seem to breathe the same air and eat much the same food that we do, Mr. Pitt," Mrs. Bernardi changed her tack, "I suppose we'll be physically comfortable on your planet for the rest of our lives. Our children will be born there and our children's children, and eventually they'll forget all about Earth and think it was only a legend."

"But you did expect to settle permanently on Venus, didn't you?" the vine asked, bewilderedly. "Or for a long visit, anyway. So I don't really see that it makes much difference if you go to Jrann-Pttt's Alpha Centauri place. So much nicer to be living with friends, I should think."

"But Alpha Centauri is so very far away," Mrs. Bernardi sighed. "There wouldn't be much chance of our ever getting back."

"Look!" Mortland exclaimed. "The river's branching. Which fork do we take?"

*   *   *   *   *

Jrann-Pttt, who had been dabbling his arms idly in the translucent violet-blue water, withdrew them hastily as nine green eyes, obviously belonging to the same individual, rose to the surface and regarded him with more than casual interest. He consulted his compass. "Left."

"Contrarily!" the mosquito-bat suddenly squeaked, pointing a small rod at his companions. "Rightward."

There was a stunned silence.

"Monster!" Mortland cried in reproach. "You can talk! How could you deceive us like that?"

"Can talk," the creature retorted. "Me not intelligent life-form, ha! Who talks last talks best. Have not linguistic facility of inferior life-forms, but can communicate rudely in your language."

"Remember," Mortland cautioned, "there are ladies present."

"Have been lying low and laughing to self—ha, ha!—at witlessness of lowerly life-forms."

"But why?" Mrs. Bernardi demanded distractedly. "Haven't we been kind to you?"

"You be likewise well treated in our zoo," it assured her. "All of you. Our zoo finest in Galaxy. And clean, too."

"Now really, sir, I must protest—" Professor Bernardi began, trying to extricate a blaster unobtrusively from the pile of gear in which the too-confident terrestrials had cached their weapons.

Monster gestured with his rod. "This is lethal weapon. Do not try hindrancing me. Hate damage fine specimens. Captain, go rightward."

"Oh, is that so!" Greenfield retorted hotly. "Let me tell you, you—you insect!"

"George!" Miss Anspacher clutched his arm. "Do what it says. For my sake, George!"

"Oh, all right," he muttered. "Just for you, then. Told you not to trust any of 'em," he went on, reluctantly poling the raft in the ordered direction. "Foreigners!"

"Fine zoo," the mosquito-bat insisted. "Very clean. Run with utmost efficientness. Strict visiting hours."

*　　*　　*　　*　　*

"And there goes Plan D," the vine said lightly. There was a hint of laughter in its voice. Jrann-Pttt stared at it in consternation. "Are you also from the Alpha Centauri system, sir?" It turned its attention to the mosquito-bat. "Naturally I'm curious to know where I'm going," it explained, "since I seem definitely to be included in your gracious invitation."

"Alpha Centauri, hah!" the mosquito-bat snorted. "I from what Earthlets laughingly term Sirius. Alpha Centauri merely little star."

"Now see here!" Jrann-Pttt sprang to his feet. Criminal he might be, but he was not going to sit there and have his sun insulted!

"Gentlemen! Gentlemen!" Miss Anspacher cried. "No use getting yourself killed, Jrann-Pttt!"

"Correctly," Monster approved. "Elementary intelligence displayed. Why damage fine specimens?"

From one prison into another, the saurian mentalized bitterly.

Yes, returned Dfar-Lll, *and it's all your fault*. The junior lizard burst into tears. *I wish I had let Merglyt-Ruuu do what he wanted. I would have been better off.*

"Sirius," the vine repeated. "That's even farther away than Alpha Centauri, isn't it? I never thought I would get that far away from the swamp! This really will be an adventure!"

"How do you know—" Professor Bernardi began.

"Frankly," it went on, "I don't see why you chaps are so put out by the whole thing. What's the difference between Alpha Centauri and Sirius anyway? Matter of a few light-years, but otherwise a star's a star for all that."

"To Jrann-Pttt, we wouldn't have been specimens," Mrs. Bernardi said, belatedly recognizing the advantages of Alpha Centauri.

"No, not specimens," the vine told her easily. "I don't suppose you know he had no intention of taking you back to his system. He wanted you to help him kill the officers of his ship so they couldn't look for him and the other escaped prisoner or report back to his planet. Then he was going to put the ship out of commission and found his own colony here with you as his slaves. I'd just as soon be a specimen as a slave. Sooner. Better to reign in a zoo than serve in a swamp!"

"Just how do you know all this?" Miss Anspacher demanded.

"It's obvious enough," Bernardi said gloomily. "Another telepath." *How can we compete or even cope with creatures like these? What a fool I was to think I could outwit them.*

"Telepathy just tricksomeness," the mosquito-bat put in jealously. "I have no telepathy, yet superior to all."

"But why should Mr. Pitt want to kill his officers?" Mrs. Bernardi asked querulously. "He's the commandant, isn't he? Or is he a professor? I never got that straight."

"He was one of the criminals on the ship," the vine told her. "What you might call a confidence man. This is about the only system in the Galaxy where he isn't wanted. He did tell you the truth, though, when he said they were sent on an expedition to collect zoological specimens. Dangerous work," it sighed, "and so his people use criminals for it. They were sent out in small detachments. Our friend here killed his guard in a fight over a female prisoner, which was why–"

"But what happened to the female prisoner?" Miss Anspacher's eye caught Dfar-Lll's. "Oh, no!" she gasped.

"Why not?" Dfar-Lll demanded. "I'm as much of a female as you are. Maybe even more."

The captain leaned close to Miss Anspacher. "No one can be more feminine than you are, Dolores," he whispered.

"But he–she's so young!" Mrs. Bernardi wailed.

The vine made an amused sound. "Don't you have juvenile delinquents on Earth?"

"Oh, what does all that matter now?" Jrann-Pttt said sullenly. "We're all going to a Sirian zoo, anyway."

"Correctly," approved the monster-bat. "Finest zoo. Clean. Commodious cages. Reasonable visiting hours. Very nice."

Mrs. Bernardi began to cry.

"Now," the vine comforted her, "a zoo's not so bad. After all, most of us spend our lives in cages of one kind or another, and without the basic security a zoo affords–"

"But we don't know we're in cages," Mrs. Bernardi sobbed. "That's the important thing."

Professor Bernardi looked at the vine. "But why are you–" he began, then halted. "Perhaps I don't want an answer," he said. There was no hope at all left in him, now that there was no doubt.

"You are wise," the vine agreed quietly. Algol arose from Mr. Bernardi's lap and rubbed against its thick pale green stem. He knew. The mosquito-bat looked at both of them restlessly.

The yellow haze had deepened to old gold. Now it was beginning to turn brown.

"It's twilight," Miss Anspacher observed. "Soon it will be dark."

"Perhaps we'll sail right past his ship in the night," Mortland suggested hopefully.

The mosquito-bat gave a snort. "Ship has lights. All modern convenients."

Suddenly the air seemed to have grown chilly–colder than it had any right to be on that torrid planet. All around them, it was dark and very quiet.

"I think I do see lights," Mortland said.

"Must be ship," Monster replied. And somehow the rest of them could sense the uneasiness in the thin, piping, alien voice. "Must be!"

"Your ship's a very large one then," Bernardi commented as they rounded a bend and a whole colony of varicolored pastel lights sprang up ahead of them.

"Not my ship!" the mosquito-bat exclaimed in a voice pierced with anguish. "Not my ship!"

Before them rose the fantastic, twisting, convoluting, turning spires of a tall, marvelous, glittering city.

"You will find that the streets actually are filled with chlorophyll," the vine said. "And I know you'll be happy here, all of you. You see, we can't have you going back to your planets now. No matter how good your intentions were, you'd destroy us. You do see that, don't you?"

"You may be right," Bernardi agreed dispiritedly, "although that doesn't cheer us any. But what will you do with us?"

"You'll be provided with living quarters comparable to those on your own planets," the vine told him, "and you'll give lectures just as if you were in a university—only you'll be much more secure. I assure you—" its voice was very gentle now—"you'll hardly know you're in a zoo."

The Vilbar Party

Originally Published in *Galaxy Science Fiction*
January 1955

Illustrated by Sandford Kossin

*"Nuts to you!" was what Narli knew Earthmen
would tell him ... only it was frismil nuts!*

THE VILBAR PARTY

"The Perzils are giving a vilbar party tomorrow
night," Professor Slood said cajolingly. "You *will* come
this time, won't you, Narli?"

Narli Gzann rubbed his forehead fretfully. "You know
how I feel about parties, Karn." He took a frismil nut out
of the tray on his desk and nibbled it in annoyance.

"But this is in your honor, Narli–a farewell party. You
must go. It would be–it would be unthinkable if you
didn't." Karn Slood's eyes were pleading. He could not
possibly be held responsible for his friend's anti-social
behavior and yet, Narli knew, he would somehow feel at
fault.

Narli sighed. He supposed he would have to conform
to public sentiment in this particular instance, but he
was damned if he would give in gracefully. "After all,
what's so special about the occasion? I'm just leaving to
take another teaching job, that's all." He took another
nut.

"That's *all*!" Slood's face swelled with emotion. "You
can't really be that indifferent."

"Another job, that's all it is to me," Narli persisted.
"At an exceptionally high salary, of course, or I wouldn't
dream of accepting a position so inconveniently located."

Slood was baffled and hurt and outraged. "You have
been honored by being the first of our people to be offered
an exchange professorship on another planet," he said
stiffly, "and you call it 'just another job.' Why, I would
have given my right antenna to get it!"

Narli realized that he had again overstepped the invisible boundary between candor and tactlessness. He poked at the nuts with a stylus.

"Honored by being the first of our species to be offered a guinea-pigship," he murmured.

He had not considered this aspect of the matter before, but now that it occurred to him, he was probably right.

"Oh, I don't mind, really." He waved away the other's sudden commiseration. "You know I like being alone most of the time, so I won't find that uncomfortable. Students are students, whether they're Terrestrials or Saturnians. I suppose they'll laugh at me behind my back, but then even here, my students always did that."

He gave a hollow laugh and unobtrusively put out one of his hands for a nut. "At least on Earth I'll know why they're laughing."

There was pain on Slood's expressive face as he firmly removed the nut tray from his friend's reach. "I didn't think of it from that angle, Narli. Of course you're right. Human beings, from what I've read of them, are not noted for tolerance. It will be difficult, but I'm sure you'll be able to—" he choked on the kindly lie—"win them over."

Narli repressed a bitter laugh. Anyone less likely than he to win over a hostile alien species through sheer personal charm could hardly be found on Saturn. Narli Gzann had been chosen as first exchange professor between Saturn and Earth because of his academic reputation, not his personality. But although the choosers had probably not had that aspect of the matter in mind, the choice, he thought, was a wise one.

As an individual of solitary habits, he was not apt to be much lonelier on one planet than another.

And he had accepted the post largely because he felt that, as an alien being, he would be left strictly alone. This would give him the chance to put in a lot of work on his definitive history of the Solar System, a monumental project from which he begrudged all the time he had to spend in fulfilling even the minimum obligations expected of a professor on sociable Saturn.

The salary was a weighty factor, too—not only was it more than twice what he had been getting, but since there would be no necessity for spending more than enough for bare subsistence he would be able to save up a considerable amount and retire while still comparatively young. It was pleasant to imagine a scholarly life unafflicted by students.

He could put up with a good deal for that goal.

But how could he alleviate the distress he saw on Karn's face? He did not consciously want to hurt the only person who, for some strange reason, seemed to be fond of him, so he said the only thing he could think of to please: "All right, Karn, I'll go to the Perzils tomorrow night."

It would be a deadly bore—parties always were—and he would eat too much, but, after all, the thought that it would be a long time before he'd ever see any of his own kind again would make the affair almost endurable. And just this once it would be all right for him to eat as much as he wanted. When he was on Earth out of reach of decent food, he would probably trim down considerably.

*   *   *   *   *

"I just *know* you're going to love Earth, Professor Gzann," the hostess on the interplanetary liner gushed.

"I'm sure I shall," he lied politely. She smiled at him too much, over-doing her professional cordiality; underneath the effusiveness, he sensed the repulsion. Of course he couldn't blame her for trying not to show her distaste for the strange creature—the effort at concealment was, as a matter of fact, more than he had expected from a Terrestrial. But he wished she would leave him alone to meditate. He had planned to get a lot of meditation done on the journey.

"You speak awfully good English," she told him.

He looked at her. "I am said to have some scholarly aptitude. I understand that's why I was chosen as an exchange professor. It does seem reasonable, doesn't it?"

She turned pink–a sign of embarrassment with these creatures, he had learned. "I didn't mean to–to question your ability, Professor. It's just that–well, you don't look like a professor."

"Indeed?" he said frostily. "And what do I look like, then?"

She turned even rosier. "Oh–I–I don't know exactly. It's just that–well...." And she fled.

He couldn't resist flicking his antennae forward to catch her *sotto voce* conversation with the co-pilot; it was so seldom you got the chance to learn what others were saying about you behind your back. "But I could hardly tell him he looks like a teddy bear, could I?"

"He probably doesn't even know what a teddy bear is."

"Perhaps I don't," Narli thought resentfully, "but I can guess."

With low cunning, the Terrestrials seemed to have ferreted out the identity of all his favorite dishes and kept serving them to him incessantly. By the time the ship made planetfall on Earth, he had gained ten grisbuts.

"Oh, well," he thought, "I suppose it's all just part of the regular diplomatic service. On Earth, I'll have to eat crude native foods, so I'll lose all the weight again."

President Purrington of North America came himself to meet Narli at the airfield because Narli was the first interplanetary exchange professor in history.

"Welcome to our planet, Professor Gzann," he said with warm diplomatic cordiality, wringing Narli's upper right hand after a moment of indecision. "We shall do everything in our power to make your stay here a happy and memorable one."

"I wish you would begin by doing something about the climate," Narli thought. It was stupid of him not to have realized how hot it would be on Earth. He was really going to suffer in this torrid climate; especially in the tight Terrestrial costume he wore over his fur for the sake of conformity. Of course, justice compelled him to admit to himself, the clothes wouldn't have become so snug if he hadn't eaten quite so much on board ship.

Purrington indicated the female beside him. "May I introduce my wife?"

"Ohhh," the female gasped, "isn't he *cute!*"

The President and Narli stared at her in consternation. She looked abashed for a moment, then smiled widely at Narli and the press photographers.

"Welcome to Earth, dear Professor Gzann!" she exclaimed, mispronouncing his name, of course. Bending down, she kissed him right upon his fuzzy forehead.

Kissing was not a Saturnian practice, nor did Narli approve of it; however, he had read enough about Earth to know that Europeans sometimes greeted dignitaries in this peculiar way. Only this place, he had been given to understand, was not Europe but America.

"I am having a cocktail party in your honor this afternoon!" she beamed, smoothing her flowered print dress down over her girdle. "You'll be there at five sharp, won't you, dear?"

"Delighted," he promised dismally. He could hardly plead a previous engagement a moment after arriving.

"I've tried to get all the things you like to eat," she went on anxiously, "but you will tell me if there's anything special, won't you?"

"I am on a diet," he said. He must be strong. Probably the food would be repulsive anyhow, so he'd have no difficulty controlling his appetite. "Digestive disorders, you know. A glass of Vichy and a biscuit will be...."

He stopped, for there were tears in Mrs. Purrington's eyes. "Your tummy hurts? Oh, you poor little darling!"

"Gladys!" the President said sharply.

There were frismil nuts at Mrs. Purrington's cocktail party and vilbar and even slipnis broogs ... all imported at fabulous expense, Narli knew, but then this was a government affair and expense means nothing to a government since, as far as it is concerned, money grows on taxpayers. Some of the native foods proved surprisingly palatable, too—pate de foie gras and champagne and little puff pastries full of delightful surprises. Narli was afraid he was making a zloogle of himself. However, he thought, trying not to catch sight of his own portly person in the mirrors that walled the room, the lean days were just ahead.

Besides, what could he do when everyone insisted on pressing food on him? "Try this, Professor Gzann." "Do try that, Professor Gzann." ("Doesn't he look cunning in his little dress suit?") They crowded around him. The women cooed, the men beamed, and Narli ate. He would be glad when he could detach himself from all this cloying diplomacy and get back to the healthy rancor of the classroom.

*   *   *   *   *

At school, the odor of chalk dust, ink and rotting apple cores was enough like its Saturnian equivalent to make Narli feel at home immediately. The students would dislike him on sight, he knew. It is in the nature of the young to be hostile toward whatever is strange and alien. They would despise him and jeer at him, and he, in his turn, would give them long, involved homework assignments and such difficult examinations that they would fail....

Narli waddled briskly up to his desk which had, he saw, been scaled down to Saturnian size, whereas he had envisioned himself struggling triumphantly with ordinary Earth-sized, furniture. But the atmosphere was as hot and sticky and intolerable as he had expected. Panting as unobtrusively as possible, he rapped with his pointer. "Attention, students!"

Now should come the derisive babble ... but there was a respectful silence, broken suddenly by a shrill feminine whisper of, "Oooo, he's so adorable!" followed by the harsh, "Shhh, Ava! You'll embarrass the poor little thing."

Narli's face swelled. "I am your new professor of Saturnian Studies. Saturn, as you probably know, is a major planet. It is much larger and more important than Earth, which is only a minor planet."

The students obediently took this down in their notebooks. They carefully took down everything he said. Even a bout of coughing that afflicted him half-way through seemed to be getting a phonetic transcription. From time to time, they would interrupt his lecture with questions so pertinent, so well-thought out and so courteous that all he could do was answer them.

His antennae lifted to catch the whispers that from time to time were exchanged between even the best-behaved of the students. "Isn't he precious?" "Seems like a nice fellow—sound grasp of his subject." "Sweet little thing!" "Unusually interesting presentation." "Doesn't he remind you of Winnie the Pooh?" "Able chap." "Just darling!"

After class, instead of rushing out of the room, they hovered around his desk with intelligent, solicitous questions. Did he like Earth? Was his desk too high? Too low? Didn't he find it hot with all that fur? Such lovely, soft, fluffy fur, though. "Do you mind if I stroke one of your paws–*hands*–Professor?" ("So cuddly-looking!")

He said yes, as a matter of fact, he was hot, and no, he didn't mind being touched in a spirit of scientific investigation.

He had a moment of uplift at the teachers' cafeteria when he discovered lunch to be virtually inedible. The manager, however, had been distressed to see him pick at his food, and by dinner-time a distinguished chef with an expert knowledge of Saturnian cuisine had been rushed from Washington. Since the school food was inedible for all intelligent life-forms, everyone ate the Saturnian dishes and praised Narli as a public benefactor.

*   *   *   *   *

That night, alone in the quiet confines of his small room at the Men's Faculty Club, Narli had spread out his notes and was about to start work on his history when there was a knock at the door. He trotted over to open it, grumbling to himself.

The head of his department smiled brightly down at him. "Some of us are going out for a couple of drinks and a gabfest. Care to come along?"

Narli did not see how he could refuse and still carry the Saturnian's burden, so he accepted. Discovering that gin fizzes and Alexanders were even more palatable than champagne and more potent than vilbar, he told several Saturnine locker-room stories which were hailed with loud merriment. But he was being laughed *at*, not *with*, he knew. All this false cordiality, he assured himself, would die down after a couple of days, and then he would be able to get back to work. He must curb his intellectual impatience.

In the morning, he found that enrollment in his classes had doubled, and the room was crowded to capacity with the bright, shining, eager faces of young Terrestrials athirst for learning. There were apples, chocolates and imported frismil nuts on his desk, as well as a pressing invitation from Mrs. Purrington for him to spend all his weekends and holidays at the White House. The window was fitted with an air-conditioning unit which, he later discovered, his classes had chipped in to buy for him, and the temperature had been lowered to a point where it was almost comfortable. All the students wore coats.

When he went out on the campus, women—students, teachers, even strangers—stopped to talk to him, to exclaim over him, to touch him, even to kiss him. Photographers were perpetually taking pictures, some of which turned up in the Student Union as full-color postcards. They sold like Lajl out of season.

Narli wrote in Saturnian on the back of one: "Having miserable time; be glad you're not here," and sent it to Slood.

There were cocktail parties, musicales and balls in Narli's honor. When he tried to refuse an invitation, he was accused of shyness and virtually dragged to the affair by laughing members of the faculty. He put on so much weight that he had to buy a complete new Terrestrial outfit, which set him back a pretty penny. As a result, he had to augment his income by lecturing to women's clubs. They slobbered appallingly.

*   *   *   *   *

Narli's students did all their homework assiduously and, in fact, put in more work than had been assigned. At the end of the year, not only did all of them pass, but with flying colors.

"I hope you'll remember, Professor Gzann," the President of the University said, "that there will always be a job waiting for you here—a non-exchange professorship. Love to have you."

"Thank you," Narli replied politely.

Mrs. Purrington broke into loud sobs when he told her he was leaving Earth. "Oh, I'll miss you so, Narli! You will write, won't you?"

"Yes, of course," he said grimly. That made two hundred and eighteen people to whom he'd had to promise to write.

It was fortunate he was traveling as a guest of the North American government, he thought as he supervised the loading of his matched interplanetary luggage; his eight steamer baskets; his leather-bound *Encyclopedia Terrestria*, with his name imprinted in gold on each volume; his Indian war-bonnet; his oil painting of the President; and his six cases of champagne—all parting gifts—onto the liner. Otherwise the fee for excess luggage would take what little remained of his bank account. There had been so many expenses—clothes and hostess gifts and ice.

Not all his mementoes were in his luggage. A new rare-metal watch gleamed on each of his four furry wrists; a brand-new trobskin wallet, platinum key-chain, and uranium fountain pen were in his pocket; and a diamond and curium bauble clasped a tie lovingly handpainted by a female student. The argyles on his fuzzy ankles had been knitted by another. Still another devoted pupil had presented him with a hand-woven plastic case full of frismil nuts to eat on the way back.

*   *   *   *   *

"Well, Narli!" Slood said, his face swelling with joy. "Well, well! You've put on weight, I see."

Narli dropped into his old chair with a sigh. Surely Slood might have picked something else to comment on first—his haggardness, for instance, or the increased spirituality of his expression.

"Nothing else to do on Earth in your leisure moments but eat, I suppose," Slood said, pushing over the nut tray. "Even their food. Have some frismils."

"No, thank you," Narli replied coldly.

Slood looked at him in distress. "Oh, how you must have suffered! Was it very, very bad, Narli?"

Narli hunched low in his chair. "It was just awful."

"I'm sure they didn't mean to be unkind," Slood assured him. "Naturally, you were a strange creature to them and they're only—"

"*Unkind?*" Narli gave a bitter laugh. "They practically killed me with kindness! It was fuss, fuss, fuss all the time."

"Now, Narli, I do wish you wouldn't be quite so sarcastic."

"I'm *not* being sarcastic. And I wasn't a strange creature to them. It seems there's a sort of popular child's toy on Earth known as a—" he winced—"teddy bear. I aroused pleasant childhood memories in them, so they showered me with affection and edibles."

Slood closed his eyes in anguish. "You are very brave, Narli," he said almost reverently. "Very brave and wise and good. Certainly that would be the best thing to tell our people. After all, the Terrestrials are our allies; we don't want to stir up public sentiment against them. But you can be honest with *me*, Narli. Did they refuse to serve you in restaurants? Were you segregated in public vehicles? Did they shrink from you when you came close?"

Narli beat the desk with all four hands. "I was hardly ever given the chance to be alone! They crawled all over me! Restaurants begged for my trade! I had to hire private vehicles because in public ones I was mobbed by admirers!"

"Such a short time," Slood murmured, "and already suspicious of even me, your oldest friend. But don't talk about it if you don't want to, Narli.... Tell me, though, did they sneer at you and whisper half-audible insults? Did they—"

"You're right!" Narli snapped. "I *don't* want to talk about it."

Slood placed a comforting hand upon his shoulder. "Perhaps that's wisest, until the shock of your experience has worn off."

Narli made an irritable noise.

"The Perzils are giving a vilbar party tonight," Slood said. "But I know how you feel about parties. I've told them you're exhausted from your trip and won't be able to make it."

"Oh, you did, did you?" Narli asked ironically. "What makes you think you know how I feel about parties?"

"But—"

"There's an interesting saying on Earth: 'Travel is so broadening.'" He looked down at his bulges with tolerant amusement. "In more than one way, in case the meaning eludes you. Very sound psychologically. I've discovered that I *like* parties. I *like* being *liked*. If you'll excuse me, I'm going to inform the Perzils that I shall be delighted to come to their party. Care to join me?"

"Well," Slood mumbled, "I'd like to, but I have so much work—"

"Introvert!" said Narli, and he began dialing the Perzils.

By EVELYN E. SMITH

HELPFULLY YOURS

ORIGINALLY PUBLISHED IN *GALAXY SCIENCE FICTION*
FEBRUARY 1955

ILLUSTRATED BY ILLUSTRATED BY ED EMSHWILLER

*Come down to Earth—and stay there!" is a
humiliating order for somebody with wings!*

Helpfully Yours

Tarb Morfatch had read all the information on
Terrestrial customs that was available in the *Times*
morgue before she'd left Fizbus. And all through the
journey she'd studied her *Brief Introduction to Terrestrial
Manners and Mores* avidly. Perhaps it was a bit
overinspirational in spots, but it had facts in it, too.

So she knew that, since the natives were non-alate,
she was not to take wing on Earth. She had, however,
forgotten to correlate the knowledge of their winglessness
with her own vertical habits. As a result, on leaving the
tender that had ferried her down from the Moon, she
looked up instead of right and narrowly escaped death at
the jaws of a raging groundcar that swerved out onto the
field.

She recognized it as a taxi from one of the pictures in
the handbook. It was a pity, she thought sadly as she was
knocked off her feet, that all those lessons she had so
carefully learned were to go to waste.

But it was only the wind of the car's passage that had
thrown her down. As she struggled to get up, hampered
by her awkward native skirts, the door of the taxi flew
open. A tall young man—a Fizbian—burst out, the soft
yellowish-green down on his handsome face bristling with
fright until each feather stood out separately.

"Miss Morfatch! Are you all right?"

"Just—just a little shaky," she murmured, brushing
dirt from her rosy leg feathers. *Too young to be Drosmig;
too good-looking to be anyone important, she thought
glumly. Must be the office boy.*

To her surprise, he didn't help her up. Probably it would violate some native taboo if he did, she deduced. The handbook hadn't mentioned anything that seemed to apply, but, after all, a little book like that couldn't cover everything.

*   *   *   *   *

She could see the young man was embarrassed–his emerald crest was waving to and fro.

"I'm Stet Zarnon," he introduced himself awkwardly.

The Managing Editor! The handsome young employer of her girlish dreams! But perhaps he had a wife on Fizbus–no, the Grand Editor made a point of hiring people without families to use as a pretext for expensive vacations on the Home Planet.

As she opened her mouth to say something brilliantly witty, to show she was no ordinary female but a creature of spirit and fire and intelligence, a sudden cacophony of shrill cries and explosions arose, accompanied by bursts of light. Her feathers stood erect and she clung to her employer with both feathered legs.

"If these are the friendly diplomatic relations Earth and Fizbus are supposed to be enjoying," she said, "I'm not enjoying them one bit!"

"They're only taking pictures of you with native equipment," he explained, pulling away from her. What was the matter with him? "You're the first Fizbian woman ever to come to Terra, you know."

She certainly did know–and, what was more, she had made the semi-finals for Miss Fizbus only the year before. Perhaps he had some Terrestrial malady he didn't want her to catch. Or could it be that in the four years he had spent in voluntary exile on this planet, he had come to prefer the native females? Now it was her turn to shrink from him.

He was conversing rapidly in Terran with the chattering natives who milled about them. Although Tarb had been an honors student in Terran back at school, she found herself unable to understand more than an occasional word of what they said. Then she remembered that they were not at the world capital, Ottawa, but another community, New York. Undoubtedly they were all speaking some provincial dialect peculiar to the locality.

And nobody at all booed in appreciation, although, she told herself sternly, she really couldn't have expected them to. Standards of beauty were different in different solar systems. At least they were picking up as souvenirs some of the feathers she'd shed in her tumble, which showed they took an interest.

Stet turned back to her. "These are fellow-members of the press."

She was able to catch enough of what he said next in Terran to understand that she was being formally introduced to the aboriginal journalists. Although you could never call the natives attractive, with their squat figures and curiously atrophied vestigial wings–*arms*, she reminded herself–they were very Fizboid in appearance and, with their winglessness cloaked, could have creditably passed for singed Fizbians.

Moreover, they seemed friendly; at any rate, the sounds they uttered were welcoming. She began to make the three ritual *entrechats*, but Stat stopped her. "Just smile at them; that'll be enough."

It didn't seem like enough, but he was the boss.

*   *   *   *   *

"Thank the stars we're through with that," he sighed, as they finally were able to escape their confreres and get into the taxi. "I suppose," he added, wriggling inside the clumsy Terrestrial jacket which, cut to fit over his wings, did nothing either to improve his figure or to make him look like a native, "it was as much of an ordeal for you as for me."

"Well, I am a little bewildered by it all," Tarb admitted, settling herself as comfortably as possible on the seat cushions.

"No, don't do that!" he cried. "Here people don't crouch on seats. They sit," he explained in a kindlier tone. "Like this."

"You mean I have to bend myself in that clumsy way?"

He nodded. "In public, at least."

"But it's so hard on the wings. I'm losing feathers foot over claw."

"Yes, but you could...." He stopped. "Well, anyhow, remember we have to comply with local customs. You see, the Terrestrials have those things called arms instead of legs. That is, they have legs, but they use them only for walking."

She sighed. "I'd read about the arms, but I had no idea the natives would be so–so primitive as to actually use them."

"Considering they had no wings, it was very clever of them to make use of the vestigial appendages," he said hotly. "If you take their physical limitations into account, they've done a marvelous job with their little planet. They can't fly; they have very little sense of balance; their vision is exceedingly poor–yet, in spite of all that, they have achieved a quite remarkable degree of civilization." He gestured toward the horizontal building arrangements visible through the window. "Why, you could almost call those streets. As a matter of fact, the natives do."

At the moment, she could take an interest in Terrestrial civilization only as it affected her personally. "But I'll be able to relax in the office, won't I?"

"To a certain extent," he replied cautiously. "You see, we have to use a good deal of native help because–well, our facilities are limited...."

"Oh," she said.

Then she remembered that she was on Terra at least partly to demonstrate the pluck of Fizbian femininity. Back on Fizbus, most of the *Times* executives had been dead set against having a woman sent out as Drosmig's assistant. But Grupe, the Grand Editor, had overruled them. "Time we broke with tradition," he had said. He'd felt she could do the job, and, by the stars, she would justify his faith in her!

"Sounds like rather a lark," she said hollowly.

Stet brightened. "That's the girl!" His eyes, she noticed, were emerald shading into turquoise, like his crest. "I certainly hope you'll like it here. Very wise of Grupe to send a woman instead of a man, after all. Women," he went on quickly, "are so much better at working up the human interest angle. And Drosmig is out of commission most of the time, so it's you who'll actually be in charge of 'Helpfully Yours.'"

She herself in charge of the column that had achieved interstellar fame in three short years! Basically, it had been designed to give guidance, advice and, if necessary, comfort to those Fizbians who found themselves living on Terra, for the Fizbus *Times* had stood for public service from time immemorial. As Grupe had put it, "We don't run this paper for ourselves, Tarb, but for our readers. And the same applies to our Terrestrial edition."

With the growing development of trade and cultural relations between the two planets, the Fizbians on Earth were an ever-increasing number. But they were not the only readers of "Helpfully Yours." Reprinted in the parent paper, it was read with edification and pleasure all over Fizbus. Everyone wanted to learn more about the ancient and other-worldly Terran culture.

The handbook, *A Brief Introduction to Terrestrial Manners and Mores*, owed much of its content to "Helpfully Yours." A grateful, almost fulsome, introductory note had said so. But the column truly deserved all the praise that had been lavished upon it by the handbook. How well she had studied the thoughtful letters that filled it and the excellent and well-reasoned advice–erring, if it erred at all, on the side of overtolerance–that had been given in return. Of course, on Earth, spiritual adjustment apparently was more important than the physical; you could tell that from the questions that were asked. A number of the letters had been reprinted in an appendix to the manual.

New York

Dear Senbot Drosmig:

When in contact with Terrestrial culture, I find myself constantly overawed and weighed down by the knowledge of my own inadequacy. I cannot seem to appreciate the local art forms as disseminated by the juke box, the comic strip, the tabloid.

How can I help myself toward a greater understanding?

Hopefully yours,
Gnurmis Plitt

*   *   *   *   *

Dear Mr. Plitt:

Remember, Orkv was not excavated in a week. It took the Terrestrials many centuries to develop their exquisite and esoteric art forms. How can you expect to comprehend them in a few short years? Expose yourself to their art. Work, study, meditate.

Understanding will come, I promise you.

Helpfully yours,
Senbot Drosmig

*   *   *   *   *

Paris

Dear Senbot Drosmig:

To think that I am enjoying the benefits of Terra while my wife and little ones are forced to remain on Fizbus makes my heart ache. Surely it is not fair that I should have so much and they so little. Imagine the inestimable advantage to the fledgling of even a short contact with Terrestrial culture!

Why cannot my loved ones come to join me so that we can share all these wonderful spiritual experiences and be enriched by them together?

Poignantly yours,
Tpooly N'Ox

*   *   *   *   *

Dear Mr. N'Ox:.

After all, it has been only five years since Fizbian spaceships first came into contact with Terra. In keeping with our usual colonial policy—so inappropriate and anachronistic when applied to a well-developed civilization like Terra's—at first only males are allowed to go to the new world until it is made certain over a period of years that the planet is safe for mothers and future mothers of Fizbus.

But Stet Zarnon himself, the celebrated and capable editor of the Terran edition of *The Fizbus Times*, has taken up your cause, and I promise you that eventually your loved ones will be able to join you.

Meanwhile, work, study, meditate.

Helpfully yours,
Senbot Drosmig

*   *   *   *   *

Ottawa

Dear Senbot Drosmig:

Having just completed a two-year tour of duty on Earth as part of a diplomatic mission, I am regretfully leaving this fair planet. What books, what objects of art, what, in short, souvenirs shall I take back to Fizbus which will give our people some small idea of Earth's rich cultural heritage and, at the same time, serve as useful and appropriate gifts for my friends and relatives back Home?

Inquiringly yours,
Solgus Zagroot

*   *   *   *   *

Dear Mr. Zagroot:

Take back nothing but your memories. They will be your best souvenirs.

Out of context, any other mementos might convey little, if anything, of the true beauty and advanced spirituality of Terrestrial culture, and you might cheapen them were you to use them crassly as souvenirs. Furthermore, it is possible that you, in your ignorance, might unwittingly select some items that give a distorted and false idea of our extrafizbian friends.

The Fizbian-Earth Cultural Commission, sponsored by *The Fizbian Times*, in conjunction with the consulate, is preparing a vast program of cultural interchange. Leave it to them to do the great work, for you can be sure they will do it well.

And be sure to tell your fellow-laborers in the diplomatic vineyards that it is wiser not to send unapproved Terran souvenirs back Home. They might cause a fatal misunderstanding between the two worlds. Tell them to spend their time on Earth in working, studying and meditating, rather than shopping.

Helpfully yours,
Senbot Drosmig

*   *   *   *   *

And now she–Tarb Morfatch–herself was going to be the guiding spirit that brought enlightenment and uplift to countless thousands on Terra and millions on Fizbus. Her name wouldn't appear on the columns, but the reward of having helped should be enough. Besides, Drosmig was due to retire soon. If she proved herself competent, she would take over the column entirely and get the byline. Grupe had promised faithfully.

But what, she wondered, had put Drosmig "out of commission"?

The taxi drew up before a building with a vulgar number of floors showing above ground.

"Ah—before we—er—meet the others," Stet suggested, twitching his crest, "I was wondering whether you would care to—er—have dinner with me tonight?"

This roused Tarb from her speculations. "Oh, I'd love to!" *A date with the boss right away!*

Stet fumbled in his garments for appropriate tokens with which to pay the driver. "You—you're not engaged or anything back Home, Miss Morfatch?"

"Why, no," she said. "It so happens that I'm not."

"Splendid!" He made an abortive gesture with his leg, then let her get out of the taxi by herself. "It makes the natives stare," he explained abashedly.

"But why shouldn't they?" she asked, wondering whether to laugh or not. "How could they help but stare? We are different." *He must be joking.* She ventured a smile.

He smiled back, but made no reply.

The pavement was hard under her thinly covered soles. Now that walking looked as if it would present a problem, the ban on wing use loomed more threateningly. She had, of course, walked before—on wet days when her wings were waterlogged or in high winds or when she had surface business. However, the sidewalks on Fizbus were soft and resilient. Now she understood why the Terrestrials wore such crippling foot armor, but that didn't make her feel any better about it.

A box-shaped machine took the two Fizbians up to the twentieth story in twice the time it would have taken them to fly the same distance. Tarb supposed that the offices were in an attic instead of a basement because exchange difficulties forced the *Times* to such economy. She wondered ruefully whether her own expense account would also suffer.

But it was no time to worry about such sordid matters; most important right now was making a favorable impression on her co-workers. She did want them to like her.

Taking out her compact, she carefully polished her eyeballs. The man at the controls of the machine practically performed a ritual *entrechat.*

"Don't do that!" Stet ordered in a harsh whisper.

"But why not?" she asked, unable to restrain a trace of belligerence from her voice. He hadn't been very polite himself. "The handbook said respectable Terran women make up in public. Why shouldn't I?"

He sighed. "It'll take time for you to catch on, I suppose. There's a lot the handbook doesn't–can't–cover. You'll find the setup here rather different from on Fizbus," he went on as he kicked open the door neatly lettered *THE FIZBUS TIMES* in both Fizbian and Terran. "We've found it expedient to follow the local newspaper practice. For instance–" he indicated a small green-feathered man seated at a desk just beyond the railing that bisected the room horizontally–"we have a Copy Editor."

"What does he do?" she asked, confused.

"He copies news from the other papers, of course."

"And what are *you* doing tonight, Miss Morfatch?" the Copy Editor asked, springing up from his desk to execute the three ritual entrechats with somewhat more verve than was absolutely necessary.

"Having dinner with me," Stet said quickly.

"Pulling rank, eh, old bird? Well, we'll see whether position or sterling worth will win out in the end."

As the rest of the staff crowded around Tarb, leaping and booing as appreciatively as any girl could want, she managed to snatch a rapid look around. The place wasn't really so very much different from a Fizbian newsroom, once she got over the oddity of going across, not up and down, with the desks–queerly shaped but undeniably desks–arranged side by side instead of one over the other. There were chairs and stools, no perches, but that was to be expected in a wingless society. And it was noisy. Even though the little machines had stopped clattering when she came in, a distant roaring continued, as if, concealed somewhere close by, larger, more sinister machines continued their work. A peculiar smell hung in the air– not unpleasant, exactly, but strange.

She sniffed inquiringly.

"Ink," Stet said.

"What's that?"

"Oh, some stuff the boys in the back shop use. The feature writers," he went on quickly, before she could ask what the "back shop" was, "have private offices where they can perch in comfort."

He led the way down a corridor, opening doors. "Our drama editor." He indicated a middle-aged man with faded blue feathers, who hung head downward from his perch. "On the lobster-trick last night writing a review, so he's catching fifty-one twinkles now."

"Enchanted, Miss Morfatch," the critic said, opening one bright eye. "By a curious chance, it so happens that tonight I have two tickets to–"

"Tonight she's going out with me."

"Well, I can get tickets to any play, any night. And you haven't laughed unless you've seen a Terrestrial drama. Just say the word, chick."

Stet got Tarb out of the office and slammed the door shut. "Over here is the office of our food editor," he said, breathing hard, "whom you'll be expected to give a claw to now and then, since your jobs overlap. Can't introduce you to him right now, though, because he's in the hospital with ptomaine poisoning. And this is the office you'll share with Drosmig."

Stet opened the door.

Underneath the perch, Senbot Drosmig, dean of Fizbian journalists, lay on the rug in a sodden stupor, letters to the editor scattered thickly over his shriveled person. The whole room reeked unmistakably of caffeine.

Tarb shrank back and twined both feet around Stet's. This time he did not repulse her. "But how can a–an educated, cultured man like Senbot Drosmig sink to such depths?"

"It's hard for anyone with even the slightest inclination toward the stuff to resist it here," Stet replied somberly. "I can't deny it; the sale of caffeine is absolutely unrestricted on Earth. Coffee shops all over the place. Coffee served freely at even the best homes. And not only coffee ... caffeine is insiduously present in other of their popular beverages."

Her eyes bulged sideways. "But how can a so-called civilized people be so depraved?"

"Caffeine doesn't seem to affect them the way it does us. Their nervous systems are so very uncomplicated, one almost envies them."

Drosmig stirred restlessly under his blanket of correspondence. "Go back ... Fizbus," he muttered. "Warn you ... 'fore ... too late ... like me."

Tarb's rose-pink feathers stood on end. She looked apprehensively at Stet.

"Senbot can't go back because he's in no shape to take the interstel drive." The young editor was obviously annoyed. "He's old and he's a physical wreck. But that certainly doesn't apply to you, Miss Morfatch." He looked long and hard into her eyes.

"Few years on planet," Drosmig groaned, struggling to his wings, "'ply to anybody."

His feathers, Tarb noticed, were an ugly, darkish brown. She had never seen any one that color before, but she'd heard rumors that too much caffeine could do that to you. At least she hoped it was only the caffeine.

"For your information, he was almost as bad as this when he came!" Stet snapped. "Frankly, that's why he was sent here—to get rid of his unfortunate addiction. Grupe had no idea, when he assigned him to Earth, that there was caffeine on the planet."

The old man gave a sardonic laugh as he clumsily made his way to the perch and gripped it with quivering toes.

"That is, I don't *think* he knew," Stet said dubiously.

Tarb reached over and picked a letter off the floor. The Fizbian characters were clumsy and ill-made, as if someone had formed them with his feet. Could there be such poverty here that individuals existed who could not afford a scripto? The letter didn't read like any that had ever been printed in the column—at least none that had been picked up in the Fizbus edition:

*   *   *   *   *

New York

Dear Senbot Drosmig:

I am a subaltern clerk in the shipping department of the FizbEarth Trading Company, Inc. Although I have held this post for only three months, I have already won the respect and esteem of my superiors through my diligence and good character. My habits are exemplary: I do not gamble, sing, or take caffeine.

Earlier today, while engaged in evening meditation at my modest apartments, I was aroused by a peremptory knock at the door. I flung it open. A native stood there with a small case in his hand.

"Is the house on fire?" I asked, wondering which of my few humble possessions I should rescue first.

"No," he said. "I would like to interest you in some brushes."

"Are the offices of the FizbEarth Trading Company, Inc., on fire?"

"Not to my knowledge," he replied, opening his case. "Now I have here a very nice hairbrush—"

I wanted to give him every chance. "Have you come to tell me of any disaster relative to the FizbEarth Trading Company, to myself, or to anyone or anything else with whom or with which I am connected?"

"Why, no," he said. "I have come to sell you brushes. Now here is a little number I know you'll like. My company developed it with you folks specially in mind. It's—"

"Do you know, sir, that you have wantonly interrupted me in the midst of my meditations, which constitutes an established act of privacy violation?"

"Is that a fact? Now this little item is particularly designed for brushing the wings—"

At that point, I knocked him down and punched him into insensibility with my feet. Then I summoned the police. To my surprise, they arrested me instead of him.

I am writing this letter from jail. I do not like to ask my employers to get me out because, even though I am innocent, you know how a thing like this can leave a smudge on the record.

What shall I do?

Anxiously yours,
Fruzmus Bloxx

*   *   *   *   *

"What should he do?" Tarb asked, handing Stet the paper. "Or is the question academic by now? The letter's five days old."

Stet sighed. "I'll find out whether the consulate has been notified. Native police usually do that, you know. Very thoughtful fellows. If this Bloxx hasn't been bailed out already, I'll see that he is."

"But how will we answer his letter? Advise him to sue for false arrest?"

Stet smiled. "But he has no grounds for false arrest. He is guilty of assault. The native was entirely within his rights in trying to sell him a brush. Now–" he put out a foot–"brace yourself. Privacy violation is not a crime on Terra. It is perfectly legal. In fact, it does not exist as such!"

At that point, everything went maroon.

When Tarb came to, she found herself lying upon Drosmig's desk. A skin-faced native woman was offering her water and clucking.

"Are you all right, Tarb–Miss Morfatch?" Stet demanded anxiously.

"Yes. I–I think so," she murmured, raising herself to a crouch.

"Better ... have died," Drosmig groaned from his perch. "Fate worse ... death ... awaits you."

Tarb tried to smile. "Sorry to have been so much trouble." She stuck out her tongue at both Stet and the native.

The woman drew in her breath.

"Miss Morfatch," Stet reminded Tarb, "sticking out the tongue is not an apology on Terra; it is an insult. Fortunately, Miss Snow happens to be perhaps the only Terran who would not be offended. She has become thoroughly acquainted with us and our odd little customs. She even–" he beamed at the Terran female–"has learned to speak our language."

"Hail to thee, O visitor from the stars," Miss Snow said in Fizbian. "May thy sojourn upon Earth be an incessant delight and may peace and plenty shower their gifts in abundance upon thee."

Tarb put her hand to her aching head. "I'm very glad to meet you," she said, glad she did not have to get up to make the ritual *entrechats*.

"Miss Snow is my right foot," Stet said, "but I'm going to be noble and let her act as your secretary until you can learn to operate a typewriter."

"Secretary? Typewriter?"

"Well, you see, there are no scriptos or superscriptos on Earth and we can't import any from Home because the natives–" Miss Snow smiled–"don't have the right kind of power here to run psychic installations. All prosifying has to be done directly on prosifying machines or–" he paused–"by foot."

"Catch her!" Miss Snow exclaimed in Terran.

Everything had gone maroon for Tarb again. As she fell, she could hear a sudden thump. It was, she later discovered, Drosmig falling off his perch again–the result of insecure grip, she was given to understand, rather than excessive empathy.

*　　*　　*　　*　　*

"I didn't mean, of course, to give you the impression that we actually produce the individual copies of the papers ourselves," Stet explained over the dinner table that night. "We have native printers who do that. They've turned out some really remarkable Fizbian type fonts."

"Very clever of them," Tarb said, knowing that was what she was expected to say. She glanced around the restaurant. In their low-cut evening garments, the Terrestrial females looked much less Fizboid than they had during the day. All that naked-looking skin; one would think they'd want to cover it. Probably they were sick with jealousy of her beautiful rose-colored down–what they could see of it, anyway.

"Of course, our real problem is getting proofreaders. The proofing machines won't operate here either, of course, and so we need human personnel. But what Fizbian would do such degrading work? We had thought of convict labor, but–"

"Why mustn't I take off my wrap?" Tarb interrupted. "No one else is wearing one."

Stet coughed. "You'll feel much less self-conscious about your wings if you keep it on. And try not to use your feet so conspicuously. I'm sure everyone understands you need them to eat with, but–"

"But I'm not in the least self-conscious about my wings. On Fizbus, they were considered rather nice-looking, if I do say so myself."

"It's better," he said firmly, "not to emphasize the differences between the natives and ourselves. You didn't object to wearing a Terrestrial costume, did you?"

"No, I realize I must make some concessions to native prudery, but–"

"Matter of fact, I've been thinking it would be a good idea for you to wear a stole or a cape or something in the daytime when you go to and from the office. You wouldn't want to make yourself or the *Times* conspicuous, I'm sure.... No, waiter, no coffee. We'll take champagne."

"I want to try coffee," Tarb said mutinously. "Champagne! You'd think I was a fledgling, giving me that bubbly stuff!"

He looked at her. "Now don't be silly, Miss Morfatch ... Tarb. I can't let you indulge in such rash experiments. You realize I am responsible for you."

Tarb muttered darkly into her *coupe maison.*

Stet raised his eyebrows. "What did you say?"

"I was only wondering whether you'd remembered to check on whether that young man–Bloxx–ever did get out of jail."

Stet snapped his toes. "Glad you reminded me. Completely slipped my mind. Let's go and see what happened to him, shall we?"

*　　*　　*　　*　　*

As they rose to leave, a dumpy Earthwoman rushed up to them, enthusiastically babbling in Terran. Seizing Tarb's foot, she clung to it before the Fizbian girl could do anything to prevent her. Tarb had to spread her wings wide to retain her balance. Her cloak flew off and an adjoining table of diners disappeared beneath it.

Stet and the headwaiter rushed to the rescue with profuse apologies, Stet's crest undulating as if it concealed a nest of snakes. But Tarb was too much frightened to be calmed.

"Is this a hostile attack?" she shrieked frantically at Stet. "Because the handbook never said shaking feet was an Earth custom!"

"No, no, she's a friend!" Stet yelled, leaving the diners still struggling with the cloak as he sped back to her. "And shaking feet isn't an Earth custom; she thinks it's a Fizbian one. You see.... Oh, hell, never mind—I'll explain the whole thing to you later. But she's just greeting you, trying to put you at your ease. It's Belinda Romney, a very important Terrestrial. She owns the Solar Press—you must have heard of it even on Fizbus–biggest news service on the planet. Absolutely wouldn't do to offend her. Mrs. Romney, may I present Miss Morfatch?"

The woman beamed and continued to gush endlessly.

"Tell her to let go my foot!" Tarb demanded. "It's getting so it feels carbonated."

He smiled deprecatingly. "Now, Tarb, we mustn't be rude–"

For the first time in her life, Tarb spoke Terran to a Terrestrial. She formed the words slowly and carefully: "Sorry we must leave, but we have to go to jail."

She looked to Stet for approval ... and didn't get it. He started to explain something quickly to the woman. Every time she'd heard him speak Terran, Tarb thought, he seemed to be introducing, explaining or apologizing.

It turned out that, through some oversight, the usually thoughtful Terran police department had neglected to inform the Fizbian consul that one of his people had been incarcerated, for the young man had already been tried, found guilty of assault plus contempt of court, and sentenced to pay a large fine. However, after Stet had given his version of the circumstances to a sympathetic judge, the sum was reduced to a nominal one, which the *Times* paid.

"But I don't see why you should have paid anything at all," Bloxx protested ungratefully. "I didn't do anything wrong. You should have made an issue of it."

"According to Earth laws, you did do wrong," Stet said wearily, "and this is Earth. What's more, if we take the matter up, it will naturally get into print. You don't want your employers to hear about it, do you–even if you don't care about making Fizbians look ridiculous to Terrestrials?"

"I suppose I wouldn't like FizbEarth to find out," Bloxx conceded. "As it is, I'll have to do some fast explaining to account for my not having shown up for nearly a week. I'll say I caught some horrible Earth disease–that'll scare them so much, they'll probably beg me to take another week off. Though I do wish you fellows over at the *Times* would answer your mail sooner. I'm a regular subscriber, you know."

*   *   *   *   *

"But the same kind of thing's going to happen over and over again, isn't it, Stet?" Tarb asked as a taxi took them back to the hotel in which most of the *Times* staff was domiciled. "If privacy doesn't exist on Earth, it's bound to keep occurring."

"Eh?" Stet took his attention away from her toes with some difficulty. "Some Earth people like privacy, too, but they have to fight for it. Violations aren't legally punishable–that's the only difference."

"Then surely the Terrestrials would understand about us, wouldn't they?" she asked eagerly. "If they knew how strongly we felt about privacy, maybe they wouldn't violate it–not as much, anyway. I'm sure they're not vicious, just ignorant. And you can't just keep on getting Fizbians out of jail each time they run up against the problem. It would be too expensive, for one thing."

"Don't worry," he said, pressing her toes. "I'll take care of the whole thing."

"An article in the paper wouldn't really help much," she persisted thoughtfully, "and I suppose you must have run at least one already. It would explain to the Fizbians that Terrestrials don't regard invasion of privacy as a crime, but it wouldn't tell the Terrestrials that Fizbians do. We'll have to think of–"

"You're surely not going to tell me how to run my paper on your first day here, are you?"

He tried to take the sting out of his words by twining his toes around hers, but she felt guilty. She had been presumptuous. Probably there were lots of things she couldn't understand yet–like why she shouldn't polish her eyeballs in public. Stet had finally explained to her that, while Terrestrial women did make up in public, they didn't scour their irises, ever, and would be startled and horrified to see someone else doing so.

"But I was horrified to see them raking their feathers in public!" Tarb had contended.

"Combing their hair, my dear. And why not? This is their planet."

That was always his answer. *I wonder*, she speculated, *whether he would expect a Terrestrial visitor to Fizbus to fly ... because, after all, Fizbus is our planet.* But she didn't dare broach the question.

However, if it was presumptuous of her to make helpful suggestions the first day, it was more than presumptuous of Stet to ask her up to his rooms to see his collection of rare early twentieth-century Terrestrial milk bottles and other antiques. So she just told him courteously that she was tired and wanted to go to roost. And, since the hotel had a whole section fitted up to suit Fizbian requirements, she spent a more comfortable night than she had expected.

She awoke the next day full of enthusiasm and ready to start in on the great work at once. Although she might have been a little too forward the previous night, she knew, as she took a reassuring glance in the mirror, that Stet would forgive her.

*   *   *   *   *

In the office, she was, at first, somewhat self-conscious about Drosmig, who hung insecurely from his perch muttering to himself, but she soon forgot him in her preoccupation with duty. The first letter she picked up— although again oddly unlike the ones she'd read in the paper on Fizbus—seemed so simple that she felt she would have no difficulty in answering it all by herself:

Heidelberg

Dear Senbot Drosmig:

I am a professor of Fizbian History at a local university. Since my salary is a small one, owing to the small esteem in which the natives hold culture, I must economize wherever I can in order to make both ends meet. Accordingly, I do my own cooking and shop at the self-service supermarket around the corner, where I have found that prices are lower than in the service groceries and the food no worse.

However, the manager and a number of the customers have objected to my shopping with my feet. They don't so much mind my taking packages off the shelves with them, but they have been quite vociferous on the subject of my pinching the fruit with my toes. Unripe fruit, however, makes me ill.

What shall I do?

Sincerely yours,
Grez B'Groot

Tarb dictated an unhesitating reply:

Dear Professor B'Groot:
Why don't you explain to the manager of the store that Fizbians have wings and feet rather than arms and hands?

I'm sure his attitude and the attitudes of his customers will change when they learn that your pinching the fruit with your feet is not mere pedagogical eccentricity, but the regular practice on our planet. Point out to him that your feet are covered and, therefore, more sanitary than the bare hands of his other customers.

And always put on clean socks before you go shopping.

Helpfully yours,
Senbot Drosmig

Miss Snow raised pale eyebrows.

"Is something wrong?" Tarb asked anxiously. "Should I have put in that bit about work, study, meditate? It seems inappropriate somehow."

"Oh, no, not that. It's just that your letter—well, violates Mr. Zarnon's precept that, in Rome, one must do as the Romans do."

"But this isn't Rome," Tarb replied, bewildered. "It's New York."

"He didn't make the saying up," Miss Snow replied testily. "It's a Terrestrial proverb."

"Oh," Tarb said.

She resented this creature's trying to tell her how to do her job. On the other hand, Tarb was wise enough to realize that Miss Snow, unpleasant though she might be, probably did know Stet well enough to be able to predict his reactions.

So Tarb not only was reluctant to show Stet what she had already done, but hesitated about answering another and even more urgent letter that had just been brought in by special messenger. She tried to compromise by submitting the letters to Drosmig—for, technically speaking, it was he who was her immediate superior—but he merely groaned, "Tell 'em all to drop dead," from his perch and refused to open his eyes.

In the end, Tarb had to take the letters to Stet's office. Miss Snow trailed along behind her, uninvited. And, since this was a place of business, Tarb could not claim a privacy violation. Even if it weren't a place of business, she remembered, she couldn't—not here on Earth. Advanced spirituality, hah!

Advanced pain in the pinions!

Stet read the first letter and her answer smilingly. "Excellent, Tarb–" her hearts leaped–"for a first try, but I'd like to suggest a few changes, if I may."

"Well, of course," she said, pretending not to notice the smirk on Miss Snow's face.

"Just write this Professor B'Goot that he should do his shopping at a grocery that offers service and practice his economies elsewhere. A professor, of all people, is expected to uphold the dignity of his own race–the idea, sneering at a culture that was thousands of years old when we were still building nests! Terrestrials couldn't possibly have any respect for him if they saw him prodding kumquats with his toes."

"It's no sillier than writing with one's vestigial wings!" Tarb blazed.

"Well!" Miss Snow exclaimed in Terran. "Well, *really*!"

Tarb started to stick out her tongue, then remembered. "I didn't mean to offend you, Miss Snow. I know it's your custom. But wouldn't you understand if I typewrote with my feet?"

Miss Snow tittered.

"If you want the honest truth, hon, it would make you look like a feathered monkey."

"If you want the honest truth about what you look like to me, dearie–it's a plucked chicken!"

"Tarb, I think you should apologize to Miss Snow!"

"All right!" Tarb stuck out her tongue. Miss Snow promptly thrust out hers in return.

"Ladies, ladies!" Stet cried. "I think there has been a slight confusion of folkways!" He quickly changed the subject. "Is that another letter you have there, Tarb?"

"Yes, but I didn't try to answer it. I thought you'd better have a look at it first, since Miss Snow didn't seem to think much of the job I did with the other one."

"Miss Snow always has the *Times'* welfare at heart," Stet remarked ambiguously, and read:

Chicago

Dear Senbot Drosmig:

I am employed as translator by the extraterrestrial division of Burns and Deerhart, Inc., the well-known interstellar mail-order house. As the company employs no other Fizbians and our offices are situated in a small rural community where no others of our race reside, I find myself rather lonely. Moreover, being a bachelor, with neither chick nor child on Fizbus, I have nothing to look forward to upon my return to the Home Planet some day.

Accordingly, I decided to adopt a child to cheer my declining years. I dispatched an interstellargram to a reliable orphanage on Fizbus, outlining my hopes and requirements in some detail. After they had satisfied themselves as to my income, strength of character, etc., they sent me a fatherless and motherless egg in cold storage, which I was supposed to hatch upon arrival.

However, when the egg came to Earth, it was impounded by Customs. They say it is forbidden to import extrasolar eggs. I have tried to explain to them that it is not at all a question of importation but of adoption; however, they cannot or will not understand.

Please tell me what to do. I fear that they may not be keeping the egg at the correct Fizbian freezing point–which, as you know, is a good deal lower than Earth's. The fledgling may hatch by itself and receive a traumatic shock that might very well damage its entire psyche permanently.

Frantically yours,

Glibmus Gluyt

"Oh, for the stars' sake!" Stet exploded. "This is really too much! Viz our consul, Miss Snow. That egg must go back to Fizbus at once, before any Terrestrials hear of it! And I must notify the government back on the Home Planet to keep a close check on all egg shipments. Something like this must certainly not occur again."

"Why shouldn't the Terrestrials hear of it?" Tarb asked, outraged. "And I think it's mean of you to send back a poor little orphan egg like that when it has a chance of getting a good home."

"An egg!" Miss Snow repeated incredulously. "You mean you really...?" She gave me one mad little hoot of laughter and then stopped and strangled slightly. Her face turned purple in her efforts to restrain mirth. *Really, Tarb* thought, *she looks so much better that color.*

Stet's crest twitched violently. "I hope–" he began. "I do hope you will keep this ... knowledge to yourself, Miss Snow."

"But of course," she assured him, calming down. "I'm dreadfully sorry I was so rude. Naturally I wouldn't dream of telling a soul, Mr. Zarnon. You can trust me."

"I'm sure I can, Miss Snow."

Tarb almost choked with indignation. "You mean you've been keeping the facts of our life from Terrestrials? As if they were fledglings ... no, even fledglings are told these days."

"One could hardly blame him for it, Miss Morfatch," Miss Snow said. "You wouldn't want people to know that Fizbians laid eggs, would you?"

"And why not?"

"Tarb," Stet intervened, "you don't know what you're talking about."

"Oh, don't I? You're ashamed of the fact that we bear our children in a clean, decent, honorable way instead of–" She stopped. "I'm being as bad as you two are. Probably the Terrestrials' way of reproduction doesn't seem dirty to them—but, since they do reproduce *that* way, they could scarcely find our way objectionable!"

"Tarb, that's not how a young girl should talk!"

"Oh, go lay an egg!" she said, knowing that she had overstepped the limits of propriety, but unable to let him get away with that. "I hope to be a wife and mother some day," she added, "and I only hope that when that time comes, I'll be able to lay good eggs."

"Miss Morfatch," Stet said, keeping control of his temper with a visible effort, "that will be enough from you. If common decency doesn't restrain you, please remember that I am your employer and that *I* set the policies on *my* paper. You'll do what you're told and keep a civil tongue in your head or you'll be sent back to Fizbus. Do I make myself clear?"

"You do, indeed," Tarb said. How could she ever have thought he was charming and handsome? Well, perhaps he still was handsome, but fine feathers do not make fine deeds. And, if it came to that, it wasn't his paper.

"We have the same thing on Terra," Miss Snow murmured sympathetically to Stet. "These young whippersnappers think they can start in running the paper the very first day. Why, Belinda Romney herself— she's a distant cousin of mine, you know—told me—"

"Miss Snow," Tarb said, "I hope for the sake of Earth that you are not a typical example of the Terrestrial species."

"And you, hon," Miss Snow retorted, "don't belong on a paper, but in a chicken coop."

"Ladies!" Stet said helplessly. "Women," he muttered, "certainly do not belong on a newspaper. Matter of fact, they don't belong anywhere; their place is in the home only because there's nowhere else to put them."

Both females glared at him.

*   *   *   *   *

During the next fortnight, Tarb gained fluency in Terran and also learned to operate a Terrestrial typewriter equipped with Fizbian type—mostly so that she could dispense with the services of the invaluable Miss Snow. She didn't like typing, though—it chipped her toenails and her temper. Besides, Drosmig kept complaining that the noise prevented him from sleeping and she preferred him to sleep rather than hang there making irrelevant and, sometimes, unpleasantly relevant remarks.

"Longing for the old scripto, eh?" one of the cameramen smiled as he lounged in the open doorway of her office. Although she was fond of fresh air, Tarb realized that she would have to keep the door shut from now on. Too many of the younger members of the staff kept booing at her as they passed, and now they had formed the habit of dropping in to offer her advice, encouragement and invitations to meals. At first, the attention had pleased her—but now she was much too busy to be bothered; she was going to turn out acceptable answers to those letters or die trying.

"Well, if the power can't be converted, it can't," she said grimly. "Griblo, I do wish you'd be a dear and flutter off. I—"

He snorted. "Who says the power can't be converted? Stet, huh?"

She took her feet off the keys and looked at him. "Why do you say 'Stet' that way?"

"Because that's a lot of birdseed he gives you about not being able to convert Earth power. Could be done all right, but he and the consul have it all fixed up to keep Fizbian technology off the planet. Consul's probably being paid off by the International Association of Manufacturers and Stet's in it for the preservation of indigenous culture—and maybe a little cash, too. After all, those rare antique collections of his cost money."

"I don't believe it!" Tarb snapped. "Griblo, please—I have so much work to get through!"

"Okay, chick, but I warn you, you're going to have your bright-eyed illusions shattered. Why don't you wake up to the truth about Stet? What you should do is maybe eschew the society of all journalists entirely, and a sordid lot they are, and devote yourself to photographers—splendid fellows, all."

"Please shut the door behind you!"

The door slammed.

Tarb gazed disconsolately at the letter before her. Would she ever be able to answer letters to Stet's satisfaction? The purpose of the whole column was service—but did she and Stet mean the same thing by the same word? Or, if they did, whom was Stet serving?

She was paying too much attention to Griblo's idle remarks. Obviously he was a sorehead—had some kind of grudge against Stet. Perhaps Stet was a bit too autocratic, perhaps he had even gone native to some extent, but you couldn't say anything worse about him than that. All in all, he wasn't a bad bird and she mustn't let herself be influenced by rumormongers like Griblo.

*   *   *   *   *

Tarb got up and took the letter to Stet. He was in his office dictating to Miss Snow. *After all,* Tarb could not repress the ugly thought, *why should he care about the scriptos? He'll never have to use a typewriter.*

And he was perfectly nice about being interrupted. The only thing he didn't like was being contradicted. *I'm getting bitter,* she told herself in surprise. *And at my age, too. I wonder what I'll be like when I'm old.*

This thought alarmed her and so she smiled very sweetly at Stet as she murmured, "Would you mind reading this?" and gave him the letter.

"Run into another little snag, eh?" he said affably, giving her foot a gentle pat with his. "Well, let's see what we can do about it."

Montreal

Dear Senbot Drosmig:

I am a chef at the Cafe Inter-stellaire, which, as everyone knows, is one of the most chic eating establishments on this not very chic planet. During my spare moments, I am a great amateur of the local form of entertainment known as television. I am especially fascinated by the native actress Ingeborg Swedenborg, who, in spite of being a Terran, compares most favorably with our own Fizbian footlight favorites.

The other day, while I am in the kitchen engaged in preparing the ragout celeste a la fizbe for which I am justly celebrated on nine planets, I hear a stir outside in the dining room. I strain my ears. I hear the cry, "It is Ingeborg Swedenborg!"

I cannot help myself. I rush to the doorway. There, behold, the incomparable Ingeborg herself! She follows the headwaiter to a choice table. She is even more ravishing in real life than on the screen. On her, it does not matter that she has no feathers save on the head—even skin looks good. Overcome by involuntary ardor, I boo at her. Whereupon I am violently assailed by a powerfully built native whom I have not previously noticed to be escorting her.

I am rescued before he can do me any permanent damage, though, if you wish the truth, it will be a long time before I can fly again. However, I am given notice by the cold-hearted management. Now I am without a job. And what is more, if on this planet one is not permitted to express one's instinctive and natural admiration for a beautiful

> *woman, then all I have to say is that it is a lousy*
> *planet and I wiggle my toes at it. How do I go*
> *about getting deported?*
>
> *Impatiently yours,*
> *Rajois Sludd*

"Oh, I suppose it serves him right," Tarb said quickly, before Stet could comment, "but don't you think it would be a good idea if the *Times* got up a Fizbian-Terrestrial handbook of its own? It's the only solution that I can see. The regular one, I recognize now, is more than inadequate, with all that spiritual gup–" Miss Snow drew in her breath sharply–"and not much else. All these problems are bound to arise again and again. Frankly speaking, Stet, your solutions only take care of the individual cases; they don't establish a sound intercultural basis."

He grunted.

"What's more," she went on eagerly, "we could not only give copies to every Fizbian planning to visit Earth, but also print copies in Terran for Terrestrials who are interested in learning more about Fizbus and the Fizbians. In fact, all Terrans who come in contact with us should have the book. It would help both races to understand each other so much better and–"

"Unnecessary!" Stet snapped, so violently that she stopped with her mouth open. "The standard handbook is more than adequate. Whatever limitations it may have are deliberate. Setting down in cold print all that ... stuff you want to have included would make a point of things we prefer not to stress. I wouldn't want to have the Terrestrials humor me as if I were a fledgling or a foreigner."

He leaped out of his chair and paced up and down the office. One would think he had forgotten he ever could fly.

"But you are a foreigner, Stet," Tarb said gently. "No matter what you do or say, Terrestrials and Fizbians are–well, worlds apart."

"Spiritually, I am much closer to the Terrestrials than–but you wouldn't understand." He and Miss Snow nodded sympathetically at each other. "And you might be interested to know that I happen to be the author of all that 'spiritual gup.' I wrote the handbook–as a service to Fizbus, I might point out. I wasn't paid for it."

"Oh, dear!" Tarb said. "Oh, *dear*! I really and truly am sorry, Stet."

He brushed her apologies aside. "Answer that letter. Ignore the question about deportation entirely." He ran a foot through his crest. "Just tell the fellow to see our personnel manager. We could use a chef in the company dining room. Haven't tasted a decent celestial ragout–at a price I could afford–since I left Fizbus."

"Would you want me to print that reply in the column?" she asked. "'If you lose your job because you're unfamiliar with Terrestrial customs, come to the *Times*. We'll give you another job at a much lower salary.'"

"Of course not! Send your answer directly to him. You don't think we put any of those letters you've been answering in the column, do you? Or any that come in at all, for that matter. I have to write all the letters that are printed–and answer them myself."

"I should have recognized the style," Tarb said. "So this is the service the *Times* offers to its subscribers. Nothing that would be of help. Nothing that could prevent other Fizbians from making the same mistake. Nothing that could be controversial. Nothing that would help Terrestrials to understand us. Nothing, in short, but a lot of birdseed!"

"Impertinence!" Miss Snow remarked. "You shouldn't let her talk to you like that, Mr. Zarnon."

"Tarb!" Stet roared, casting an impatient glance at Miss Snow. "How dare you talk to me in that way? And all this is none of your business, anyway."

"I'm a Fizbian," she stated, "and it certainly is my business. I'm not ashamed of having wings. I'm proud of them and sorry for people who don't have them. And, by the stars, I'm going to fly. If skirts are improper to wear for flying, then I can wear slacks. I saw them in a Terrestrial fashion magazine and they're perfectly respectable."

"Not for working hours," Miss Snow sniffed.

"I have no intention of flying during working hours," Tarb snapped back. "Even you should be able to see that the ceiling's much too low."

Stet ran a foot through his crest again. "I hate to say this, Tarb, but I don't feel you're the right person for this job. You mean well, I'm sure, but you're too–too inflexible."

"You mean I have principles," she retorted, "and you don't." Which wasn't entirely true; he had principles–it was just that they were unprincipled.

"That will be enough, Tarb," he said sternly. "You'd better go now while I think this over. I'd hate to send you back to Fizbus, because I'd–well, I'd miss you. On the other hand...."

Tarb went back to her office and drafted a long interstel to a cousin on Fizbus, explaining what she would like for a birthday present. "And send it special delivery," she concluded, "because I am having an urgent and early birthday."

*　　*　　*　　*　　*

"Tarb Morfatch!" Stet howled, a few months later. "What on Earth are you doing?"

"Dictating into my scripto," Tarb said cheerfully. "Some of the boys from the print shop helped fix it up for me. They were very nice about it, too, considering that the superscriptos will probably throw them out of work. You know, Stet, Terrestrials can be quite decent people."

"Where did you get that scripto?"

"Cousin Mylfis sent it to me for my birthday. I must have complained about wearing out my claws on a typewriter and he didn't understand that scriptos won't work on Earth. Only they do." She beamed at her employer. "All it needed was a transformer. I guess you're just not mechanically minded, Stet."

He clenched his feet. "Tarb, Terrestrials aren't ready for our technology. You've done a very unwise thing in having that scripto sent to you. And I've done a very unwise thing in keeping you here against my better judgment."

"Maybe the Terrestrials aren't ready," she said, ignoring his last remark, "but I'm not going to wear my feet to the bone if I can get a gadget that'll do the same thing with no expenditure of physical energy." She placed a foot on his. "I don't see how a thing like this could possibly corrupt the Terrestrials, Stet. It's made a better, brighter girl out of me already."

"Hear, hear!" said Drosmig hoarsely from his perch.

"Shut up, Senbot. You just don't understand, Tarb. If you'll only–"

"But I'm afraid I do understand, Stet. And I won't send my scripto back."

"May I come in?" Miss Snow tapped lightly on the door frame. "Is what I hear true?"

"About the scripto?" Tarb asked. "It certainly is. All you have to do is talk into it and the words appear on the paper. Guess that makes you obsolete, doesn't it, Miss Snow?"

"And high time, too," commented Drosmig. "Never liked the old biddy."

"Senbot...." Stet began, and stopped. "Oh, what's the use trying to talk reasonably to either of you! Tarb, come back to my office with me."

She could not refuse and so she followed. Miss Snow, torn between curiosity and the scripto, hesitated and then made after them.

"I've decided to take you off the column—for this morning, anyway—and send you on an outside assignment," Stet told Tarb. "The consul's wife is coming to Earth today. Once she heard there was another woman on Terra, nothing could stop her. Consul seems to think it's my fault, too," he added moodily. "Won't believe I had nothing to do with hiring you. I told the Home Office not to send a woman, that she'd disrupt the office, and you sure as hell have."

"But I thought you said in your letters that you were doing everything in your power to bring Fizbian womenfolk to their men on Terra!" Tarb pointed out malevolently.

"Yes," he confessed. "We must please our readers. You know that. Anyway, all that's irrelevant right now. What I want you to do is go meet the consul's wife. Nice touch, having the only other Fizbian woman here be the one to interview her. Human interest angle for the Terrestrial papers. Shouldn't be surprised if Solar Press picked it up—they like items of that kind for fillers. Take Griblo along with you and make sure he has film in his camera this time."

"Yes, sir," Tarb said. "Anything you say, sir."

He pretended not to notice her sarcasm. "I have a list of the questions you should ask her." He fixed her with his eye. "You stick to them, do you hear me? I don't want anything controversial." He rummaged among the papers on his desk. "I know I had it half an hour ago. Sit down, will you, Tarb? Stop hopping around."

"If I can't have a perch, I want a stool," Tarb said. "This is a private office and I think it's a gross affectation for you to have those silly, uncomfortable chairs in it."

"If you would have your wings clipped like Mr. Zarnon's—" Miss Snow began before Stet could stop her.

"Stet, you *didn't*!"

His crest thrashed back and forth. "They'll grow back again and it's so much more convenient this way. After all, I can't use them here and I do have to associate with

Terrestrials and use their equipment. The consul has had his wings clipped also and so have several of our more prominent industrialists–"

"Oh, *Stet!*" Tarb wailed. "I was beginning to think some pretty hard things about you, but I wouldn't ever have dreamed you'd do anything as awful as that!"

"Why should I have to apologize to you?" he raged. "Who do you think you are, anyway? You're an incompetent little fool. I should have fired you that first day. I've let you get away with so much only because you have a pretty face. You've only been on Earth a couple of months; how can you presume to think you know what's good and what's bad for the Fizbians here?"

"I may not know what's good," she retorted, "but I certainly do know what's bad. And that's you, Stet–you and everything you stand for. You not only don't have the courage of your convictions, you don't even have any convictions. You're ashamed of being a Fizbian, ashamed of anything that makes Fizbians different from Terrestrials, even if it's something better, something that most Terrans would like to have. You're a damned hypocrite, Stet Zarnon, that's what you are–professing to help our people when actually you're hurting them by trying to force them into the mold of an alien species."

She brushed back her crest. "I take it I'm fired," she said more quietly. "Do you want me to interview the consul's wife first or leave right away?"

It took Stet a moment to bring his voice under control. "Interview her first. We'll talk this over when you get back."

*   *   *   *   *

It was pleasant to be away from the office, she thought as the taxi pulled toward the airfield, and doing wingwork again, even if it proved to be the first and last time on this planet. Griblo sat hunched in a corner of the seat, too preoccupied with the camera, which, even after two years, he hadn't fully mastered, to pay attention to her.

Outside, it was raining, the kind of thin drizzle that, on Fizbus or Earth, could go on for days. Tarb had brought along the native umbrella she had purchased in the hotel gift shop–a delightful contraption that was supposed to keep off the rain and didn't, and was supposed to collapse and did, but at the wrong moments. She planned to take it back with her when she returned to Fizbus. Approved souvenir or not, it was the same beautiful purple as her eyes. And, besides, who had made the ruling about approved souvenirs? Stet, of course.

"No reason why we couldn't have autofax brought from Home," Griblo suddenly grumbled.

Tarb pulled herself back from her thoughts. "I suppose Stet wouldn't let you," she said. "But now that one scripto's here," she went on somewhat complacently, "he'll have to–"

"Keep this planet charming and unspoiled, he says," Griblo interrupted ungratefully. "Its spiritual values will be corrupted by too much contact with a crass advanced technology. And, of course, he's got the local camera manufacturers solidly behind him. I wonder whether they advertise in the *Times* because he helps keep autofax off Terra or whether he keeps the autofax off Terra because they advertise in the *Times*."

"But what does he care about advertising? He may talk as if he owned the *Times*, but he doesn't."

Griblo gave a nasty laugh. "No, he doesn't, but if the Terran edition didn't show a profit, it'd fold quicker than you can flip your wings and he'd have to go back to nasty old up-to-date Fizbus as a lowly sub-editor. And he wouldn't like that one bit. Our Stet, as you may have noticed, is fond of running things to suit himself."

"But Mr. Grupe told me that the *Times* isn't interested in money. It's running this edition of the paper only as a service to–oh, I suppose all that was a lot of birdseed, too!"

"Grupe!" Griblo snorted. "The sanctimonious old buzzard! He's a big stockholder on the paper. Bet you didn't know that, did you? All they're out for is money. Fizbian money, Terrestrial money—so long as it's cash."

"Tell me, Griblo," Tarb asked, "what does 'When in Rome, do as the Romans do' mean?"

Griblo grinned sourly. "Stet's favorite motto." He moved along the seat closer to her. "I'll tell you what it means, chicken. When on Earth, don't be a Fizbian."

*   *   *   *   *

The consul's wife, an old mauve creature, did not seem overpleased to see Tarb, since the younger, prettier Fizbian definitely took the spotlight away from her. The press had, of course, seen Tarb before, but at that time they hadn't been able to communicate directly with her and they didn't, she now found out, think nearly as much of Stet as he did of them.

Tarb couldn't attempt to deviate much from Stet's questions, for the consul's wife was not very cooperative and the consul himself watched both women narrowly. He was a good friend of Stet's, Tarb knew, and apparently Stet had taken the other man into his confidence.

When the interviews were over and the consular party had left, Tarb remained to chat with the Terrestrial journalists. Despite Griblo's worried objections, she joined them in the Moonfield Restaurant, where she daringly partook of a cup of coffee and then another and another.

After that, things weren't very clear. She dimly remembered the other reporters assuring her that she shouldn't disfigure her lovely wings with a stole ... and then pirouetting in the air over the bar to prolonged applause ... and then she was in the taxi again with Griblo shaking her.

"Wake up, Tarb—we're almost at the office! Stet'll have me plucked for this!"

Tarb sat up and pushed her crest out of her eyes. The sky was growing dark. They must have been gone a long time.

"I'll never hear the end of this," Griblo moaned. "Why, if only he could get someone to fill my place, Stet would fire me like a shot! Not that I wouldn't quit if I could get another job."

"Oh, it'll be mostly me he'll be mad at." Tarb pulled out her compact. Stet had warned her not to polish her eyeballs in public, but the ground with him! Her head hurt. And her feathers, she saw in the mirror, had turned almost beige. She looked horrible. She felt horrible. And Stet would probably think she was horrible.

"When Stet's mad," Griblo prophesied darkly, "he's mad at *everybody*!"

And Stet *was* mad. He was waiting in the newsroom, his emerald-blue eyes blazing as if he had not only polished but lacquered them.

"What's the idea of taking six hours to cover a simple story!" he shouted as soon as the door began to open. "Aside from the trivial matter of a deadline to be met— Griblo, *where's Tarb*? Nothing's happened to her, has it?"

"Naaah," Griblo said, unslinging his camera. "She took a short cut, only she got held up by a terrace. Snagged her umbrella on it, I believe. I heard her yelling when I was waiting for the elevator; I didn't know nice girls knew language like that. She should be up any minute now.... There she is."

He pointed to a window, through which the lissome form of the young feature writer could be seen, tapping on the glass in order to attract attention.

"Somebody better open it for her," the cameraman suggested. "Probably not meant to open from the outside. Not many people come in that way, I guess."

*   *   *   *   *

Open-mouthed, the whole newsroom stared at the window. Finally the Copy Editor got up and let a dripping Tarb in.

"Nearly thought I wouldn't make it," she observed, shaking herself in a flurry of wet pink feathers. The rest of the staff ducked, most of them too late. "Umbrella didn't do much good," she continued, closing it. It left a little puddle on the rug. "My wings got soaked right away." She tossed her wet crest out of her eyes. "Golly, but it's good to fly again. Haven't done it for months, but it seems like years." Her eye caught Miss Snow's. "You don't know what you're missing!"

"Tarb," Stet thundered, "you've been drinking coffee! *Griblo!*" But the cameraman had nimbly sought sanctuary in the dark-room.

"You'd better go home, Tarb." When Stet's eye tufts met across his nose, he was downright ugly, she realized. "Griblo can give me the dope and I'll write up the story myself. I can fill it out with canned copy. And you and I will discuss this situation in the morning."

"Won't go home when there's work to be done. Duty calls me." Giving a brief and quite recognizable imitation of a Terrestrial trumpet, Tarb stalked down the corridor to her office.

Drosmig looked up from his perch, to which he was still miraculously clinging at that hour. "So it got you, too?... Sorry ... nice girl."

"It hasn't got me," Tarb replied, picking up a letter marked *Urgent.* "I've got it." She scanned the letter, then made hastily for Stet's office.

He sat drumming on his desk with the antique stainless steel spatula he used as a paperknife.

"Read this!" she demanded, thrusting the letter into his face. "Read this, you traitor—sacrificing our whole civilization to what's most expedient for you! Hypocrite! Cad!"

"Tarb, listen to me! I'm—"

"Read it!" She slapped the letter down in front of him. "Read it and see what you've done to us! Sure, we Fizbians keep to ourselves and so the only people who know anything about us are the ones who want to sell us brushes, while the people who want to help us don't know a damn thing about us and—"

"Oh, all right! I'll read it if you'll only keep quiet!" He turned the letter right-side up.

Johannesburg

Dear Senbot Drosmig:

I represent the Dzoglian Publishing Company, Inc., of which I know you have heard, since your paper has seen fit to give our books some of the most unjust reviews on record. However, be that as it may, I have opened an office on Earth with the laudable purpose of effecting an interchange of respective literatures, to see which Terrestrial books might most profitably be translated into Fizbian, and which of the authors on our own list might have potential appeal for the Earth reader.

Dealing with authors is, of course, a nerve-racking business and I soon found myself in dire need of mental treatment. What was my horror to find that this primitive, although charming, planet had no neurotones, no psychoscopes, not even any cerebrophones–in fact, no psychiatric machines at all! The very knowledge of this brought me several degrees closer to a breakdown.

Perhaps I should have consulted you at this juncture, but I admit I was a bit of a snob. "What sort of advice can a mere journalist give me," I thought, "that I could not give myself?" So, more for amusement than anything else, I determined to consult a native practitioner. "After all," I said to myself, "a good laugh is a step forward on the road to recovery."

Accordingly, I went to see this native fellow. They work entirely without machines, I understand, using something like witchcraft. At the same time, I thought I might pick up some material for a jolly little book on primitive customs which I could get some unknown writer to throw together inexpensively. Strong human interest items like that always have great reader-appeal.

The native chap–doctor, he calls himself–was most cordial, which he should have been at the price I was paying him. One thing I must say about these natives–backward they may be, but they have a very shrewd commercial sense. You can't even imagine the trouble I had getting those authors to sign even remotely reasonable contracts ... which in part accounts for my mental disturbance, I suppose.

Well, anyway, I handed the native a privacy waiver carefully filled out in Terran. He took it, smiled and said, "We'll discuss this afterward. My contact lenses have disappeared; I suppose one of my patients has stolen them again. Can't see a thing without them."

So we sat down and had a bit of a chat. He seemed remarkably intelligent for a native; never interrupted me once.

"You are definitely in great trouble," he told me when I'd finished. "You need to be psycho-analyzed."

"Good, good," I said. "I see I've come to the right shop."

"Now just lie down and make yourself comfortable."

"Lie down?" I repeated, puzzled. I have an excellent command of Terran, but every now and then an idiom will throw me. "I tell the truth, sir, and when I am required by force of circumstances to lie, I lie up."

"No," he said, "not that kind of lying. You know, the kind you do at night when you go to sleep."

"Oh, I get you," I said idiomatically. Without further ado, I flung off my ulster and flew up to a thingummy hanging from the ceiling–chandelier, I believe, is the native term–flipped upside down, and hung from it by my toes. Wasn't the Presidential Perch, by any means, but it wasn't bad at all. "What do I do next?" I inquired affably.

"My dear fellow," the chap said, whipping out a notebook from the recesses of his costume, "how long have you had this delusion that you are a bird–or is it a bat?"

"Sir," I said as haughtily as my position permitted, "I am neither a bird nor a bat. I am a Fizbian. Surely you have heard of Fizbians?"

"Yes, yes, of course. They come from another country or planet or something. Frankly, politics is a bit outside my sphere. All I'm interested in is people—and Fizbians are people, aren't they?"

"Yes, certainly. If anything, it's you who.... Yes, they are people."

"Well, tell me then, Mr. Liznig, when was it you first started thinking you were a bat or a bird?"

I tried to control myself. "I am neither a bird nor a bat! I am a Fizbian! I have wings! See?" I fluttered them.

He peered at me. "I wish I could," he said regretfully. "Without my glasses, though, I'm as blind as a bat—or a bird."

Well, the long and the short of it is that the natives are planning to certify me as insane and incarcerate me, pending the doctor's decision as to whether my delusion is that I am a bird or a bat. They are using my privacy waiver as commitment papers.
Save me, Senbot Drosmig, for I feel that if I have to wait for the doctor's glasses to be delivered, I shall indeed go mad.

Distractedly yours,
Tgos Liznig

"I'll handle this myself," Stet said crisply. "I'll tell the consul to advise the Terran State Department that this man should be deported as an undesirable alien. That'll solve the problem neatly. We can't have this contaminating the pure stream of Terrestrial literature with–"

"But aren't you going to explain to them that he's perfectly sane?" Tarb gasped.

"No need to bother. He'll be grateful enough to get off the planet. Besides, how do I know he is perfectly sane?"

"Stet Zarnon, you're perfectly horrid!"

"And you, Tarb Morfatch, are disgustingly drunk. Now you go right home and sleep it off. I know I was too harsh with you–my fault for letting you go out alone with Griblo in the first place when you've been here only a few months. Might have known those Terran journalists would lead you astray. Nice fellows, but irresponsible." He flicked out his tongue. "There, I've apologized. Now will you go home?"

"Home!" Tarb shrieked. "Home when there's work to be done and–"

"–and you're not going to be the one to do it, Tarb," he said, attempting to seize her foot, which she pulled away, "I was going to tell you tomorrow, but you might as well know tonight. I've taken you off the column for good. I have a better job for you."

She looked at him. "A better job? Are you being sarcastic? What as?"

"As my wife." He got up and came over to her. She stood still, almost stunned. "That solves the whole problem tidily. An office is no place for you, darling– you're really a simple home-girl at heart. Newspaper work is too strenuous for you; it upsets you and makes you nervous and irritable. I want you to stay home and take care of our house and hatch our eggs– unostentatiously, of course."

"Why, you–" she spluttered.

He put his foot over her mouth. "Don't give me your answer now. You're in no condition to think. Tell me tomorrow."

*   *   *   *   *

It rained all night and continued on into the morning. Tarb's head ached, but she had to make an appearance at the office. First she vizzed an acquaintance she had made the day before; then she took her umbrella and set forth.

As she kicked open the door to the newsroom, all sound ceased. Voices stopped abruptly. Typewriters halted in mid-click. Even the roar of the presses downstairs suddenly seemed to mute. Every head turned to look at Tarb.

Humph, she thought, removing her plastic oversocks, *so suppose I was a little oblique yesterday. They needn't stare at me. They never stare at Drosmig. Just because I'm a woman, I suppose!* The gate crashed loudly behind her.

"Oh, Miss Morfatch," Miss Snow called. "Mr. Zarnon said he wanted to see you as soon as you came in. It's urgent." And she giggled.

"Really?" Tarb said. "Well, he'll just have to wait until I've wrung out my wings." Sooner or later, she would have to face Stet, but she wanted to put it off as long as possible.

She opened the door to her office and halted in amazement. For, seated on a stool behind the desk, haggard but vertical, was Senbot Drosmig, busily reading letters and blue-penciling comments on them with his feet.

"Good morning, my dear," he said, giving her a wan smile. "Surprised to see me functioning again, eh?"

"Well–yes." She opened her dripping umbrella mechanically and stood it in a corner. "How–"

"I realized last night that all that happened to you was my fault. You were my responsibility and I failed you."

"Oh, don't be melodramatic, Senbot. I wasn't your responsibility and you didn't fail me. Not that I'm not glad to see you up and doing again, but–"

"But I did fail you!" the aged journalist insisted. "And, in the same way, I failed my people. I shouldn't have given in. I should have fought Zarnon as you, my dear, tried to do. But it isn't too late!" The fire of the crusader lit up in his watery old eyes. "I can still fight him and his sacred crows–his Earthlings! If I have to, I can go over his head to Grupe. Grupe may not understand Stet's moral failings, but he certainly will comprehend his commercial ones. Grupe owns stock in other Fizbian enterprises besides the *Times*. Autofax, for example."

"Oh, Senbot!" Tarb wailed. "The whole thing's such an awful mess!"

"I don't think it'll be necessary to threaten that far," he comforted her. "Stet is no fool. He knows which side of his breadnut is peeled."

"I'm sure you'll do a wonderful job," she exclaimed, impulsively giving a ritual *entrechat*. "And I wish I could stay and help you, but...."

"I know, my dear."

"You do?" She was puzzled. "But how did the news get around so quickly?"

He shrugged. "The Terrestrial grapevine is almost as efficient as the Fizbian. Didn't you notice any change in the–ah–atmosphere when you came in?"

"Oh, was that the reason?" Tarb laughed merrily. "Somehow it never occurred to me that they could have heard so soon."

"But the morning editions have been out for hours."

The door to the office was flung open. Stet stormed in, bristling with a most unloverlike rage.

"Miss Morfatch–" he waved a crumpled copy of the *Terrestrial Tribune* at her–"when I give an order, I expect to be obeyed! Didn't Miss Snow tell you to report directly to my office the instant you came in? Although that's a question I don't have to ask; I know Miss Snow, at least, is someone I can trust."

"I was coming to see you, Stet," Tarb said soothingly. "Right away."

"Oh, you were, were you? And have you seen this?" Stet fairly threw the paper at her. Smack in the middle of the front page was a picture of herself in full flight over the airfield bar. Not a very good picture, but what could you expect with Terrestrial equipment? When the autofax came, perhaps she would be done justice.

FIZBIAN NEWSHEN GIVES EARTH A FLUTTER

"Though No Mammal, I Pack a Lot of Uplift," Says Beautiful Fizbian Gal Reporter

"I feel that you Terrans and we Fizbians can get along much better," lovely Tarb Morfatch, Fizbus *Times* feature writer, told her fellow-reporters yesterday at the Moonfield Restaurant, "if we learn to understand each other's differences as well as appreciate our similarities.

"With commerce between the two planets expanding as rapidly as it has been," Miss Morfatch went on, "it becomes increasingly important that we make sure there is no clash of mores between us. Where adaptation is impossible, we must both adjust. 'When in Rome, do as the Romans do' is an outmoded concept in the complex interstellar civilization of today. The Romans must learn to accept us as we are, and vice versa.

"Forgive me if I've offended you by my frankness," she said, sticking out her tongue in the charming gesture of apology that is acquiring such a vogue on Earth, Belinda Romney and many other socialites having enthusiastically adopted it, "but you've violated our privacy so many times, I feel I'm entitled to hurt your feelings just a teeny-weeny bit...."

"Those Terran journalists," Tarb said admiringly. "Never miss a trick, do they? Am I in all the other papers too, Stet? Same cheesecake?"

"You've made an ovulating circus out of us–that's what you've done!"

"Nonsense. Good strong human interest stuff; it'll make us lovable as chicks all over the planet. Gee–" she read on–"did I say all that while I was caffeinated? I ought to turn out some pretty terrific copy sober."

"And to think you, the woman I had asked to make my wife, did this to me."

"Oh, that's all right, Stet," Tarb said without looking up from the paper. "I wasn't going to accept you, anyway."

"Good for you, Tarb," Drosmig approved.

"You're going back to Fizbus on the next liner–do you hear me?" Stet raged.

She smiled sunnily. "Oh, but I'm not, Stet. I'm going to stay right here on Earth. I like it. You might say the spiritual aura got me."

He snorted. "How can you possibly stay? You don't have an independent income and this is an expensive planet. Besides, I won't let you stay on Earth. I have considerable influence, you know!"

"Poor Stet." She smiled at him again. "I'm afraid the Fizbian press–the Fizbian consul even–are pretty small pullets beside the Solar Press Syndicate. You see, I came in this morning only to resign."

He stared at her.

"Yesterday," she informed him, "I was offered another position–as feature writer for the SP. I hadn't decided whether or not to accept when I reported back last evening, but you made up my mind for me, so I called them this morning and took the job. My work will be to explain Fizbians to Terrans and Terrans to Fizbians—as I wanted to do for the *Times*, Stet, only you wouldn't let me."

"It's no use saying anything to you about loyalty, I suppose?"

"None whatsoever," she said. "I owe the *Times* no loyalty and I'm doing what I do out of loyalty to Fizbus ... plus, of course, a much higher salary."

"I'm glad for you, Tarb," Drosmig said sincerely.

"Be glad for yourself, Senbot, because Stet will have to let you conduct the column your way from now on. Either it'll supplement my work in the Terrestrial papers or he'll look like a fool. And you do hate looking like a fool, don't you, Stet?"

He didn't answer.

"Better give up, Stet." She turned to Drosmig. "Well, good-by, Senbot—or, rather, so long. I'm sure we'll be seeing each other again. Good-by, Stet. No hard feelings, I hope?"

He neither moved nor spoke.

"Well ... good-by, then," she said.

The door closed. Stet stared after her. The forgotten umbrella dripped forlornly in the corner.

The Doorway
Originally Published In *Fantastic Universe*
September 1955

A discerning critic once pointed out that Edgar Allen Poe possessed not so much a distinctive style as a distinctive manner. So startlingly original was his approach to the dark castles and haunted woodlands of his own somber creation that he transcended the literary by the sheer magic of his prose. Something of that same magic gleams in the darkly-tapestried little fantasy presented here, beneath Evelyn Smith's eerily enchanted wand.

THE DOORWAY

"It is my theory," Professor Falabella said, helping himself to a cookie, "that no one ever really makes a decision. What really happens is that whenever alternative courses of action are called for, the individuality splits up and continues on two or more divergent planes, very much like the parthenogenesis of a unicellular animal ... Delicious cookies these, Mrs. Hughes."

"Thank you, Professor," Gloria simpered. "I made them myself."

"You must give us the recipe," said one of the ladies—and the others murmured agreement, glad to get their individualities on a plane they could understand.

"Since most decisions are hardly as momentous as the individual imagines," Professor Falabella continued, "and since the imagination of the average individual is very limited, many of these different planes—or, as they are colloquially known, space-time continuums—may exist in close, even tangential relationship."

Gloria rose unobtrusively and took the teapot to the kitchen for a refill. Her husband stood by the sink moodily drinking whiskey out of the bottle so as to avoid having to wash a glass afterward.

"Bill, you're not being polite to our guests. Why don't you go out and listen to Professor Falabella?"

"I can hear him perfectly well from here," Bill muttered—and indeed the professor's mellifluous tones pervaded every nook and cranny of the thin-walled house. "Long-winded cultist! What is he a professor of, I'd like to know."

"Professor Falabella is *not* a cultist!" affirmed Gloria angrily. "He's a great philosopher."

Bill Hughes said something unprintable. "If I'd married Lucy Allison," he continued unkindly, "she'd never have filled the house with long-haired cultists on my so-called day of rest."

Gloria's soft chin trembled, and her blue eyes filled with tears. She was beginning to put on weight, he noticed. "I've been hearing nothing but Lucy Allison, Lucy Allison, Lucy Allison for the past year. Y-you said yourself she looked like a horse."

"Horses," he observed, "have sense."

He was being brutal, but he couldn't help it and didn't want to. Professor Falabella was only the most long-winded of a long series of mystics Gloria was forever dragging into the house. *The trouble with the half-educated*, he thought bitterly, *is that they seek culture in the most peculiar places.*

"I'll bet she would have let me have peace on Sunday," he said. "It just goes to show what happens when you marry a woman solely for her looks." He drained the bottle; then hurled it into the garbage pail with a resounding crash.

Gloria's shoulders shook as she filled the kettle. "I wish I'd decided to be an old maid," she sobbed.

A very unlikely possibility, he thought. Even now, shopworn as she was, Gloria could have a fairly wide range of suitors should something happen to him. She looked sexy, but how deceiving appearances could be!

Professor Falabella was still talking as Bill and Gloria emerged from the kitchen. "I believe that it is possible for an individual who exists on a limited plane of imagination to transpose from one plane to an adjacent one without difficulty ... Great Heavens, what was that?"

Something had whisked past the archway leading into the foyer.

"Don't pay any attention," Gloria smiled nervously. "The house is haunted."

"My dear," one of the ladies offered, "I know of the most marvelous exterminator—"

"The house," Gloria assured her coldly, "really *is* haunted. We've been seeing things ever since we moved in."

And she really believed it, Bill thought. Believed that the house was haunted, that is. Of course he had seen things too—but he was enlightened enough to know that ghosts don't exist, even if you do see them.

Professor Falabella cleared his throat. "As I was saying, it is possible to send the individual through another—well, dimension, as some popular writers would have it, to one of his other spatial existences on the same temporal plane. It is merely necessary for him to find the Door."

"Nonsense!" Bill interrupted. "Holy, unmitigated nonsense!"

Every head swivelled to look at him. Gloria restrained tears with an effort.

"Brute," someone muttered.

But ridicule apparently only stimulated the professor. He beamed. "You don't believe me. Your imagination cannot extend to the comprehension of the multifariousness of space."

"Nonsense," Bill said again, but less confidently.

"I believe that I have discovered the Doorway," Professor Falabella continued, "and the Way is Open. However, most people fear to penetrate the unknown, even though it is to enter another phase of their own existence. I do admit that the shock of spatial transference, no matter how slight, combined with the concrete awareness of a previous spatial relationship would be perhaps too much for the keenly sensitive individualism ..."

Bill opened his mouth.

"I know what you're about to say, young man!"

"You don't have to be a mind reader to know that," Bill assured him. His consonants were already a little slurred and he knew Gloria was ashamed of him. It served her right. He'd been ashamed of her for years.

Professor Falabella smiled. His teeth were very sharp and white. "Very well, Mr. Hughes, since you are a skeptic, perhaps you will not object to being the subject of our experiment yourself?"

"What kind of an experiment?" Bill asked suspiciously.

"Merely to go through the Door. Any door can become the Doorway, if it is transposed into the proper spatial dimension. That door, for instance." Professor Falabella waved his hand toward the doorway of what Gloria liked to call "Bill's study."

"You mean you just want me to open the door and go into that room?" Bill asked incredulously. "That's all?"

"That is all. Of course, you go with the awareness that it is the threshold of another plane and that you step voluntarily from this existence to an adjacent one."

"Sure," Bill said. He had just remembered there was a nearly full bottle of Calvert in the bottom drawer of the desk. "Sure. Anything to oblige."

"Very well. Go to the door, and keep remembering that of your own free will you are passing from this plane to the next."

"Look out, everybody!" Bill called raucously, as he pulled open the door. "I'm coming in on the next plane!"

No one laughed.

He stepped over the threshold, shutting the door firmly behind him. A wonderful excuse to get away from those blasted women. He'd climb out of the window as soon as he'd collected the whiskey and give them a nervous moment thinking he'd really passed into another existence. It would serve Gloria right.

For a moment, as he crossed, he had a queer sensation. Maybe there was something in what Professor Falabella said. But no, there he was in the study. All that mumbo jumbo was getting him down, that was all. He was a nervous man—only nobody appreciated the fact.

Taking a cigarette out of the pack in his pocket, he reached for the lighter on his desk. It wasn't there. Time and time again he'd told Gloria not to touch his things, and always she'd disobeyed him. Company was coming and she must tidy up. Cooking and cleaning—that was all she was good for. But this was carrying tidiness too far; she'd even removed the ashtrays.

And where did that glass block paperweight come from? He'd had a penguin in a snowstorm and he'd been happy with it. This was too much. He'd tell Gloria off. Stealing a man's penguin!

He opened the door into the living room and bumped into Lucy Allison. "Don't you think you've been in there long enough, Bill?" she asked acridly. "I'm sure your guests would appreciate catching a glimpse of you."

"Why, hello, Lucy," he said, surprised. "I didn't know Gloria had invited you—"

"Gloria, Gloria, Gloria!" Lucy cut across his sentence. "You've been talking about nothing but that dumb little blonde for months." Because of the people in the room beyond, her voice was pitched low, but her pale eyes glittered unpleasantly behind her spectacles. "I wish you had married her. You'd have made a fine pair."

Gently, caressingly, the short hairs on the back of Bill's neck rose.

"Come back in here," Lucy said, hauling him back into the living room where a number of people who had been enjoying the domestic fracas suddenly broke into loud and animated chatter. "Dr. Hildebrand was telling us all about nuclear fission."

"Can't find an ashtray," Bill muttered, seizing on something tangible. "Can't find an ashtray in the whole darn place."

"We've been over this millions of times, Bill. You know–" she smiled at the guests, a smile that carefully excluded Bill. "–I'm allergic to smoke, but I never can get my husband to remember he isn't to smoke inside the house."

"Now take the neutron, for example," Dr. Hildebrand said through a mouthful of pate. "What is the neutron? It is only ... What was that?"

The wraith of Gloria crossed the foyer and disappeared. Bill took a step forward; then stood still.

Lucy smiled self-consciously. "That's nothing at all. The house is merely haunted."

Everyone laughed.

"Forgot something," Bill muttered, and dashed back into the study. He yanked open the bottom drawer of the desk. Sure enough, there was a bottle of Schenley, nearly a third full. "There are some advantages," he thought as he tilted it to his lips, "in having a limited imagination."

THE VENUS TRAP

ORIGINALLY PUBLISHED IN *GALAXY SCIENCE FICTION*
JUNE 1956

ILLUSTRATED BY DICK FRANCIS

*One thing Man never counted on to take along
into space with him was the Eternal Triangle—
especially a true-blue triangle like this!*

THE VENUS TRAP

"What's the matter, darling?" James asked anxiously. "Don't you like the planet?"

"Oh, I love the planet," Phyllis said. "It's beautiful."

It was. The blue–really blue–grass, blue-violet shrubbery and, loveliest of all, the great golden tree with sapphire leaves and pale pink blossoms, instead of looking alien, resembled nothing so much as a fairy-tale version of Earth.

Even the fragrance that filled the atmosphere was completely delightful to Terrestrial nostrils–which was unusual, for most other planets, no matter how well adapted for colonization otherwise, tended, from the human viewpoint, anyway, to stink. Not that they were not colonized nevertheless, for the population of Earth was expanding at too great a rate to permit merely olfactory considerations to rule out an otherwise suitable planet. This particular group of settlers had been lucky, indeed, to have drawn a planet as pleasing to the nose as to the eye–and, moreover, free from hostile aborigines.

As a matter of fact, the only apparent evidence of animate life were the small, bright-hued creatures winging back and forth through the clear air, and which resembled Terrestrial birds so closely that there seemed no point to giving them any other name. There were insects, too, although not immediately perceptible– but the ones like bees were devoid of stings and the butterflies never had to pass through the grub stage but were born in the fullness of their beauty.

However, fairest of all the creatures on the planet to James Haut–just then, anyhow–was his wife, and the expression on her face was not a lovely one.

"You do feel all right, don't you?" he asked. "The light gravity gets some people at first."

"Yes, I guess I'm all right. I'm still a little shaken, though, and you know it's not the gravity."

*   *   *   *   *

He would have liked to take her in his arms and say something comforting, reassuring, but the constraint between them had not yet been worn off. Although he had sent her an ethergram nearly every day of the voyage, the necessarily public nature of the messages had kept them from achieving communication in the deeper sense of the word.

"Well, I suppose you did have a bit of a shock," he said lamely. "Somehow, I thought I had told you in my 'grams."

"You told me plenty in the 'grams, but not quite enough, it seems."

Her words didn't seem to make sense; the strain had evidently been a little too much. "Maybe you ought to go inside and lie down for a while."

"I will, just as soon as I feel less wobbly." She brushed back the long, light brown hair which had got tumbled when she fainted. He remembered a golden rather than a reddish tinge in it, but that had been under the yellow sun of Earth; under the scarlet sun of this planet, it took on a different beauty.

"How come the preliminary team didn't include–*it* in their report?" she asked, avoiding his appreciative eye.

"They didn't know. We didn't find out ourselves until we'd sent that first message to Earth. I suppose by the time we did relay the news, you were on your way."

"Yes, that must have been it."

The preliminary exploration team had established the fact that the planet was more or less Earth-type, that its air was breathable, its temperature agreeably springlike, its mineral composition very similar to Earth's, with only slight traces of unknown elements, that there was plenty of drinkable water and no threatening life-forms. Human beings could, therefore, live on it.

It remained for the scout team to determine whether human beings would *want* to live on it—whether, in fact, they themselves would want to, because, if so, they had the option of becoming the first settlers. That was the way the system worked and, in the main, it worked well enough.

After less than two weeks, this scout team had beamed back to Earth the message that the planet was suitable for colonization, so suitable that they would like to give it the name of Elysium, if there was no objection.

There would be none, Earth had replied, so long as the pioneers bore in mind the fact that six other planets had previously been given that name, and a human colony currently existed on only one of those. No need to worry about a conflict of nomenclature, however, because the name of that other planet Elysium had subsequently been changed by unanimous vote of settlers to Hades.

*   *   *   *   *

After this somewhat sinister piece of information, Earth had added the more cheerful news that the wives and families of the scouts would soon be on their way, bringing with them the tools and implements necessary to transform the wilderness of the frontier into another Earth. In the meantime, the men were to set up the packaged buildings with which all scout ships were equipped, so that when the women came, homes would be ready for them.

The men set to work and, before the month was out, they discovered that Elysium was neither a wilderness nor a frontier. It was populated by an intelligent race which had developed its culture to the limit of its physical abilities–actually well beyond the limit of what the astounded Terrestrials could have conceived its physical abilities to be–then, owing to unavoidable disaster, had started to die out.

The remaining natives were perspicacious enough to see in the Terrestrials' coming not a threat but a last hope of revivifying their own moribund species. Accordingly, the Earthmen were encouraged to go ahead building on the sites originally selected, the only ban being on the type of construction materials used–and a perfectly reasonable one under the circumstances.

James had built his cottage near the largest, handsomest tree in the area allotted to him; since there were no hostile life-forms, there was no need for a closely knit community. Everyone who had seen it agreed that his house was the most attractive one of all, for, although it was only a standard prefab, he had used taste and ingenuity to make it a little different from the other unimaginative homes.

And now Phyllis, for whom he had performed all this labor of love, for whom he had waited five long months–the tedium of which had been broken only by the intellectual pleasure of teaching English to a sympathetic native neighbor–Phyllis seemed unappreciative. She had hardly looked at the inside of the cottage, when he had shown her through, and now was staring at the outside in a blank sort of way.

The indoctrination courses had not, he reflected, reconciled her to the frontiersman's necessarily simple mode of living–which was ironic, considering that one of her original attractions for him had been her apparent suitability for the pioneer life. She was a big girl, radiantly healthy, even though a little green at the moment.

*   *   *   *   *

He just managed to keep his voice steady. "You don't like the house—is that it?

"But I *do* like it. Honestly I do." She touched his arm diffidently. "Everything would be perfect if only—"

"If only what? Is it the curtains? I'm sorry if you don't like them. I brought them all the way from Earth in case the planet turned out to be habitable. I thought blue was your favorite color."

"Oh, it is, it is! I'm mad about the curtains."

Perhaps it wasn't the house that disappointed her; perhaps it was he himself who hadn't lived up to dim memory and ardent expectation.

"If you want to know what *is* bothering me—" she glanced up apprehensively, lowering her voice as she did—"it's that tree. It's stuck on you; I just know it is."

He laughed. "Now where did you get a preposterous idea like that, Phyl? You've been on the planet exactly twenty-four hours and—"

"—and I have, in my luggage, one hundred and thirty-two ethergrams talking about practically nothing but Magnolia this, Magnolia that. Oh, I had my suspicions even before I landed, James. The only thing I didn't suspect was that she was a *tree*!"

"What are you talking about, honey? Magnolia and I—we're just friends."

"Purely a platonic relationship, I assure you," the tree herself agreed. It would have been silly for her to pretend not to have overheard, since the two were still standing almost directly underneath her. "Purely platonic."

"She's more like a sister to me," James tried to explain.

*   *   *   *   *

Phyllis stiffened. "Frankly, if I had imagined I was going to have a tree for a sister-in-law, I would have thought before I married you, James." Bursting into tears, she ran inside the cottage.

"Sorry," he said miserably to Magnolia. "It's a long trip out from Earth and an uncomfortable one. I don't suppose the other women were especially nice to her, either. Faculty wives mostly and you know how they are.... No, I don't suppose you would. But she shouldn't have acted that way toward you."

"Not your fault," Magnolia told him, sighing with such intensity that he could feel the humidity rise. "I know how you've been looking forward to her arrival. Rather a letdown, isn't it?"

"Oh, I'm sure it'll be all right." He tried to sound confident. "And I know you'll like Phyllis when you get to know her."

"Possibly, but so far I'm afraid I must admit–since there never has been any pretense between us–that she is a bit of a disappointment. I–and my sisters also–had expected your females, when they came, to be as upright and true blue as you. Instead, what are they? Shrubs."

The door to the cottage flew open. "A shrub, am I!" Phyllis brandished an axe which, James winced to recall, was an item of the equipment he had ordered from Earth before the scout team had learned that the trees were intelligent. "I'll shrub you!"

"Phyllis!" He wrested the axe from her grip. "That would be murder!"

"'Woodman,' as the Terrestrial poem goes," the tree remarked, "'spare that tree! Touch not a single bough! In youth it sheltered me and I'll protect it now!'"

Good of her to take the whole thing so calmly–rather, to pretend to take it so calmly, for he knew how sensitive Magnolia really was–but he was afraid this show of moral courage would not diminish Phyllis's dislike for her; those without self-control seldom appreciate those who have it.

"If you'll excuse us," he said, putting his arm around his wife's heaving shoulders, "I'd better see to Phyllis;

she's a little upset. Holdover from spacesickness, I expect. Poor girl, she's a long way from home and frightened."

"I understand, Jim," Magnolia told him, "and, remember, whatever happens, you can always count on me."

* * * * *

"I must say you're not a very admirable representative of Terrestrial womanhood!" James snapped, as soon as the door had slammed behind him and his wife, leaving them alone together in the principal room of the cottage. "Insulting the very first native you meet!"

"I did not either insult her. All I said was, 'What beautiful flowers—do you suppose the fruit is edible?' How was I to know it—*she* could understand? Naturally I wouldn't dream of eating her fruit now. It would probably taste nasty anyway. And how do you think *I* felt when a *tree* answered me back? You don't care that I fainted dead away, and I've never fainted before in my life. All you care about is that old vegetable's feelings! It was bad enough, feeling for five months that someone had come between us, but to find out it wasn't some*one* but some*thing*—!"

"Phyllis," he said coldly, "I'll thank you to keep a civil tongue in your head."

Dropping into the overstuffed chair, his wife dabbed at her eyes with a handkerchief. "She wasn't so very polite to me!"

"Look, Phyllis—" he strove to make his voice calm, adult, reasonable—"you happened to have hit on rather a touchy point with her. Those trees are dioecious, you know, like us, and she isn't mated. And, well, she has rather a lot of xylem zones—rings, you know."

"Are you trying to tell me she's old?"

"Well, she's no sapling any more. And, consideration aside, you know it's government's policy for us to establish good relations with any intelligent life-form we have to share a planet with. You weren't in there trying."

Phyllis put away her handkerchief with what he hoped would be a final sniff. "I suppose I shouldn't have acted that way," she conceded.

"Now you're talking like my own dear Phyllis," James said tenderly, though, as a matter of fact, he had a very remote idea of what his own dear Phyllis was like. He had met her only a couple of months before the scout mission was scheduled, and so their courtship had been brief, and the actual weeks of marriage even briefer. He had remembered Phyllis as beautiful–and she was beautiful. He had not, however, remembered her as pig-headed–and pig-headed she was, too.

"How come she hasn't a mate? I didn't think trees were choosy."

*   *   *   *   *

He wouldn't take exception to that statement, uncharitable though it was; after all, someone whose only acquaintance with trees had been with the Terrestrial variety would naturally be incapable of appreciating the total tree at its highest development.

"It's a great tragedy," he told her in a hushed tone. "There was a blight some years back and most of the male trees died off, except for a few on the other side of the planet–well out of bee-shot, even if the females there would let the females here have any pollen, which they absolutely won't."

"I don't blame them," Phyllis said coldly. Of course she would identify at once with the trees whose domestic lives seemed to be threatened.

"It's not that so much. It's that the male trees produce so little pollen."

"This would be a good place for people with hay fever then, wouldn't it?"

"And even when there is fruit, so much of it tends to be parthenocarpous—no seeds." He sighed. "The entire race is dying out."

"How is it you know so much about botany?" she asked suspiciously. "It's not your field."

"I don't know so very much, really," he smiled. "I had to learn a little, if I wanted to work the land, so I borrowed an elementary text from Cutler." Had he been a trifle idealistic in quitting his snug, if uninspiring, job on the faculty to join in this Utopian venture? So many of the other men at the university had enrolled, it had seemed a splendid idea until Phyllis's arrival.

"Daddy never had any trouble working his land and he doesn't know a thing about botany. You've been boning up on it just to please *her*!"

"Phyllis! How can you jump to conclusions without a shred of evidence?" Not that she wouldn't be able to collect such evidence later, because the allegation happened to be correct. *If, instead of coming to Elysium, I had merely gone to China, would she have thought it so odd that I studied Chinese? Then why, where the natives are trees, shouldn't I study botany? The woman is unreasonable.*

*   *   *   *   *

"And will her—people let you farm?"

Now he could show her how cogently and comprehensively he could answer a logical question. "That aspect of the situation will be all right, dear, because only the trees are an intelligent species and, even of them, some aren't so bright. They won't have any more objection to our eating the other fruit and vegetables than we would have to an extraterrestrial's eating our eggs and chickens, for example. We're going to try to introduce some Earth plants here, though, as the higher forms of vegetation are dying out and we're afraid the lower might follow. Pity it's too late for a sound conservation program."

*   *   *   *   *

Phyllis said grimly, "She doesn't think it's too late for a sound conservation program. She still has hopes–far-fetched, maybe, and I'm not so sure they are. Mark my words, James, she's got designs on *you*."

"Don't be idiotic," he protested. "That would be–" he attempted to introduce a light note–"it would be miscegenation."

"These foreigners can't be expected to have our standards." And she burst into tears again. "A fine thing to go through that miserable five-month trip only to find out a tree has alienated my husband's affections."

"Oh, come on, Phyl!" He still was trying for a smile. "What would a tree see in me?"

"I'm beginning to wonder what I saw in you. You never loved me; you just wanted a wife to come out and colonize with you and b-b-breed."

What could he say? It was almost true. Phyllis was a beautiful girl and he loved her, but, if he had planned to remain as an instructor with the Romance Languages Department instead of joining the scout mission, he knew he would never have asked her to be his wife ... for her sake, of course, as well as his own. He should say something to reassure her, but the words wouldn't come.

"I don't like it here," Phyllis sobbed. "I don't like blue leaves. I don't like blue grass. I like them green, the way they're supposed to be. I hate this nasty planet. It's all wrong. I want to go home."

She was very young–less than eight years younger than he, true, but he was mature for his age. They didn't know each other very well. And, finally, there were more men than women on the planet and he had noticed that the bachelors had seemed readily disposed, upon her arrival the day before, to overlook the fact that she had no college degree. So he must be patient with her.

"There's nothing wrong about it, dear. The plants here synthesize cyanophyll instead of chlorophyll; that's why the leaves are blue instead of green. And, of course, there are different mineral constituents of the soil–more aluminum and copper, for instance, than on Earth, and some elements we haven't quite isolated yet. So, you see, they're bound to be a little different from Terrestrial trees."

"A little different I wouldn't mind," she said sulkily, "but they're a lot different without being nearly alien enough."

"Look, Phyllis–*dear*–those trees have been very hospitable, very kind. We owe them a lot. They themselves suggested that we come here and live with them in, so to speak, symbiosis."

"That's a fine idea!"

*   *   *   *   *

He beamed. "I knew you'd understand after I had explained it to you."

"We provide the brains and they provide the furniture."

"Phyllis! What a thing to say!"

"I've heard of man-eating trees before. I suppose there could be man-loving ones, too."

"Phyllis, these trees are as gentle and sweet as–as–" He didn't know how he could explain it to her. No one who had never been friends with a tree could appreciate the true beauty of the xylemic character. "Why, we even offered to go over to the other side of the planet and fetch some pollen for them, but they wouldn't hear of it. Unfortunately, they'd rather die than be mated to anyone they had never met."

"What a perfectly disgusting idea!"

"I don't think so. Trees can be idealistic–"

"You fetching pollen for her, I mean. Naturally she wouldn't want pollen from a tree on the other side of the planet. She wants *you!*"

"Don't be silly. Incompatibility usually exists between the pollen of one species and the stigmata of another. Besides," he added patiently, "I haven't got pollen."

"You'd better not, or it won't be her who'll have the stigmata."

"Phyllis–" he sat down on the arm of her chair and tried to embrace her–"you know that you're the only life-form I love."

"Please, James." She pushed him away. "I guess I love you, too, in spite of everything ... but I don't want to make a public spectacle of myself."

"What do you mean now?"

"That tree would know everything that goes on. She's telepathic."

"Where did you get a ridiculous idea like that? What kind of rubbish have you been reading?"

"All right, tell me: how else did she learn to speak such good English?"

"It's because she's of a very high order of intelligence. And I suppose–" he laughed modestly–"because I'm such a good teacher."

"I don't care how good a teacher you are–a tree couldn't learn to speak a language so well in five months. She must be telepathic. It's the only explanation."

*   *   *   *   *

"Give her time," the tree advised later, as James came out on the lawn to talk to his only friend on the planet.

He hadn't seen much of the other scouts since the house-building frenzy had started, and visits among the men had decreased. The base camp, where the bachelors and the older married couples lived, was located a good distance away from his land, for he had raised his honeymoon cottage far from the rest; he had wanted to have his Phyllis all to himself. In the idyll he had visualized for the two of them, she would need no company but his. Little had he imagined that, within twenty-four hours of her arrival, he would be looking for company himself.

"I suppose so," he said, kicking at a root. "Oh, I'm sorry, Maggie; I didn't think."

"That's all right," Magnolia said bravely. "It didn't really hurt. That female has got you all upset, you poor boy."

James muttered a feeble defense of his wife.

"Jim, forgive me if I speak frankly," the tree went on in a low rustle, "but do you think she's really worthy of you?"

"Of course she is!"

"Surely on your planet you could have found a mate more admirable, high-minded, exemplary—more, in short, like yourself. Or are all the human females inferior specimens like Phyllis?"

"They're—she suits me," James said doggedly.

"Of course, of course. It's very noble of you to defend her; you would have disappointed me if you had said anything else, and I honor you for it, James."

He kicked at one of the pebbles. The tree meant well, he knew, yet, like so many well-meaning friends, she succeeded only in dispiriting him. It was almost like being back at the faculty club.

"I don't suppose a clod like her would have brought any more books along," the tree changed the subject. James's own library had been insufficient to slake the tree's intellectual thirst, so he had gone all over the planet to borrow books for Magnolia. Dr. Lakin, at Base, who had formerly taught English literature, possessed a fine collection which he had been reluctant to lend until he had learned that they were not for James but for a tree. At that, he had fetched the books himself, since he was anxious to meet her.

"A lot of the trees here have learned the English language," he had told James, "but none seems to have developed a taste for its literature. Your Magnolia is undoubtedly a superior specimen. Excellent natural taste, too—perhaps a little unformed when it comes to poetry and the more sophisticated aspects of life, but she'll learn, she'll learn."

*   *   *   *   *

Unfortunately, the same, James knew, could hardly be said of his wife. "Phyllis did bring some books," he told Magnolia.

"For you, no doubt. That was kind of her. I'm sure she has many good qualities which will unfold one by one, as her meristems start differentiating. I hope you don't feel I've been too—well, personal, Jim. I was only trying to help. If I've gone too far...."

"Of course not, Maggie. After all—" he laughed bitterly—"I do know you better than I know her."

"We *have* been good friends, haven't we, Jim? It was rather nice—these five months we spent alone together. For the first time in my life, I have never regretted being so far from my sisters. 'And this our life, exempt from public haunt, finds tongues in trees, books in the running brooks, sermons in stones, and good in everything.'"

Her blue leaves shone violet in the scarlet rays of the setting sun; the gold of her trunk was lit with red radiance. She was the most beautiful creature he had ever seen ... but she was a tree, not a woman.

"I'm sure she'll fit in after a while," Magnolia continued. "Perhaps she isn't well. She seems to guttate an awful lot. Do you suppose she's been overwatered?"

"That wasn't guttation," James said heavily. "It was tears. It means she's unhappy."

"Unhappy? Perhaps she won't fit in on this planet, in which case she should by all means go back to Earth. It's cruel and unfair to keep an intelligent—loosely speaking—life-form anywhere against her will, don't you think?"

"She'll be happy here," James vowed. "I'll *make* her happy."

"Well, I certainly hope you can manage it! By the way, do you suppose you'll have a chance to read me the books she brought, or will she be keeping you too busy?"

"I'll never be too busy to read to you, Magnolia."

"That's very nitrogenous of you, Jim. Our—intellectual communions have meant a lot to me. I'd hate to have to give them up."

"So would I," he said. "But there won't be any need to. Phyllis will understand."

"I certainly hope so. I so admire your English literature. It's so deeply cognizant of the really meaningful things in life. And if your coming to this planet has served only to add poetry to our cultural heritage, it would be reason enough to welcome you with open limbs. For it was a truly perceptive versifier who wrote the immortally simple lines: 'Poems are made by fools like me, but only God can make a tree.'

"And such a charming tune to go with it, too," Magnolia went on. "We have always sung the music that the wind and the rain have taught us, but, until you came, we never thought of putting words and melody together to form one glorious whole. 'A tree that may in summer wear,'" she caroled in a pleasing contralto, "'a nest of robins in her hair.' By the way, Jim, ever since reading that poem, I've been meaning to ask you precisely what are robins and do you think they'd look well in my hair, by which, I suppose the bard refers, in a somewhat pedestrian flight of fancy, to leaves?"

"They're a kind of bird," he said drearily.

"Birds—nesting in my hair! I wouldn't think of allowing it. But then I suppose Terrestrial birds are quite different from ours? More housebroken, shall we say?"

"Everything's different," James said and, for an irrational moment, he hated everything that was blue that should have been green, everything sweet that should have been vicious, everything intelligent that should have been mindless.

*   *   *   *   *

Since matters could not grow much worse, they improved to a degree. After a day or two had passed, Phyllis, being a conscientious girl, came to realize how wrong it had been for her as a Terrestrial immigrant to show overt hostility toward a native of the planet that had welcomed her.

"But how can she be a—a person?" Phyllis wanted to know, when they were inside the cottage, for she had learned to hold her tongue when they were near Magnolia or any of her sisters, who, though they could not speak the language as fluently as she, understood it very well and eavesdropped at every possible opportunity in order, they said, to improve their accents. "She's a tree. A plant. And plants are just vegetables." She stabbed her needle energetically through the tablecloth she was embroidering.

"You mustn't project Terrestrial attitudes upon Elysian ones," James said, patiently looking up from his book. "And don't underestimate Magnolia's capabilities. She has sense organs, and motor organs, too. She can't move from where she is, because she's rooted to the ground, but she's capable of turgor movements, like certain Terrestrial forms of vegetation—for example, the sensitive plant or blue grass."

"Blue grass," Phyllis exclaimed. "I'm sick of blue grass. I want green grass."

"However, these trees have conscious control of their *pulvini*, whereas the Earth's plants don't, and so they can do a lot of things that Earth plants can't."

"It sounds like a dirty word to me."

"*Pulvini* merely means motor organs."

"Oh."

*   *   *   *   *

He closed his book, which was a more advanced botany text, covered with the jacket of a French novel in order to spare Phyllis's feelings. "Darling, can't you get it through your pretty head that they're intelligent life-forms? If it'll make it easier for you to think of them as human beings who happen to look like trees, then do that."

"That's exactly what I *am* doing. And I'm quite sure she thinks of you as a tree who happens to look like a human being."

"Phyllis, sometimes I think you're being deliberately difficult. Do you know one of the reasons why I took such pains to teach Magnolia English? It was that I hoped she would be a companion for you, that you could talk to each other when I had to be away from home."

"Why do you call her Magnolia? She isn't a lot like one."

"Isn't she? I thought she was. You see, I don't know so much botany, after all." Actually, he had picked that name for the tree because it expressed both the arboreal and the feminine at the same time—and also because it was one of the loveliest names he knew. But he couldn't tell Phyllis that; there would be further misunderstanding. "Of course she has a name in her own language, but I can't pronounce it."

"They *do* have a language of their own then?"

"Naturally, though they don't get much chance to speak it, since they've grown so few and far apart that verbal communication has become difficult. They communicate by a network of roots that they've developed."

"I don't think that's so clever."

"I merely said ... oh, what's the use of trying to explain everything to you? You just don't want to understand."

*   *   *   *   *

Phyllis put down her needlework and closed her eyes. "James," she said, opening them again, "it's no use pretending. I've been trying to be sympathetic and understanding, but I can't do it. That tree—I've forced myself to be nice to her, but the more I see of her, the more convinced I am that she's trying to steal you from me."

Phyllis was beginning to poison his mind, he thought, because it had seemed to him also, in his last conversation with Magnolia, that he had discerned more than ordinary warmth in her attitude toward him ... and perhaps a trace of spite toward his wife?

Preposterous! The tree had only been trying to cheer him up as any friend might reasonably do. After all, a tree and a man.... Nonsense! One had an anabolic metabolism, one a catabolic.

But this was a different kind of tree. She spoke, she read, she was capable of conscious turgor movements. And he, he had often thought secretly, was a different kind of man. Whereas Phyllis....

But that was disloyalty—to the type as well as the individual. The tree could be a companion to him, but she could not give him sons to work his land; she could not give him daughters to populate his planet; moreover, she did not, could not possibly know what human love meant, while Phyllis could at least learn.

"Look, dear," he said, sitting down beside his wife on the couch and taking her hand in his. She didn't draw away this time. "Suppose that what you say is true—not that it is, of course. Just because the tree has a crush on me doesn't mean I necessarily have a crush on her, does it?"

His wife looked up at him, her rose-red lips parted, her moss-gray eyes shining. "Oh, if only I could believe that, James!"

"Anyhow, she doesn't know what the whole thing's about, poor kid!"

"Poor *kid*!"

"Phyllis, you know you're prettier than any tree." That was not literally true, but reason was useless; he had to make his point in terms she could understand. "And, remember, she's got a lot of rings–she must be centuries old–while you are only nineteen."

"Twenty," Phyllis corrected. "I had a birthday on the ship."

"Well, you certainly must allow me to wish you a happy birthday, darling."

She was in his arms at last; he was about to kiss her, and the tree seemed very remote, when she drew back. "But are you sure she doesn't–she isn't–she can't be watching us?"

"Darling, I swear it!" "*Lady, by yonder blessed moon I swear, that tips with silver all these fruit-tree tops*".... But he had sense enough not to say it, and Elysium had not one blessed moon, but three, and everything was all right.

For a while anyway.

*   *   *   *   *

"I see your wife is developing a corm," the tree remarked, as James paused for a chat. He hadn't much time to be sociable those days, for there was such a lot of work to be done, so many preparations to be made, so many things to be requisitioned from Earth. The supply ships were beginning to come now, bringing necessities and an occasional luxury for those who could afford it.

"She's pregnant," James explained. "Happened before I left Earth."

"How do you mean?"

"She's about to fruit. Didn't I read that zoology book to you?"

"Yes, but–oh, James, it all seems so vulgar! To fruit without ever having bloomed–how squalid!"

"It all depends on how you look at it," he said. "I–that is, we had hoped that when the baby came, you would be godmother to it. You know what that is, don't you?"

"Of course I do. You read *Cinderella* to me. I know it's a great honor. But I'm afraid I must decline."

"Why? I thought you were my–our friend."

"Jim, there is something I must confess: my feelings toward you are not merely those of a friend. Although Phyllis doesn't have too many rings of intellect, she is a female, so she knew all along." Magnolia's leaves rustled diffidently. "I feel toward you the way I never felt toward any intelligent life-form, but only toward the sun, the soil, the rain. I sense a tropism that seems to incline me toward you. In fact, I'm afraid, Jim, in your own terms, I love you."

"But you're a tree! You can't love me in my own terms, because trees can't love in the way people can, and, of course, people can't love like trees. We belong to two entirely different species, Maggie. You can't have listened to that zoology book very attentively."

"Our race is a singularly adaptable one or we wouldn't have survived so long, Jim, or gone so far in our particular direction. It's lack of fertility, not lack of enterprise, that's responsible for our decline. And I think your species must be an adaptable one, too; you just haven't really tried. Oh, James, let us reverse the classical roles–let me be the Apollo to your Daphne! Don't let Phyllis stand in our way. The Greek gods never let a little thing like marriage interfere with their plans."

*   *   *   *   *

"But I love Phyllis," he said in confusion. "I love you, too," he added, "but in a different way."

"Yes, I know. More like a sister. However, I have plenty of sisters and I don't need a brother."

"We're starting a conservation program," he tried to comfort her. "We have every hope of getting some pollen from the other side of the planet once we have explained to the trees there how far we can make a little go, and you've got to accept it; you mustn't be silly about it."

"It isn't the same thing, Jim, and you know it. One of the penalties of intelligence is a diffusiveness of the natural instincts. I would rather not fruit at all than–"

"Magnolia, you just don't understand. No matter how much you–well, pursue me, I can never turn into a laurel tree."

"I didn't–"

"Or any kind of tree! Look, some more books were just sent over from Base."

Magnolia gave a rueful rustle. "Just were sent? Didn't they come over a month ago?"

James flushed. "I know I haven't had a chance to do much reading to you in the last few weeks, Maggie–or any at all, in fact–but I've been so busy. After the baby's born, things will be much less hectic and we'll be able to catch up."

"Of course, James. I understand. Naturally your family comes first."

"One of the books that came was an advanced zoology text that might make things a little clearer."

"I should very much like to hear it. When you have the time to spare, that is."

"Tell you what," he said. "I'll get the book and read you the chapter on the reproductive system in mammals. Won't take more than an hour or so."

"If you're in a hurry, it can wait."

"No," he told her. "This will make me feel a little less guilty about having neglected you."

*   *   *   *   *

"Whereupon the umbilical cord is severed," he concluded, "and the human infant is ready to take its place in the world as a separate entity. Now do you understand, Magnolia?"

"No," she said. "Where do the bees come in?"

"I thought you were in such a hurry to get to Base, James," Phyllis remarked sweetly from the doorway, wiping her reddening hands on a dish towel.

"I am, dear." He slipped the book behind his back; it was possible that, in her present state of mind—induced, of course, by her delicate condition—Phyllis might misunderstand his motive in reading that particular chapter of that particular book to that particular tree. "I just stopped

for a chat with Magnolia. She's agreed to be godmother to the baby."

"How very nice of her. Earth Government will be so pleased at such a *fine* example of rapport with the natives. You might even get a medal. Wouldn't that be nice?... James," she hurried on, before he could speak, "you still haven't found any green-leafed plants on the planet, have you? Have you looked everywhere? Have you looked *hard*?"

"Haven't I told you time and time again, Mrs. Haut," the tree said, "that there aren't any–that there can't be any? It's impossible to synthesize chlorophyll from the light rays given off by our sun–only cyanophyll. What do you want with a green-leafed plant, anyway?"

Phyllis's voice broke. "I think I'd lose my mind if I was convinced that I'd never see a green leaf again. All this awful blue, blue, blue, all the time, and the leaves never fall, or, if they do, there are new ones right away to take their place. They're always there–always blue."

"We're everblue," Magnolia explained. "Sorry, but that's the way it is."

"Jim, I hate to hurt your feelings, but I just have to take down those curtains. The colors–I can't stand it!"

*   *   *   *   *

"Pregnant women sometimes get fanciful notions," James said to the tree. "It's part of the pregnancy syndrome. Try not to pay any attention."

"Kindly don't explain me to a tree!" Phyllis cried. "I have a right to prefer green, don't I?"

"There is, as your proverb says, no accounting for strange tastes," the tree murmured. "However–"

"We're going to have a formal christening," James interrupted, for the sake of the peace. "We thought we should, since ours will be the first baby born on the planet. Everybody on Elysium will come–that is, all the human beings. Only because they *can* come, you know; we'd love to have the trees if they were capable of locomotor movement. You'll get to widen your social contacts, Maggie. Dr. Lakin and Dr. Cutler will probably be here; I know you'll be glad to see Dr. Lakin again, and you've been anxious to meet Dr. Cutler. They've been asking after you, too. I think Dr. Lakin is planning to write a monograph on you for the *Journal of the*

American Association of Professors of English Literature–
with your permission, of course."

"Christening–that's one of your native festivals, isn't
it? It should be most interesting."

"That's right," Phyllis murmured. "It will be
Christmas soon. I'd almost forgotten. It'll be the first
Christmas I've ever spent away from home. And there
won't be any snow or–or anything." She started to
guttate–to cry again.

"Cheer up, honey," Jim said. "It won't be as bad as you
think, because I didn't forget Christmas was coming.
There's something specially nice for you on its way from
Earth; I only hope it gets here on time." Phyllis sniffled.
"Maybe we'll have a Christmas party, too. Would you like
that?" But she remained unresponsive.

He turned to the tree. "Christening's entirely
different, though," he explained. "It's–I guess naming the
fruit would be the best way to describe it."

"Is that so?" Magnolia said. "What kind of fruit do you
expect to have, Mrs. Haut? Oranges? Bananas? As your
good St. Luke says, the tree is known by its fruit. You
look as if yours might be a watermelon."

"Why, the–idea!" Phyllis choked. "Are you going to
stand there, James, and let that *vegetable* insult me?"

"I'm sure she didn't mean to," he protested. "She got
confused by–that zoology book I read her."

The door slammed behind his weeping wife.

"I don't think you quite understand, Maggie," he said.
"In fact, sometimes I almost think you, too, don't want to
understand."

"I know what kind of fruit it's going to be," the tree
concluded triumphantly. "Sour apples."

*   *   *   *   *

"Ouch," exclaimed Magnolia, "that tickles! There's
more to acting as a Christmas tree than I had anticipated
from your glowing descriptions, Jim."

"Here, dear," Phyllis said, "maybe you'd better let me put the decorations on her."

"You can't get on the ladder in your condition," he said, apprehensive not only for her welfare but for the tree's. Phyllis had not taken kindly to the idea of having Magnolia as official Christmas tree, suggesting that, if she must participate in the ceremonies, it might be better in the capacity of Yule log. However, Jim knew Magnolia would be offended if any other tree were chosen to be decorated.

"I'll manage all right," he assured his wife. "If you want to be useful, you might put on some coffee and make sandwiches or something. The bachelors are coming over from Base with that equipment that arrived yesterday, and they'll probably be glad of a snack before turning in."

"The coffee's already on and the canapes made," Phyllis smiled. "And I've baked cookies, too, and whipped up a batch of penuche. What kind of a Christmas party do you think it would be without refreshments?"

"Very efficient, isn't she?" Magnolia remarked, as the battery-powered lights that James had affixed to her began to wink on, for the deep red-violet dusk had already fallen and the first moon was rising. "Have you thought, Mrs. Haut, that if you fruit today, it will save the expense of another festival?"

"I don't expect to fruit for another two months," Phyllis said coldly, "and why shouldn't we have another festival? We can afford it and I like parties. I haven't been to one since the day I landed."

"Is the life out here getting a little quiet for you, petiole?" the tree asked solicitously. "It must be hard when one has no intellectual resources upon which to draw."

*   *   *   *   *

Phyllis held her peace for ten seconds; then, "I wonder where those boys can be," she said. "I hope they bring some pickles along. I asked to have some sent, but I'm accustomed to having no attention paid to what I want."

"There's a surprise coming for you, Phyllis," James could not help telling her again, hoping to arouse some semblance of interest. "Something I know you'll love.... And for you, too," he said courteously to Magnolia.

"You mean the same surprise for both, or a surprise apiece?" the tree asked.

"Oh, one for each, of course."

"I see the lights of the 'copter now!" Phyllis cried and, running out into the middle of the lawn, began waving her handkerchief. He hadn't seen her so pleasantly excited for a long time.

"I don't suppose I'll need to turn on the landing lights," he said to Magnolia. "You should do the trick."

"Am I all finished?" she rustled anxiously. "I do wish I could see myself. How do I look?"

"Splendid. I've never had as beautiful a Christmas tree as you, Maggie," he told her with complete honesty. "Not even on Earth."

"I'm glad, Jim, but I still wish I could be more to you than just a Christmas tree."

"Shh. The others might hear."

For the helicopter had landed and the visitors were pouring out, with shouts of admiration. Not only the bachelors had come—and in full force—but some of the older men from Base, who apparently felt they could manage to do without their wives for twelve hours, even if those hours included Christmas Eve. He wondered where he and Phyllis could put them all, but some could sleep outside, if need be, for it was never cold on Elysium. The winds were gentle and the rains light and fragrant.

*   *   *   *   *

While the visitors were crowding around Phyllis and the tree, James rooted eagerly through the packages they had brought, until he found what he wanted. Then he rushed over to the group. "I know I should wait until tomorrow, but I want to give the girls their presents now." The other men smiled sympathetically, almost as joyful as he. "Merry Christmas, Magnolia!" He hoped Phyllis would understand that it was etiquette which dictated that the alien life-form should get her gift first.

"Thank you," the tree said. "I am deeply touched. I don't believe anyone ever gave me a present before. What is it?"

"Liquid plant food—vitamins and minerals, you know. For you to drink."

"What fun!" she exclaimed in pretty excitement. "Pour some over me right now!"

"Not so fast, Jim, boy!" Dr. Cutler, the biologist, snatched the jug from James' hand. "First you-all better let me take a sample of this here stuff back to Base to test on a lower life-form, so's I can make sure it won't do anything bad to Miss Magnolia. Might have iron in it and I have a theory that iron may not be beneficial for the local vegetation."

"Oh, thank you!" the tree rustled. "It's so very thoughtful of you, Doctor, but I'm sure Jim would never give me anything that would injure me."

"I'm sure he isn't fixing to do a thing like that, ma'am, but he's no botanist."

"And for you, Phyllis...." James handed his wife the awkward bundle to unwrap for herself.

She tore the papers off slowly. "Oh, Jim, darling, it's– it's–"

"You wanted a bit of green, so I ordered a plant from Earth. You like it? I hope you do."

"Oh, *Jim*!" She embraced him and the pot simultaneously. "More than *anything*!"

"It won't stay green," Magnolia observed. "Either it'll turn blue or it'll die. Puny-looking specimen, isn't it?"

"Well," said James, "it's only a youngster. I guess this Christmas is too early, but next Christmas there ought to be berries. It's a holly plant, Phyl."

"Holly," she repeated, her voice shaking a little. "*Holly*." She and Dr. Cutler exchanged glances.

"I told you, Miz Phyllis, ma'am–he may know the first thing about botany, but he doesn't know anything after that."

"Jim," Phyllis said, linking her free arm through his, "I misjudged you. Dr. Cutler is right. You don't know so very much about botany, after all."

*   *   *   *   *

He looked at her blankly. Her voice was trembling, and not with tears this time. "I love this little plant; it's just what I wanted ... but there aren't ever going to be any berries, because, to have berries, you have to have two plants. And the right two. Holly's di–dio–it's just like us."

"Oh," James said, feeling thoroughly inadequate. "I'm sorry."

"But you mustn't be sorry. I'm going to plant it here on Elysium, and I hope it will stay green in spite of what she says, and it'll have blossoms anyway ... and it was very, very sweet of you, dear."

She kissed his cheek.

"Is this one a boy or a girl?" Magnolia asked.

"You-all can't tell till it blooms, Miss Magnolia, ma'am," Dr. Cutler informed her.

"Maybe I can. Hand it up here, please."

Phyllis paused for an irresolute moment, then, smiling nervously at her guests, obliged.

"It's a boy," Magnolia announced, after a minute. "A boy." She gave back the pot reluctantly. "Phyllis," she said, "you and I have never been friends and I admit that it's been my fault just as much as yours."

"As much as mine?" Phyllis echoed. "I like that–" and was going to go on when she obviously recollected that they had company, and stopped.

"So I know it's presumptuous of me to ask you a favor."

"Yes, Magnolia?" Phyllis said, her fine cornsilk eyebrows arched a trifle. "What is this favor?"

"When you plant the little fellow–you said you were going to, anyhow–would you plant him near me?"

Phyllis looked down at the plant she held cradled in her arms and then up at the tree. "Of course, Magnolia," she said, frowning slightly. "I didn't realize...." Her voice began to tremble. "I *have* been pretty rotten, haven't I?" She looked toward James, but he turned his glance away.

"Just because you were a plant," Phyllis continued, "didn't mean I had to be a b-b-beast. It must have been awful for you, seeing me like this, practically crowing over you, and knowing that you yourself would never have the chance to be a m-m-m-mother."

"'Full many a flower is born to blush unseen,'" Magnolia said sadly, "'and waste its sweetness on the desert air.'"

*   *   *   *   *

Phyllis was crying unashamedly now. "I'll plant him right next to you–Maggie. I want you to have him. He can be your baby."

"Thank you, Phyl," Maggie said softly. "That's very ... blue of you."

"Although I think that's a jim-dandy idea," the biologist said, "and I sure wouldn't want to do anything to discourage it, being real interested in the results of an experiment like that my own self, I don't think you ought to feel so mean about it, Miz Phyllis. If all she wanted–begging your pardon, Miss Magnolia, ma'am–was a baby, why didn't she take an interest in the holly until she found out it was a male? Why wouldn't a little old girl holly have done as well?"

"Why–why, you scheming vegetable!" Phyllis exploded at Magnolia, clutching the holly plant to her protective bosom. "He's much too young for you, and I'm going to plant him far away, where he can't possibly fall into your clutches."

"Now, Miss Phyllis, we-all mustn't look at things out of their proper perspective."

"Then why did you take your hat off when you were introduced to Miss Magnolia, Cutler?" Dr. Lakin asked interestedly.

"Sir, where I come from, we respect femininity, whether it be animal, vegetable or mineral. Nonetheless, we-all got to remember, though Miss Magnolia is unquestionably a lady, she is not a woman."

Phyllis began to laugh hysterically. "You're right!" she gasped. "I had almost forgotten *she* was only a tree. And that *it* is only a little Christmas holly plant that's probably going to die, anyway–they almost always do."

"That's cruel, Phyllis," James said, "and you know it is."

"Do you really think I'm cruel? Are you going to tell the Society for the Prevention of Cruelty to Vegetables on me? But why am I cruel? I'm giving her the holly. That's what she wants, isn't it? Do you hear that, Miss Magnolia, ma'am? *He*'s all yours. We'll plant *him* next to you–right away. And I hope *he* doesn't die. I hope *he* grows up to make you a good husband."

*   *   *   *   *

"She's really quite remarkable," Dr. Lakin said to James later that same evening, after the planting ceremonies were over and the rest of the party had gone into the cottage for fresh coffee and more sandwiches and cookies and penuche. "Quite remarkable. You're a lucky man, Haut."

"Thank you, sir," James replied abstractedly. "I'm sure Phyllis will be pleased to–"

"*Phyllis!* Oh, Mrs. Haut is a very remarkable woman, of course. A handsome, strong girl; she'll make a splendid mother, I'm sure. But I was referring to Miss Magnolia. She's a credit to you, my boy. If for no other reason, your name will go down in the history of our colony as that of the guide and mentor of Miss Magnolia. That's quite a tree you have there."

James looked at the dark form of the tree–for the lights had been turned out–silhouetted against the three pale moons and the violet night. "Yes, she is," he said.

"You're fortunate to be her neighbor ... and her friend."

"Yes, I am."

"Well, I expect I'd better join the rest. Are you coming on in, Jim?"

"In a little while, sir. I thought I'd–I wanted to have a word with Magnolia. I won't be long."

"Of course, of course. I'm delighted to see that there is such an excellent relationship between you.... Good night, Miss Magnolia!" he called.

"Good night, Dr. Lakin," the tree replied, politely enough, but it was obvious that she was preoccupied with her new charge, who stood as close to her as it was possible to plant him and yet allow room for him to grow.

*   *   *   *   *

The door closed. James walked across the lawn until he was quite near Magnolia. "Maggie," he whispered, reaching out to touch her trunk–smooth it was, and hard, but he could feel the vibrant life pulsing inside it. Certainly she was not a plant, not *just* a plant, even though she was a tree. She was a native of Elysium, neither animal nor vegetable, unique unto the planet, unique unto herself. "Maggie."

"Yes, Jim. Don't you think his silhouette is so graceful there in the moonlight? He isn't really puny–just frail."

"Maggie, you're not serious about this holly?"

"What do you mean?" And still he didn't have her full attention. Would he ever have it again?

"Serious about raising him to be your–your–"

"Why not, Jim?"

"It's impossible."

"Is it? It certainly is far more possible with him, isn't it? That much I understood from your zoology books."

"I suppose so."

"Besides, I have nothing to lose, have I?"

"But even if it were possible, wouldn't it be humiliating for you? The creature's mindless!"

Magnolia's leaves rustled in the darkness. She was laughing–a little bitterly. "Your Phyllis isn't your intellectual equal, Jim, and yet you say you love her and I suppose you do. Am I not entitled to my follies also?"

But she couldn't compare Phyllis to a holly plant! It was unreasonable.

"He may die, of course," Magnolia said. "I've got to be prepared for that. The soil is different, the air is different, the sun is different. But the chances are, if he survives, he'll turn blue. And if he turns blue, who knows what other changes might be brought about? Maybe the plants on your Earth aren't inherently mindless, Jim. Maybe they just didn't have a chance. 'Know ye the land where the cypress and myrtle are emblems of deeds that are done in their clime...?' That land isn't Earth, Jim, so it might just possibly be Elysium."

*   *   *   *   *

Again he didn't say anything. What he wanted to say, he had no right to say, so he kept silent.

"It'll be a chance for me, too, Jim. At least we're both plants, he and I. That gives us a headstart."

"Yes, I suppose it does."

"Intellect doesn't count for much in the propagation of the species. Life goes on without regard for reason, and that's mainly what we're here for, to make sure that life goes on—if we're here for anything at all. Thanks to your kind, Jim, life will continue on this planet; it will certainly be your kind of life—and I hope it can be ours as well."

"Yes," he said. "I hope so, too."

And he did, but he wished it didn't have to continue in quite that way. Perhaps it was a trick of the three moons, but the holly plant's leaves seemed to have changed color.. They were no longer green, but almost blue—powder blue.

"You'd best be getting on to your party, Jim," Magnolia said. "You wouldn't want to be remiss in your duties as host. And please close the door gently when you go inside. The little holly plant's asleep."

As he closed the door carefully behind him, he heard a burst of laughter coming from the kitchen, where the guests apparently had assembled–raucous animal laughter–and, rising shrill and noisy above it, Phyllis's company laugh.

Once a Greech

Originally Published In *Galaxy Science Fiction*
April 1957

Illustrated by Alice Julia Christie Dillon

*The mildest of men, Iversen was capable of murder...
to disprove Harkaway's hypothesis that in the midst
of life, we are in life!*

Once a Greech

Just two weeks before the *S. S. Herringbone* of the Interstellar Exploration, Examination (and Exploitation) Service was due to start her return journey to Earth, one of her scouts disconcertingly reported the discovery of intelligent life in the Virago System.

"Thirteen planets," Captain Iversen snarled, wishing there were someone on whom he could place the blame for this mischance, "and we spend a full year here exploring each one of them with all the resources of Terrestrial science and technology, and what happens? On the nineteenth moon of the eleventh planet, intelligent life is discovered. And who has to discover it? Harkaway, of all people. I thought for sure all the moons were cinders or I would never have sent him out to them just to keep him from getting in my hair."

"The boy's not a bad boy, sir," the first officer said. "Just a thought incompetent, that's all–which is to be expected if the Service will choose its officers on the basis of written examinations. I'm glad to see him make good."

Iversen would have been glad to see Harkaway make good, too, only such a concept seemed utterly beyond the bounds of possibility. From the moment the young man had first set foot on the *S. S. Herringbone*, he had seemed unable to make anything but bad. Even in such a conglomeration of fools under Captain Iverson, his idiocy was of outstanding quality.

The captain, however, had not been wholly beyond reproach in this instance, as he himself knew. Pity he had made such an error about the eleventh planet's moons. It was really such a small mistake. Moons one to eighteen and twenty to forty-six still appeared to be cinders. It was all too easy for the spectroscope to overlook Flimbot, the nineteenth.

But it would be Flimbot which had turned out to be a green and pleasant planet, very similar to Earth. Or so Harkaway reported on the intercom.

"And the other forty-five aren't really moons at all," he began. "They're—"

"You can tell me all that when we reach Flimbot," Iversen interrupted, "which should be in about six hours. Remember, that intercom uses a lot of power and we're tight on fuel."

But it proved to be more than six *days* later before the ship reached Flimbot. This was owing to certain mechanical difficulties that arose when the crew tried to lift the mother ship from the third planet, on which it was based. For sentimental reasons, the IEE(E) always tried to establish its prime base on the third planet of a system. Anyhow, when the *Herringbone* was on the point of takeoff, it was discovered that the rock-eating species which was the only life on the third planet had eaten all the projecting metal parts on the ship, including the rocket-exhaust tubes, the airlock handles and the chromium trim.

"I had been wondering what made the little fellows so sick," Smullyan, the ship's doctor, said. "They went wump, wump, wump all night long, until my heart bled for them. Ah, everywhere it goes, humanity spreads the fell seeds of death and destruction—"

"Are you a doctor or a veterinarian?" Iversen demanded furiously. "By Betelgeuse, you act as if I'd crammed those blasted tubes down their stinking little throats!"

"It was you who invaded their paradise with your ship. It was you—"

"Shut up!" Iversen yelled. "Shut up, shut up, shut up, shut up!"

So Dr. Smullyan went off, like many a ship's physician before him, and got good and drunk on the medical stores.

*   *   *   *   *

By the time they finally arrived on Flimbot, Harkaway had already gone native. He appeared at the airlock wearing nothing but a brief, colorful loincloth of alien fabric and a wreath of flowers in his hair. He was fondling a large, woolly pink caterpillar.

"Where is your uniform, sir!" Captain Iversen barked, aghast. If there was one thing he was intolerant of in his command, it was sloppiness.

"This is the undress uniform of the Royal Flimbotzi Navy, sir. I was given the privilege of wearing one as a great *msu'gri*–honor–to our race. If I were to return to my own uniform, it might set back diplomatic relations between Flimbot and Earth as much as–"

"All right!" the captain snapped. "All right, all right, all right!"

He didn't ask any questions about the Royal Flimbotzi Navy. He had deduced its nature when, on nearing Flimbot, he had discovered that the eleventh planet actually had only one moon. The other forty-five celestial objects were spacecraft, quaint and primitive, it was true, but spacecraft nonetheless. Probably it was their orbital formation that had made him think they were moons. Oh, the crew must be in great spirits; they did so enjoy having a good laugh at his expense!

He looked for something with which to reproach Harkaway, and his eye lighted on the caterpillar. "What's that thing you're carrying there?" he barked.

Raising itself on its tail, the caterpillar barked right back at him.

Captain Iversen paled. First he had overlooked the spacecraft, and now, after thirty years of faithful service to the IEE(E) in the less desirable sectors of space, he had committed the ultimate error in his first contact with a new form of intelligent life!

"Sorry, sir," he said, forgetting that the creature—whatever its mental prowess—could hardly be expected to understand Terran yet. "I am just a simple spaceman and my ways are crude, but I mean no harm." He whirled on Harkaway. "I thought you said the natives were humanoid."

The young officer grinned. "They are. This is just a greech. Cuddly little fellow, isn't he?" The greech licked Harkaway's face with a tripartite blue tongue. "The Flimbotzik are mad about pets. Great animal-lovers. That's how I knew I could trust them right from the start. Show me a life-form that loves animals, I always say, and—"

"I'm not interested in what you always say," Iversen interrupted, knowing Harkaway's premise was fundamentally unsound, because he himself was the kindliest of all men, and he hated animals. And, although he didn't hate Harkaway, who was not an animal, save in the strictly Darwinian sense, he could not repress unsportsmanlike feelings of bitterness.

Why couldn't it have been one of the other officers who had discovered the Flimbotzik? Why must it be Harkaway—the most inept of his scouts, whose only talent seemed to be the egregious error, who always rushed into a thing half-cocked, who mistook superficialities for profundities, Harkaway, the blundering fool, the blithering idiot–who had stumbled into this greatest discovery of Iversen's career? And, of course, Harkaway's, too. Well, life was like that and always had been.

"Have you tested those air and soil samples yet?" Iversen snarled into his communicator, for his spacesuit was beginning to itch again as the gentle warmth of Flimbot activated certain small and opportunistic life-forms which had emigrated from a previous system along with the Terrans.

"We're running them through as fast as we can, sir," said a harried voice. "We can offer you no more than our poor best."

"But why bother with all that?" Harkaway wanted to know. "This planet is absolutely safe for human life. I can guarantee it personally."

"On what basis?" Iversen asked.

"Well, I've been here two weeks and I've survived, haven't I?"

"That," Iversen told him, "does not prove that the planet can sustain human life."

Harkaway laughed richly. "Wonderful how you can still keep that marvelous sense of humor, Skipper, after all the things that have been going wrong on the voyage. Ah, here comes the *flim'tuu*–the welcoming committee," he said quickly. "They were a little shy before. Because of the rockets, you know."

"Don't their ships have any?"

"They don't seem to. They're really very primitive affairs, barely able to go from planet to planet."

"If they *go*," Iversen said, "stands to reason *something* must power them."

"I really don't know what it is," Harkaway retorted defensively. "After all, even though I've been busy as a beaver, three weeks would hardly give me time to investigate every aspect of their culture.... Don't you think the natives are remarkably humanoid?" he changed the subject.

They were, indeed. Except for a somewhat greenish cast of countenance and distinctly purple hair, as they approached, in their brief, gay garments and flower garlands, the natives resembled nothing so much as a group of idealized South Sea Islanders of the nineteenth century.

Gigantic butterflies whizzed about their heads. Countless small animals frisked about their feet—more of the pink caterpillars; bright blue creatures that were a winsome combination of monkey and koala; a kind of large, merry-eyed snake that moved by holding its tail in its mouth and rolling like a hoop. All had faces that reminded the captain of the work of the celebrated twentieth-century artist W. Disney.

"By Polaris," he cried in disgust, "I might have known you'd find a *cute* planet!"

"Moon, actually," the first officer said, "since it is in orbit around Virago XI, rather than Virago itself."

"Would you have *wanted* them to be hostile?" Harkaway asked peevishly. "Honestly, some people never seem to be satisfied."

From his proprietary airs, one would think Harkaway had created the natives himself. "At least, with hostile races, you know where you are," Iversen said. "I always suspect friendly life-forms. Friendliness simply isn't a natural instinct."

"Who's being anthropomorphic now!" Harkaway chided.

Iversen flushed, for he had berated the young man for that particular fault on more than one occasion. Harkaway was too prone to interpret alien traits in terms of terrestrial culture. Previously, since all intelligent life-forms with which the *Herringbone* had come into contact had already been discovered by somebody else, that didn't matter too much. In this instance, however, any mistakes of contact or interpretation mattered terribly. And Iversen couldn't see Harkaway not making a mistake; the boy simply didn't have it in him.

"You know you're superimposing our attitude on theirs," the junior officer continued tactlessly. "The Flimbotzik are a simple, friendly, *shig-livi* people, closely resembling some of our historical primitives—in a nice way, of course."

"None of our primitives had space travel," Iversen pointed out.

"Well, you couldn't really call those things spaceships," Harkaway said deprecatingly.

"They go through space, don't they? I don't know what else you'd call them."

"One judges the primitiveness of a race by its cultural and technological institutions," Harkaway said, with a lofty smile. "And these people are laughably backward. Why, they even believe in reincarnation—*mpoola*, they call it."

"How do you know all this?" Iversen demanded. "Don't tell me you profess to speak the language already?"

"It's not a difficult language," Harkaway said modestly, "and I have managed to pick up quite a comprehensive smattering. I dare-say I haven't caught all the nuances—*heeka lob peeka*, as the Flimbotzik themselves say—but they are a very simple people and probably they don't have—"

"Are we going to keep them waiting," Iversen asked, "while we discuss nuances? Since you say you speak the language so well, suppose you make them a pretty speech all about how the Earth government extends the—I suppose it would be hand, in this instance—of friendship to Flimbot and—"

Harkaway blushed. "I sort of did that already, acting as your deputy. *Mpoo*—status—means so much in these simple societies, you know, and they seemed to expect something of the sort. However, I'll introduce you to the Flimflim—the king, you know—" he pointed to an imposing individual in the forefront of the crowd—"and get over all the amenities, shall I?"

"It would be jolly good of you," Iversen said frigidly.

*   *   *   *   *

It was a pity they hadn't discovered Flimbot much earlier in their survey of the Virago System, Iversen thought with regret, because it was truly a pleasant spot and a week was very little time in which to explore a world and study a race, even one as simple as the gentle Flimbotzik actually turned out to be. It seemed amazing that they should have developed anything as advanced as space travel, when their only ground conveyances were a species of wagon drawn by plookik, a species of animal.

But Iversen had no time for further investigation. The *Herringbone's* fuel supply was calculated almost to the minute and so, willy-nilly, the Earthmen had to leave beautiful Flimbot at the end of the week, knowing little more about the Flimbotzik than they had before they came. Only Harkaway, who had spent the three previous weeks on Flimbot, had any further knowledge of the Flimbotzik—and Iversen had little faith in any data he might have collected.

"I don't believe Harkaway knows the language nearly as well as he pretends to," Iversen told the first officer as both of them watched the young lieutenant make the formal speech of farewell.

"Come now," the first officer protested. "Seems to me the boy is doing quite well. Acquired a remarkable command of the language, considering he's been here only four weeks."

"Remarkable, I'll grant you, but is it accurate?"

"He seems to communicate and that is the ultimate objective of language, is it not?"

"Then why did the Flimbotzik fill the tanks with wine when I distinctly told him to ask for water?"

Of course the ship could synthesize water from its own waste products, if necessary, but there was no point in resorting to that expedient when a plentiful supply of pure H_2O was available on the world.

"A very understandable error, sir. Harkaway explained it to me. It seems the word for water, m'koog, is very similar to the word for wine, *mk'oog.* Harkaway himself admits his pronunciation isn't perfect and–"

"All right," Iversen interrupted. "What I'd like to know is what happened to the *mk'oog,* then–"

"The m'koog, you mean? It's in the tanks."

"–because, when they came to drain the wine out of the tanks to put the water in, the tanks were already totally empty."

"I have no idea," the first officer said frostily, "no idea at all. If you'll glance at my papers, you'll note I'm Temperance by affiliation, but if you'd like to search my cabin, anyway, I–"

"By Miaplacidus, man," Iversen exclaimed, "I wasn't accusing you! Of that, anyway!"

Everybody on the vessel was so confoundedly touchy. Lucky they had a stable commanding officer like himself, or morale would simply go to pot.

*   *   *   *   *

"Well, it's all over," Harkaway said, joining them up at the airlock in one lithe bound–a mean feat in that light gravity. "And a right good speech, if I do say so myself. The Flimflim says he will count the thlubbzik with ardent expectation until the mission from Earth arrives with the promised gifts."

"Just what gifts did you take it upon yourself to–" Iversen began, when he was interrupted by a voice behind them crying, "Woe, woe, woe!"

And, thrusting himself past the three other officers, Dr. Smullyan addressed the flim'puu, or farewell committee, assembled outside the ship. "Do not let the Earthmen return to your fair planet, O happily ignorant Flimbotzik," he declaimed, "lest wretchedness and misery be your lot as a result. Tell them, 'Hence!' Tell them,

'Begone!' Tell them, 'Avaunt!' For, know ye, humanity is a blight, a creeping canker–"

He was interrupted by the captain's broad palm clamping down over his mouth.

"Clap him in the brig, somebody, until we get clear of this place," Iversen ordered wearily. "If Harkaway could pick up the Flimbotzi language, the odds are that some of the natives have picked up Terran."

"That's right, always keep belittling me," Harkaway said sulkily as two of the crewmen carried off the struggling medical officer, who left an aromatic wake behind him that bore pungent testimonial to where a part, at least, of the *mk'oog* had gone. "No wonder it took me so long to find myself."

"Oh, have you found yourself at last?" Iversen purred. "Splendid! Now that you know where you are, supposing you do me a big favor and go lose yourself again while we make ready for blastoff."

"For shame," said the first officer as Harkaway stamped off. "For shame!"

"The captain's a hard man," observed the chief petty officer, who was lounging negligently against a wall, doing nothing.

"Ay, that he is," agreed the crewman who was assisting him. "That he is–a hard man, indeed."

"By Caroli, be quiet, all of you!" Iversen yelled. The very next voyage, he was going to have a new crew if he had to transfer to Colonization to do it! Even colonists couldn't be as obnoxious as the sons of space with which he was cursed.

*   *   *   *   *

It was only after the *Herringbone* had left the Virago System entirely that Iversen discovered Harkaway had taken the greech along.

"But you can't abscond with one of the natives' pets!" he protested, overlooking, for the sake of rhetoric, the undeniable fact that Harkaway had already done so and that there could be no turning back. It would expend too much precious fuel and leave them stranded for life on Virago XI^a.

"Nonsense, sir!" Harkaway retorted. "Didn't the Flimflim say everything on Flimbot was mine? *Thlu'pt shig-nliv, snusnigg bnig-nliv* were his very words. Anyhow, they have plenty more greechi. They won't miss this little one."

"But he may have belonged to someone," Iversen objected. "An incident like this could start a war."

"I don't see how he could have belonged to anyone. Followed me around most of the time I was there. We've become great pals, haven't we, little fellow?" He ruffled the greech's pink fur and the creature gave a delighted squeal.

Iversen could already see that the greechik were going to be Flimbot's first lucrative export. From time immemorial, the people of Earth had been susceptible to cuddly little life-forms, which was why Earth had nearly been conquered by the zz^{iu} from Sirius VII, before they discovered them to be hostile and quite intelligent life-forms rather than a new species of tabby.

"Couldn't bear to leave him," Harkaway went on as the greech draped itself around his shoulders and regarded Iversen with large round blue eyes. "The Flimflim won't mind, because I promised him an elephant."

"You mean the diplomatic mission will have to waste valuable cargo space on an elephant!" Iversen sputtered. "And you should know, if anyone does, just how spacesick an elephant can get. By Pherkad, Lieutenant Harkaway, you had no authority to make any promises to the Flimflim!"

"I discovered the Flimbotzik," Harkaway said sullenly. "I learned the language. I established rapport. Just because you happen to be the commander of this expedition doesn't mean you're God, Captain Iversen!"

"Harkaway," the captain barked, "this smacks of downright mutiny! Go to your cabin forthwith and memorize six verses of the Spaceman's Credo!"

The greech lifted its head and barked back at Iversen, again. "That's my brave little watch-greech," Harkaway said fondly. "As a matter of fact, sir," he told the captain, "that was just what I was proposing to do myself. Go to my cabin, I mean; I have no time to waste on inferior prose. I plan to spend the rest of the voyage, or such part as I can spare from my duties–"

"You're relieved of them," Iversen said grimly.

"–working on my book. It's all about the doctrine of *mpoola*–reincarnation, or, if you prefer, metempsychosis. The Flimbotzi religion is so similar to many of the earlier terrestrial theologies–Hindu, Greek, Egyptian, Southern Californian–that sometimes one is almost tempted to stop and wonder if simplicity is not the essence of truth."

Iversen knew that, for the sake of discipline, he should not, once he had ordered Harkaway to his cabin, stop to bandy words, but he was a chronic word-bandier, having inherited the trait from his stalwart Viking ancestors. "How can you have learned all about their religion, their doctrine of reincarnation, in just four ridiculously short weeks?"

"It's a gift," Harkaway said modestly.

"Go to your cabin, sir! No, wait a moment!" For, suddenly overcome by a strange, warm, utterly repulsive emotion, Iversen pointed a quivering finger at the caterpillar. "Did you bring along the proper food for that– that thing? Can't have him starving, you know," he added gruffly. After all, he was a humane man, he told himself; it wasn't that he found the creature tugging at his heart-strings, or anything like that.

"Oh, he'll eat anything we eat, sir. As long as it's not meat. All the species on Flimbot are herbivores. I can't figure out whether the Flimbotzik themselves are vegetarians because they practice *mpoola*, or practice *mpoola* because they're–"

"I don't want to hear another word about *mpoola* or about Flimbot!" Iversen yelled. "Get out of here! And stay away from the library!"

"I have already exhausted its painfully limited resources, sir." Harkaway saluted with grace and withdrew to his cabin, wearing the greech like an affectionate lei about his neck.

*   *   *   *   *

Iverson heard no more about *mpoola* from Harkaway—who, though he did not remain confined to his cabin when he had pursuits to pursue in other parts of the ship, at least had the tact to keep out of the captain's way as much as possible—but the rest of his men seemed able to talk of nothing else. The voyage back from a star system was always longer in relative terms than the voyage out, because the thrill of new worlds to explore was gone; already anticipating boredom, the men were ripe for almost any distraction.

On one return voyage, the whole crew had set itself to the study of Hittite with very creditable results. On another, they had all devoted themselves to the ancient art of alchemy, and, after nearly blowing up the ship, had come up with an elixir which, although not the quintessence—as they had, in their initial enthusiasm, alleged—proved to be an effective cure for hiccups. Patented under the name of *Herringbone* Hiccup Shoo, it brought each one of them an income which would have been enough to support them in more than modest comfort for the rest of their lives.

However, the adventurous life seemed to exert an irresistible lure upon them and they all shipped upon the *Herringbone* again—much to the captain's dismay, for he had hoped for a fresh start with a new crew and there seemed to be no way of getting rid of them short of reaching retirement age.

The men weren't quite ready to accept *mpoola* as a practical religion–Harkaway hadn't finished his book yet–but as something very close to it. The concept of reincarnation had always been very appealing to the human mind, which would rather have envisaged itself perpetuated in the body of a cockroach than vanishing completely into nothingness.

"It's all so logical, sir," the first officer told Iversen. "The individuality or the soul or the psyche–however you want to look at it–starts the essentially simple cycle of life as a greech–"

"Why as a greech?" Iversen asked, humoring him for the moment. "There are lower life-forms on Flimbot."

"I don't know." The first officer sounded almost testy. "That's where Harkaway starts the progression."

"Harkaway! Is there no escaping that cretin's name?"

"Sir," said the first officer, "may I speak frankly?"

"No," Iversen said, "you may not."

"Your skepticism arises less from disbelief than from the fact that you are jealous of Harkaway because it was he who made the great discovery, not you."

"Which great discovery?" Iversen asked, sneering to conceal his hurt at being so overwhelmingly misunderstood. "Flimbot or *mpoola*?"

"Both," the first officer said. "You refuse to accept the fact that this hitherto incompetent youth has at last blossomed forth in the lambent colors of genius, just as the worthy greech becomes a zkoort, and the clean-living zkoort in his turn passes on to the next higher plane of existence, which is, in the Flimbotzik scale–"

"Spare me the theology, please," Iversen begged. "Once a greech, always a greech, I say. And I can't help thinking that somehow, somewhere, Harkaway has committed some horrible error."

"Humanity is frail, fumbling, futile," Dr. Smullyan declared, coming upon them so suddenly that both officers jumped. "To err is human, to forgive divine, and I am an atheist, thank God!"

"That *mk'oog* is powerful stuff," the first officer said. "Or so they tell me," he added.

"This is more than mere *mk'oog*," Iversen said sourly. "Smullyan has been too long in space. It hits everyone in the long run–some sooner than others."

"Captain," the doctor said, ignoring these remarks as he ignored everything not on a cosmic level, which included the crew's ailments, "I am in full agreement with you. Young Harkaway has doomed that pretty little planet–"

"Moon," the first officer corrected. "It's a satellite, not a–"

"We ourselves were doomed ab origine, but the tragic flaw inherent in each one of our pitiful species is contagious, dooming all with whom we come in contact. And Harkaway is the most infectious carrier on the ship. Woe, I tell you. Woe!" And, with a hollow moan, the doctor left them to meditate upon the state of their souls, while he went off to his secret stores of oblivion.

"Wonder where he's hidden that *mk'oog*," Iversen brooded. "I've turned the ship inside out and I haven't been able to locate it."

The first officer shivered. "Somehow, although I know Smullyan's part drunk, part mad, he makes me a little nervous. He's been right so often on all the other voyages."

"Ruchbah!" Iversen said, not particularly grateful for support from such a dithyrambic source as the ship's medical officer. "Anyone who prophesies doom has a hundred per cent chance of ultimately being right, if only because of entropy."

He was still brooding over the first officer's thrust, even though he had been well aware that most of his officers and men considered him a sorehead for doubting Harkaway in the young man's moment of triumph. However, Iversen could not believe that Harkaway had undergone such a radical transformation. Even on the basis of *mpoola*, one obviously had to die before passing on to the next existence and Harkaway had been continuously alive–from the neck down, at least.

Furthermore, all that aside, Iversen just couldn't see Harkaway going on to a higher plane. Although he supposed the young man was well-meaning enough–he'd grant him that negligible virtue–wouldn't it be terrible to have a system of existence in which one was advanced on the basis of intent rather than result? The higher life-forms would degenerate into primitivism.

But weren't the Flimbotzik virtually primitive? Or so Harkaway had said, for Iversen himself had not had enough contact with them to determine their degree of sophistication, and only the spaceships gave Harkaway's claim the lie.

*   *   *   *   *

Iversen condescended to take a look at the opening chapter of Harkaway's book, just to see what the whole thing was about. The book began:

"What is the difference between life and death? Can we say definitely and definitively that life is life and death is death? Are we sure that death is not life and life is not death?

"No, we are not sure!

"Must the individuality have a corporeal essence in which to enshroud itself before it can proceed in its rapt, inexorable progress toward the Ultimate Non-actuality? And even if such be needful, why must the personal essence be trammeled by the same old worn-out habiliments of error?

"Think upon this!

"What is the extremest intensification of individuality? It is the All-encompassing Nothingness. Of what value are the fur, the feathers, the skin, the temporal trappings of imperfection in our perpetual struggle toward the final undefinable resolution into the Infinite Interplay of Cosmic Forces?

"Less than nothing!"

At this point, Iversen stopped reading and returned the manuscript to its creator, without a word. This last was less out of self-restraint than through sheer semantic inadequacy.

The young man might have spent his time more profitably in a little research on the biology or social organization of the Flimbotzik, Iversen thought bitterly when he had calmed down, thus saving the next expedition some work. But, instead, he'd been blinded by the flashy theological aspects of the culture and, as a result, the whole crew had gone metempsychotic.

This was going to be one of the *Herringbone's* more unendurable voyages, Iversen knew. And he couldn't put his foot down effectively, either, because the crew, all being gentlemen of independent means now, were outrageously independent.

However, in spite of knowing that all of them fully deserved what they got, Iversen couldn't help feeling guilty as he ate steak while the other officers consumed fish, vegetables and eggs in an aura of unbearable virtue.

"But if the soul transmigrates and not the body," he argued, "what harm is there in consuming the vacated receptacle?"

"For all you know," the first officer said, averting his eyes from Iversen's plate with a little—wholly gratuitous, to the captain's mind—shudder, "that cow might have housed the psyche of your grandmother."

"Well, then, by indirectly participating in that animal's slaughter, I have released my grandmother from her physical bondage to advance to the next plane. That is, if she was a good cow."

"You just don't understand," Harkaway said. "Not that you could be expected to."

"He's a clod," the radio operator agreed. "Forgive me, sir," he apologized as Iversen turned to glare incredulously at him, "but, according to *mpoola*, candor is a Step Upward."

"Onward and Upward," Harkaway commented, and Iversen was almost sure that, had he not been there, the men would have bowed their heads in contemplation, if not actual prayer.

*   *   *   *   *

As time went on, the greech thrived and grew remarkably stout on the Earth viands, which it consumed in almost improbable quantities. Then, one day, it disappeared and its happy squeal was heard no longer.

There was much mourning aboard the *Herringbone*—for, with its lovable personality and innocently engaging ways, the little fellow had won its way into the hearts of all the spacemen—until the first officer discovered a substantial pink cocoon resting on the ship's control board and rushed to the intercom to spread the glad tidings. That was a breach of regulations, of course, but Iversen knew when not to crowd his fragile authority.

"I should have known there was some material basis for the spiritual doctrine of *mpoola*," Harkaway declared with tears in his eyes as he regarded the dormant form of his little pet. "Was it not the transformation of the caterpillar into the butterfly that first showed us on Earth how the soul might emerge winged and beautiful from its vile house of clay? Gentlemen," he said, in a voice choked with emotion, "our little greech is about to become a zkoort. Praised be the Impersonal Being who has allowed such a miracle to take place before our very eyes. *J'goona lo mpoona*."

"Amen," said the first officer reverently.

All those in the control room bowed their heads except Iversen. And even he didn't quite have the nerve to tell them that the cocoon was pushing the *Herringbone* two points off course.

*   *   *   *   *

"Take that thing away before I lose my temper and clobber it," Iversen said impatiently as the zkoort dived low to buzz him, then whizzed just out of its reach on its huge, brilliant wings, giggling raucously.

"He was just having his bit of fun," the first officer said with reproach. "Have you no tolerance, Captain, no appreciation of the joys of golden youth?"

"A spaceship is no place for a butterfly," Iversen said, "especially a four-foot butterfly."

"How can you say that?" Harkaway retorted. "The *Herringbone* is the only spaceship that ever had one, to my knowledge. And I think I can safely say our lives are all a bit brighter and better and m'poo'p for having a zkoort among us. Thanks be to the Divine Nonentity for—"

"Poor little butterfly," Dr. Smullyan declared sonorously, "living out his brief life span so far from the fresh air, the sunshine, the pretty flowers—"

"Oh, I don't know that it's as bad as all that," the first officer said. "He hangs around hydroponics a lot and he gets a daily ration of vitamins." Then he paled. "But that's right—a butterfly does live only a day, doesn't it?"

"It's different with a zkoort," Harkaway maintained stoutly, though he also, Iversen noted, lost his ruddy color. "After all, he isn't really a butterfly, merely an analogous life-form."

"My, my! In four weeks, you've mastered their entomology as well as their theology and language," Iversen jeered. "Is there no end to your accomplishments, Lieutenant?"

Harkaway's color came back twofold. "He's already been around half a thubb," he pointed out. "Over two weeks."

"Well, the thing is bigger than a Terrestrial butterfly," Iversen conceded, "so you have to make some allowances for size. On the other hand—"

Laughing madly, the zkoort swooped down on him. Iversen beat it away with a snarl.

"Playful little fellow, isn't he?" the first officer said, with thoroughly annoying fondness.

"He likes you, Skipper," Harkaway explained. "Urg'h n gurg'h—or, to give it the crude Terran equivalent, living is loving. He can tell that beneath that grizzled and seemingly harsh exterior of yours, Captain—"

But, with a scream of rage, Iversen had locked himself into his cabin. Outside, he could hear the zkoort beating its wings against the door and wailing disappointedly.

*   *   *   *   *

Some days later, a pair of rapidly dulling wings were found on the floor of the hydroponics chamber. But of the zkoort's little body, there was no sign. An air of gloom and despondency hung over the *Herringbone* and even Iversen felt a pang, though he would never admit it without brainwashing.

During the next week, the men, seeking to forget their loss, plunged themselves into *mpoola* with real fanaticism. Harkaway took to wearing some sort of ecclesiastical robes which he whipped up out of the recreation room curtains. Iversen had neither the heart nor the courage to stop him, though this, too, was against regulations. Everyone except Iversen gave up eating fish and eggs in addition to meat.

Then, suddenly, one day a roly-poly blue animal appeared at the officers mess, claiming everyone as an old friend with loud squeals of joy. This time, Iversen was the only one who was glad to see him—really glad.

"Aren't you happy to see your little friend again, Harkaway?" he asked, scratching the delighted animal between the ears.

"Why, sure," Harkaway said, putting his fork down and leaving his vegetable macedoine virtually untasted. "Sure. I'm very happy—" his voice broke—"very happy."

"Of course, it does kind of knock your theory of the transmigration of souls into a cocked hat," the captain grinned. "Because, in order for the soul to transmigrate, the previous body's got to be dead, and I'm afraid our little pal here was alive all the time."

"Looks it, doesn't it?" muttered Harkaway.

"I rather think," Iversen went on, tickling the creature under the chin until it squealed happily, "that you didn't quite get the nuances of the language, did you, Harkaway? Because I gather now that the whole difficulty was a semantic one. The Flimbotzik were explaining the zoology of the native life-forms to you and you misunderstood it as their theology."

"Looks it, doesn't it?" Harkaway repeated glumly. "It certainly looks it."

"Cheer up," Iversen said, reaching over to slap the young man on the back—a bit to his own amazement. "No real harm done. What if the Flimbotzik are less primitive than you fancied? It makes our discovery the more worthwhile, doesn't it?"

At this point, the radio operator almost sobbingly asked to be excused from the table. Following his departure, there was a long silence. It was hard, Iversen realized in a burst of uncharacteristic tolerance, to have one's belief, even so newly born a credo, annihilated with such suddenness.

"After all, you did run across the Flimbotzik first," he told Harkaway as he spread gooseberry jam on a hard roll for the ravenous ex-zkoort (now a chu-wugg, he had been told). "That's the main thing, and a life-form that passes through two such striking metamorphoses is not unfraught with interest. You shall receive full credit, my

boy, and your little mistake doesn't mean a thing except–
"

"Doom," said Dr. Smullyan, sopping up the last of his gravy with a piece of bread. "Doom, doom, doom." He stuffed the bread into his mouth.

"Look, Smullyan," Iversen told him jovially, "you better watch out. If you keep talking that way, next voyage out we'll sign on a parrot instead of a medical officer. Cheaper and just as efficient."

Only the chu-wugg joined in his laughter.

"Ever since I can remember," the first officer said, looking gloomily at the doctor, "he's never been wrong. Maybe he has powers beyond our comprehension. Perhaps we sought at the end of the Galaxy what was in our own back yard all the time."

"Who was seeking what?" Iversen asked as all the officers looked at Smullyan with respectful awe. "I demand an answer!"

But the only one who spoke was the doctor. "Only Man is vile," he said, as if to himself, and fell asleep with his head on the table.

"Make a cult out of Smullyan," Iversen warned the others, "and I'll scuttle the ship!"

Later on, the first officer got the captain alone. "Look here, sir," he began tensely, "have you read Harkaway's book about *mpoola?*"

"I read part of the first chapter," Iversen told him, "and that was enough. Maybe to Harkaway it's eschatology, but to me it's just plain scatology!"

"But–"

"Why in Zubeneschamali," Iversen said patiently, "should I waste my time reading a book devoted to a theory which has already been proved erroneous? Answer me that!"

"I think you should have a look at the whole thing," the first officer persisted.

"Baham!" Iversen replied, but amiably enough, for he was in rare good humor these days. And he needed good humor to tolerate the way his officers and men were behaving. All right, they had made idiots of themselves; that was understandable, expected, familiar. But it wasn't the chu-wugg's fault. Iversen had never seen such a bunch of soreheads. Why did they have to take their embarrassment and humiliation out on an innocent little animal?

For, although no one actually mistreated the chu-wugg, the men avoided him as much as possible. Often Iversen would come upon the little fellow weeping from loneliness in a corner with no one to play with and, giving in to his own human weakness, the captain would dry the creature's tears and comfort him. In return, the chu-wugg would laugh at all his jokes, for he seemed to have acquired an elementary knowledge of Terran.

*   *   *   *   *

"By Vindemiatrix, Lieutenant," the captain roared as Harkaway, foiled in his attempt to scurry off unobserved, stood quivering before him, "why have you been avoiding me like this?"

"I didn't think I was avoiding you any particular way, sir," Harkaway said. "I mean does it appear like that, sir? It's only that I've been busy with my duties, sir."

"I don't know what's the matter with you! I told you I handsomely forgave you for your mistake."

"But I can never forgive myself, sir—"

"Are you trying to go over my head?" Iversen thundered.

"No, sir. I—"

"If I am willing to forgive you, you will forgive yourself. That's an order!"

"Yes, sir," the young man said feebly.

Harkaway had changed back to his uniform, Iversen noted, but he looked unkempt, ill, harrowed. The boy had really been suffering for his precipitance. Perhaps the captain himself had been a little hard on him.

Iversen modulated his tone to active friendliness. "Thought you might like to know the chu-wugg turned into a hoop-snake this morning!"

But Harkaway did not seem cheered by this social note. "So soon!"

"You knew there would be a fourth metamorphosis!" Iversen was disappointed. But he realized that Harkaway was bound to have acquired such fundamental data, no matter how he interpreted them. It was possible, Iversen thought, that the book could actually have some value, if there were some way of weeding fact from fancy, and surely there must be scholars trained in such an art, for Earth had many wholly indigenous texts of like nature.

"He's a thor'glitch now," Harkaway told him dully.

"And what comes next?... No, don't tell me. It's more fun not knowing beforehand. You know," Iversen went on, almost rubbing his hands together, "I think this species is going to excite more interest on Earth than the Flimbotzik themselves. After all, people are people, even if they're green, but an animal that changes shape so many times and so radically is really going to set biologists by the ears. What did you say the name of the species as a whole was?"

"I–I couldn't say, sir."

"Ah," Iversen remarked waggishly, "so there are one or two things you don't know about Flimbot, eh?"

Harkaway opened his mouth, but only a faint bleating sound came out.

*   *   *   *   *

As the days went on, Iversen found himself growing fonder and fonder of the thor'glitch. Finally, in spite of the fact that it had now attained the dimensions of a well-developed boa constrictor, he took it to live in his quarters.

Many was the quiet evening they spent together, Iversen entering acid comments upon the crew in the ship's log, while the thor'glitch looked over viewtapes from the ship's library.

The captain was surprised to find how much he–well, enjoyed this domestic tranquility. I must be growing old, he thought–old and mellow. And he named the creature Bridey, after a twentieth-century figure who had, he believed, been connected with another metempsychotic furor.

When the thor'glitch grew listless and began to swell in the middle, Iversen got alarmed and sent for Dr. Smullyan.

"Aha!" the medical officer declaimed, with a casual glance at the suffering snake. "The day of reckoning is at hand! Reap the fruit of your transgression, scurvy humans! Calamity approaches with jets aflame!"

Iversen clutched the doctor's sleeve. "Is he–is he going to die?"

"Unhand me, presumptuous navigator!" Dr. Smullyan shook the captain's fingers off his arm. "I didn't say he was going to die," he offered in ordinary bedside tones. "Not being a specialist in this particular sector, I am not qualified to offer an opinion, but, strictly off the record, I would hazard the guess that he's about to metamorphose again."

"He never did it in public before," Iversen said worriedly.

"The old order changeth," Smullyan told him. "You'd better call Harkaway."

"What does he know!"

"Too little and, at the same time, too much," the doctor declaimed, dissociating himself professionally from the case. "Too much and too little. Eat, drink, be merry, iniquitous Earthmen, for you died yesterday!"

"Oh, shut up," Iversen said automatically, and dispatched a message to Harkaway with the information that the thor'glitch appeared to be metamorphosing again and that his presence was requested in the captain's cabin.

The rest of the officers accompanied Harkaway, all of them with the air of attending a funeral rather than a rebirth, Iversen noted nervously. They weren't armed, though, so Bridey couldn't be turning into anything dangerous.

*   *   *   *   *

Now it came to pass that the thor'glitch's mid-section, having swelled to unbearable proportions, began to quiver. Suddenly, the skin split lengthwise and dropped cleanly to either side, like a banana peel.

Iversen pressed forward to see what fresh life-form the bulging cavity had held. The other officers all stood in a somber row without moving, for all along, Iversen realized, they had known what to expect, what was to come. And they had not told him. But then, he knew, it was his own fault; he had refused to be told.

Now, looking down at the new life-form, he saw for himself what it was. Lying languidly in the thor'glitch skin was a slender youth of a pallor which seemed excessive even for a member of a green-skinned race. He had large limpid eyes and a smile of ineffable sweetness.

"By Nopus Secundus," Iversen groaned. "I'm sunk."

"Naturally the ultimate incarnation for a life-form would be humanoid," Harkaway said with deep reproach. "What else?"

"I'm surprised you didn't figure that out for yourself, sir," the first officer added. "Even if you did refuse to read Harkaway's book, it seems obvious."

"Does it?" Smullyan challenged. "Does it, indeed? Is Man the highest form of life in an irrational cosmos? Then all causes are lost ones!... So many worlds," he muttered in more subdued tones, "so much to do, so little done, such things to be!"

"The Flimbotzik were telling Harkaway about their own life cycle," Iversen whispered as revelation bathed him in its murky light. "The human embryo undergoes a series of changes inside the womb. It's just that the Flimbotzik fetus develops outside the womb."

"Handily bypassing the earliest and most unpleasant stages of humanity," Smullyan sighed. "Oh, idyllic planet, where one need never be a child—where one need never see a child!"

"Then they were trying to explain their biology to you quite clearly and coherently, you lunkhead," Iversen roared at Harkaway, "and you took it for a religious doctrine!"

"Yes, sir," Harkaway said weakly. "I–I kind of figured that out myself in these last few weeks of intensive soul-searching. I–I'm sorry, sir. All I can say is that it was an honest mistake."

"Why, they weren't necessarily pet-lovers at all. Those animals they had with them were.... By Nair al Zaurak!"

The captain's voice rose to a shriek as the whole enormity of the situation finally dawned upon him. "You went and kidnaped one of the children!"

"That's a serious charge, kidnaping," the first officer said with melancholy pleasure. "And you, as head of this expedition, Captain, are responsible. Ironic, isn't it?"

"Told you all this spelled doom and disaster," the doctor observed cheerfully.

Just then, the young humanoid sat up—with considerable effort, Iversen was disturbed to notice. But perhaps that was one of the consequences of being born. A new-born infant was weak; why not a new-born adult, then?

"Why doom?" the humanoid asked in a high, clear voice. "Why disaster?"

"You—you speak Terran?" the captain stammered.

Bridey gave his sad, sweet smile. "I was reared amongst you. You are my people. Why should I not speak your tongue?"

"But we're not your people," Iversen blurted, thinking perhaps the youth did not remember back to his greechi days. "We're an entirely different species—"

"Our souls vibrate in unison and that is the vital essence. But do not be afraid, shipmates; the Flimbotzik do not regard the abduction of a transitory corporeal shelter as a matter of any great moment. Moreover, what took place could not rightly be termed abduction, for I came with you of my own volition—and the Flimbotzik recognize individual responsibility from the very first moment of the psyche's drawing breath in any material casing."

Bridey talked so much like Harkaway's book that Iversen was almost relieved when, a few hours later, the alien died. Of course the captain was worried about possible repercussions from the governments of both Terra and Flimbot, in spite of Bridey's assurances.

And he could not help but feel a pang when the young humanoid expired in his arms, murmuring, "Do not

grieve for me, soul-mates. In the midst of life, there is
life...."

"Funny," Smullyan said, with one of his disconcerting
returns to a professional manner, "all the other forms
seemed perfectly healthy. Why did this one go like that?
Almost as if he wanted to die."

"He was too good for this ship, that's what," the radio
operator said, glaring at the captain. "Too fine and brave
and—and noble."

"Yes," Harkaway agreed. "What truly sensitive soul
could exist in a stultifying atmosphere like this?"

All the officers glared at the captain. He glared back
with right good will. "How come you gentlemen are still
with us?" he inquired. "One would have thought you
would have perished of pure sensibility long since, then."

"It's not nice to talk that way," the chief petty officer
burst out, "not with him lying there not yet cold.... Ah," he
heaved a long sigh, "we'll never see his like again."

"Ay, that we won't," agreed the crew, huddled in the
corridor outside the captain's cabin.

Iversen sincerely hoped not, but he forbore to speak.

*　　*　　*　　*　　*

Since Bridey had reached the ultimate point in his life
cycle, it seemed certain that he was not going to change
into anything else and so he was given a spaceman's
burial. Feeling like a put-upon fool, Captain Iversen read
a short prayer as Bridey's slight body was consigned to
the vast emptiness of space.

Then the airlock clanged shut behind the last mortal
remains of the ill-fated extraterrestrial and that was the
end of it.

But the funereal atmosphere did not diminish as the
ship forged on toward Earth. Gloomy days passed, one
after the other, during which no one spoke, save to issue
or dispute an order. Looking at himself one day in the
mirror on his cabin wall, the captain realized that he was

getting old. Perhaps he ought to retire instead of still dreaming of a new command and a new crew.

And then one day, as he sat in his cabin reading the Spaceman's Credo, the lights on the *Herringbone* went out, all at once, while the constant hum of the motors died down slowly, leaving a strange, uncomfortable silence. Iversen found himself suspended weightless in the dark, for the gravity, of course, had gone off with the power. What, he wondered, had come to pass? He often found himself thinking in such terms these days.

Hoarse cries issued from the passageway outside; then he heard a squeak as his cabin door opened and persons unknown floated inside, breathing heavily.

"The power has failed, sir!" gasped the first officer's voice.

"That has not escaped my notice," Iversen said icily. Were not even his last moments to be free from persecution?

"It's all that maniac Smullyan's fault. He stored his *mk'oog* in the fuel tanks. After emptying them out first, that is. We're out of fuel."

The captain put a finger in his book to mark his place, which was, he knew with a kind of supernal detachment, rather foolish, because there was no prospect of there ever being lights to read by again.

"Put him in irons, if you can find him," he ordered. "And tell the men to prepare themselves gracefully for a lingering death."

Iversen could hear a faint creak as the first officer drew himself to attention in the darkness. "The men of the *Herringbone*, sir," he said, stiffly, "are always prepared for calamity."

"Ay, that we are," agreed various voices.

So they were all there, were they? Well, it was too much to expect that they would leave him in death any more than they had in life.

"It is well," Iversen said. "It is well," he repeated, unable to think of anything more fitting.

Suddenly the lights went on again and the ship gave a leap. From his sprawling position on the floor, amid his recumbent officers, Iversen could hear the hum of motors galvanized into life.

"But if the fuel tanks are empty," he asked of no one in particular, "where did the power come from?"

"I am the power," said a vast, deep voice that filled the ship from hold to hold.

"And the glory," said the radio operator reverently. "Don't forget the glory."

"No," the voice replied and it was the voice of Bridey, resonant with all the amplitude of the immense chest cavity he had acquired. "Not the glory, merely the power. I have reached a higher plane of existence. I am a spaceship."

"Praise be to the Ultimate Nothingness!" Harkaway cried.

"Ultimate Nothingness, nothing!" Bridey said impatiently. "I achieved it all myself."

"Then that's how the Flimbotzi spaceships were powered!" Iversen exclaimed. "By themselves–the Flimbotzik themselves, I mean–"

"Even so," Bridey replied grandly. "And this lofty form of life happens to be one which we poor humans cannot reach unassisted. Someone has to build the shell for us to occupy, which is the reason humans dwell together in fellowship and harmony–"

"You purposely got Harkaway to take you aboard the *Herringbone*," Iversen interrupted wrathfully. "You–you stowaway!"

Bridey's laugh rang through the ship, setting the loose parts quivering. "Of course. When first I set eyes upon this vessel of yours, I saw before me the epitome of all dreams. Never had any of our kind so splendid an encasement. And, upon determining that the vessel was, as yet, a soulless thing, I got myself aboard; I was born, I died, and was reborn again with the greatest swiftness consonant with comfort, so that I could awaken in this magnificent form. Oh, joy, joy, joy!"

"You know," Iversen said, "now that I hear one of you talk at length, I really can't blame Harkaway for his typically imbecilic mistake."

"We are a wordy species," Bridey conceded.

"You had no right to do what you did," Iversen told him, "no right to take over—"

"But I didn't take over," Bridey the *Herringbone* said complacently. "I merely remained quiescent and content in the knowledge of my power until yours failed. Without me, you would even now be spinning in the vasty voids, a chrome-trimmed sepulcher. Now, three times as swiftly as before, shall I bear you back to the planet you very naively call home."

"Not three times as fast, please!" Iversen was quick to plead. "The ship isn't built—we're not built to stand such speeds."

The ship sighed. "Disappointment needs must come to all—the high, the low, the man, the spaceship. It must be borne—" the voice broke—"bravely. Somehow."

"What am I going to do?" Iversen asked, turning to the first officer for advice for the first time ever. "I was planning to ask for a transfer or resign my command when we got back to Earth. But how can I leave Bridey in the hands of the IEE(E)?"

"You can't, sir," the first officer said. "Neither can we."

"If you explain," Harkaway offered timidly, "perhaps they'll present the ship to the government."

Both Iversen and the first officer snorted, united for once. "Not the IEE(E)," Iversen said. "They'd—they'd exhibit it or something and charge admission."

"Oh, no," Bridey cried, "I don't want to be exhibited! I want to sail through the trackless paths of space. What good is a body like this if I cannot use it to its fullest?"

"Have no fear," Iversen assured it. "We'll just—" he shrugged, his dreams of escape forever blighted—"just have to buy the ship from the IEE(E), that's all."

"Right you are, sir," the first officer agreed. "We must club together, every man Jack of us, and buy her. Him. It. That's the only decent thing to do."

"Perhaps they won't sell," Harkaway worried. "Maybe–"

"Oh, they'll sell, all right," Iversen said wearily. "They'd sell the chairman of the board, if you made them an offer, and throw in all the directors if the price was right."

"And then what will we do?" the first officer asked. "Once the ship has been purchased, what will our course be? What, in other words, are we to do?"

It was Bridey who answered. "We will speed through space seeking, learning, searching, until you–all of you– pass on to higher planes and, leaving the frail shells you now inhabit, occupy proud, splendid vessels like the one I wear now. Then, a vast transcendent flotilla, we will seek other universes...."

"But we don't become spaceships," Iversen said unhappily. "We don't become anything."

"How do you know we don't?" Smullyan demanded, appearing on the threshold. "How do you know what we become? Build thee more stately spaceships, O my soul!"

Above all else, Iversen was a space officer and dereliction of duty could not be condoned even in exceptional circumstances. "Put him in irons, somebody!"

"Ask Bridey why there were only forty-five spaceships on his planet!" the doctor yelled over his shoulder as he was dragged off. "Ask where the others went–where they are now."

But Bridey wouldn't answer that question.

THE MOST SENTIMENTAL MAN

ORIGINALLY PUBLISHED IN FANTASTIC UNIVERSE
AUGUST 1957

Johnson knew he was annoying the younger man, who so obviously lived by the regulations in the "Colonial Officer's Manual" and lacked the imagination to understand why he was doing this....

THE MOST SENTIMENTAL MAN

Johnson went to see the others off at Idlewild. He knew they'd expect him to and, since it would be the last conventional gesture he'd have to make, he might as well conform to their notions of what was right and proper.

For the past few centuries the climate had been getting hotter; now, even though it was not yet June, the day was uncomfortably warm. The sun's rays glinting off the bright metal flanks of the ship dazzled his eyes, and perspiration made his shirt stick to his shoulder blades beneath the jacket that the formality of the occasion had required. He wished Clifford would hurry up and get the leave-taking over with.

But, even though Clifford was undoubtedly even more anxious than he to finish with all this ceremony and take off, he wasn't the kind of man to let inclination influence his actions. "Sure you won't change your mind and come with us?"

Johnson shook his head.

The young man looked at him—hatred for the older man's complication of what should have been a simple departure showing through the pellicule of politeness. He was young for, since this trip had only slight historical importance and none of any other kind, the authorities had felt a junior officer entirely sufficient. It was clear, however, that Clifford attributed his commandership to his merits, and he was very conscious of his great responsibility.

"We have plenty of room on the ship," he persisted. "There weren't many left to go. We could take you easily enough, you know."

Johnson made a negative sign again. The rays of the sun beating full upon his head made apparent the grey that usually blended into the still-thick blond hair. Yet, though past youth, he was far from being an old man. "I've made my decision," he said, remembering that anger now was pointless.

"If it's—if you're just too proud to change your mind," the young commander said, less certainly, "I'm sure everyone will understand if ... if ..."

Johnson smiled. "No, it's just that I want to stay—that's all."

But the commander's clear blue eyes were still baffled, uneasy, as though he felt he had not done the utmost that duty—not duty to the service but to humanity—required. That was the trouble with people, Johnson thought: when they were most well-meaning they became most troublesome.

Clifford lowered his voice to an appropriately funeral hush, as a fresh thought obviously struck him. "I know, of course, that your loved ones are buried here and perhaps you feel it's your duty to stay with them...?"

At this Johnson almost forgot that anger no longer had any validity. By "loved ones" Clifford undoubtedly had meant Elinor and Paul. It was true that Johnson had had a certain affection for his wife and son when they were alive; now that they were dead they represented an episode in his life that had not, perhaps, been unpleasant, but was certainly over and done with now.

Did Clifford think that was his reason for remaining? Why, he must believe Johnson to be the most sentimental man on Earth. "And, come to think of it," Johnson said to himself, amused, "I am—or soon will be—just that."

The commander was still unconsciously pursuing the same train of thought. "It does seem incredible," he said in a burst of boyish candor that did not become him, for he was not that young, "that you'd want to stay alone on a whole planet. I mean to say—entirely alone.... There'll never be another ship, you know—at least not in your lifetime."

Johnson knew what the other man was thinking. If there'd been a woman with Johnson now, Clifford might have been able to understand a little better how the other could stick by his decision.

Johnson wriggled, as sweat oozed stickily down his back. "For God's sake," he said silently, "take your silly ship and get the hell off my planet." Aloud he said, "It's a good planet, a little worn-out but still in pretty good shape. Pity you can't trade in an old world like an old car, isn't it?"

"If it weren't so damned far from the center of things," the young man replied, defensively assuming the burden of all civilization, "we wouldn't abandon it. After all, we hate leaving the world on which we originated. But it's a long haul to Alpha Centauri—you know that—and a tremendously expensive one. Keeping up this place solely out of sentiment would be sheer waste—the people would never stand for the tax burden."

"A costly museum, yes," Johnson agreed.

How much longer were these dismal farewells going to continue? How much longer would the young man still feel the need to justify himself? "If only there were others fool enough—if only there were others with you.... But, even if anybody else'd be willing to cut himself off entirely from the rest of the civilized universe, the Earth won't support enough of a population to keep it running. Not according to our present living standards anyway.... Most of its resources are gone, you know—hardly any coal or oil left, and that's not worth digging for when there are better and cheaper fuels in the system."

He was virtually quoting from the *Colonial Officer's Manual*. Were there any people left able to think for themselves, Johnson wondered. Had there ever been? Had he thought for himself in making his decision, or was he merely clinging to a childish dream that all men had had and lost?

"With man gone, Earth will replenish herself," he said aloud. First the vegetation would begin to grow thick. Already it had released itself from the restraint of cultivation; soon it would be spreading out over the continent, overrunning the cities with delicately persistent green tendrils. Some the harsh winters would kill, but others would live on and would multiply. Vines would twist themselves about the tall buildings and tenderly, passionately squeeze them to death ... eventually send them tumbling down. And then the trees would rear themselves in their places.

The swamps that man had filled in would begin to reappear one by one, as the land sank back to a pristine state. The sea would go on changing her boundaries, with no dikes to stop her. Volcanoes would heave up the land into different configurations. The heat would increase until it grew unbearable ... only there would be no one–no human, anyway–to bear it.

Year after year the leaves would wither and fall and decay. Rock would cover them. And some day ... billions of years thence ... there would be coal and oil–and nobody to want them.

"Very likely Earth will replenish herself," the commander agreed, "but not in your time or your children's time.... That is, not in my children's time," he added hastily.

The handful of men lined up in a row before the airlock shuffled their feet and allowed their muttering to become a few decibels louder. Clifford looked at his wrist chronometer. Obviously he was no less anxious than the crew to be off, but, for the sake of his conscience, he must make a last try.

"Damn your conscience," Johnson thought. "I hope that for this you feel guilty as hell, that you wake up nights in a cold sweat remembering that you left one man alone on the planet you and your kind discarded. Not that

I don't want to stay, mind you, but that I want you to suffer the way you're making me suffer now—having to listen to your platitudes."

The commander suddenly stopped paraphrasing the Manual. "Camping out's fun for a week or two, you know, but it's different when it's for a lifetime."

Johnson's fingers curled in his palms ... he was even angrier now that the commander had struck so close to home. Camping out ... was that all he was doing—fulfilling childhood desires, nothing more?

Fortunately Clifford didn't realize that he had scored, and scuttled back to the shelter of the *Manual*. "Perhaps you don't know enough about the new system in Alpha Centauri," he said, a trifle wildly. "It has two suns surrounded by three planets, Thalia, Aglaia, and Euphrosyne. Each of these planets is slightly smaller than Earth, so that the decrease in gravity is just great enough to be pleasant, without being so marked as to be inconvenient. The atmosphere is almost exactly like that of Earth's, except that it contains several beneficial elements which are absent here—and the climate is more temperate. Owing to the fact that the planets are partially shielded from the suns by cloud layers, the temperature—except immediately at the poles and the equators, where it is slightly more extreme—is always equable, resembling that of Southern California...."

"Sounds charming," said Johnson. "I too have read the Colonial Office handouts.... I wonder what the people who wrote them'll do now that there's no longer any necessity for attracting colonists—everybody's already up in Alpha Centauri. Oh, well; there'll be other systems to conquer and colonize."

"The word conquer is hardly correct," the commander said stiffly, "since not one of the three planets had any indigenous life forms that was intelligent."

"Or life forms that you recognized as intelligent," Johnson suggested gently. Although why should there be such a premium placed on intelligence, he wondered. Was intelligence the sole criterion on which the right to life and to freedom should be based?

The commander frowned and looked at his chronometer again. "Well," he finally said, "since you feel that way and you're sure you've quite made up your mind, my men are anxious to go."

"Of course they are," Johnson said, managing to convey just the right amount of reproach.

Clifford flushed and started to walk away.

"I'll stand out of the way of your jets!" Johnson called after him. "It would be so anticlimactic to have me burned to a crisp after all this. Bon voyage!"

There was no reply.

Johnson watched the silver vessel shoot up into the sky and thought, "Now is the time for me to feel a pang, or even a twinge, but I don't at all. I feel relieved, in fact, but that's probably the result of getting rid of that fool Clifford."

He crossed the field briskly, pulling off his jacket and discarding his tie as he went. His ground car remained where he had parked it–in an area clearly marked No Parking.

They'd left him an old car that wasn't worth shipping to the stars. How long it would last was anybody's guess. The government hadn't been deliberately illiberal in leaving him such a shabby vehicle; if there had been any way to ensure a continuing supply of fuel, they would probably have left him a reasonably good one. But, since only a little could be left, allowing him a good car would have been simply an example of conspicuous waste, and the government had always preferred its waste to be inconspicuous.

He drove slowly through the broad boulevards of Long Island, savoring the loneliness. New York as a residential area had been a ghost town for years, since the greater part of its citizens had been among the first to emigrate to the stars. However, since it was the capital of the world and most of the interstellar ships–particularly the last few–had taken off from its spaceports, it had been kept up as an official embarkation center. Thus, paradoxically, it was the last city to be completely evacuated, and so, although the massive but jerry-built apartment houses that lined the streets were already crumbling, the roads had been kept in fairly good shape and were hardly cracked at all.

Still, here and there the green was pushing its way up in unlikely places. A few more of New York's tropical summers, and Long Island would soon become a wilderness.

The streets were empty, except for the cats sunning themselves on long-abandoned doorsteps or padding about on obscure errands of their own. Perhaps their numbers had not increased since humanity had left the city to them, but there certainly seemed to be more–striped and solid, black and grey and white and tawny–accepting their citizenship with equanimity. They paid no attention to Johnson–they had long since dissociated themselves from a humanity that had not concerned itself greatly over their welfare. On the other hand, neither he nor the surface car appeared to startle them; the old ones had seen such before, and to kittens the very fact of existence is the ultimate surprise.

The Queensborough Bridge was deadly silent. It was completely empty except for a calico cat moving purposefully toward Manhattan. The structure needed a coat of paint, Johnson thought vaguely, but of course it would never get one. Still, even uncared for, the bridges should outlast him–there would be no heavy traffic to weaken them. Just in case of unforeseeable catastrophe, however–he didn't want to be trapped on an island, even Manhattan Island–he had remembered to provide himself with a rowboat; a motorboat would have been preferable, but then the fuel difficulty would arise again....

How empty the East River looked without any craft on it! It was rather a charming little waterway in its own right, though nothing to compare with the stately

Hudson. The water scintillated in the sunshine and the air was clear and fresh, for no factories had spewed fumes and smoke into it for many years. There were few gulls, for nothing was left for the scavenger; those remaining were forced to make an honest living by catching fish.

In Manhattan, where the buildings had been more soundly constructed, the signs of abandonment were less evident ... empty streets, an occasional cracked window. Not even an unusual amount of dirt because, in the past, the normal activities of an industrial and ruggedly individual city had provided more grime than years of neglect could ever hope to equal. No, it would take Manhattan longer to go back than Long Island. Perhaps that too would not happen during his lifetime.

Yet, after all, when he reached Fifth Avenue he found that Central Park had burst its boundaries. Fifty-ninth Street was already half jungle, and the lush growth spilled down the avenues and spread raggedly out into the side streets, pushing its way up through the cracks it had made in the surface of the roads. Although the Plaza fountain had not flowed for centuries, water had collected in the leaf-choked basin from the last rain, and a group of grey squirrels were gathered around it, shrilly disputing possession with some starlings.

Except for the occasional cry of a cat in the distance, these voices were all that he heard ... the only sound. Not even the sudden blast of a jet regaining power ... he would never hear that again; never hear the stridor of a human voice piercing with anger; the cacophony of a hundred television sets, each playing a different program; the hoot of a horn; off-key singing; the thin, uncertain notes of an amateur musician ... these would never be heard on Earth again.

He sent the car gliding slowly ... no more traffic rules ... down Fifth Avenue. The buildings here also were well-built; they were many centuries old and would probably last as many more. The shop windows were empty, except for tangles of dust ... an occasional broken, discarded mannequin.... In some instances the glass had already cracked or fallen out. Since there were no children to throw stones, however, others might last indefinitely, carefully glassing in nothingness. Doors stood open and he could see rows of empty counters and barren shelves fuzzed high with the dust of the years since a customer had approached them.

Cats sedately walked up and down the avenue or sat genteelly with tails tucked in on the steps of the cathedral—as if the place had been theirs all along.

Dusk was falling. Tonight, for the first time in centuries, the street lamps would not go on. Undoubtedly when it grew dark he would see ghosts, but they would be the ghosts of the past and he had made his peace with the past long since; it was the present and the future with which he had not come to terms. And now there would be no present, no past, no future—but all merged into one and he was the only one.

At Forty-second Street pigeons fluttered thickly around the public library, fat as ever, their numbers greater, their appetites grosser. The ancient library, he knew, had changed little inside: stacks and shelves would still be packed thick with reading matter. Books are bulky, so only the rare editions had been taken beyond the stars; the rest had been microfilmed and their originals left to Johnson and decay. It was his library now, and he had all the time in the world to read all the books in the world—for there were more than he could possibly read in the years that, even at the most generous estimate, were left to him.

He had been wondering where to make his permanent residence for, with the whole world his, he would be a fool to confine himself to some modest dwelling. Now he fancied it might be a good idea to move right into the library. Very few places in Manhattan could boast a garden of their own.

He stopped the car to stare thoughtfully at the little park behind the grimy monument to Neoclassicism. Like

Central Park, Bryant had already slipped its boundaries and encroached upon Sixth Avenue—Avenue of the World, the street signs said now, and before that it had been Avenue of the Nations and Avenue of the Americas, but to the public it had always been Sixth Avenue and to Johnson, the last man on Earth, it was Sixth Avenue.

He'd live in the library, while he stayed in New York, that was—he'd thought that in a few weeks, when it got really hot, he might strike north. He had always meant to spend a summer in Canada. His surface car would probably never last the trip, but the Museum of Ancient Vehicles had been glad to bestow half a dozen of the bicycles from their exhibits upon him. After all, he was, in effect, a museum piece himself and so as worth preserving as the bicycles; moreover, bicycles are difficult to pack for an interstellar trip. With reasonable care, these might last him his lifetime....

But he had to have a permanent residence somewhere, and the library was an elegant and commodious dwelling, centrally located. New York would have to be his headquarters, for all the possessions he had carefully amassed and collected and begged and—since money would do him no good any more—bought, were here. And there were by far too many of them to be transported to any really distant location. He loved to own things.

He was by no means an advocate of Rousseau's complete return to nature; whatever civilization had left that he could use without compromise, he would—and thankfully. There would be no electricity, of course, but he had provided himself with flashlights and bulbs and batteries—not too many of the last, of course, because they'd grow stale. However, he'd also laid in plenty of candles and a vast supply of matches.... Tins of food and concentrates and synthetics, packages of seed should he grow tired of all these and want to try growing his own—fruit, he knew, would be growing wild soon enough.... Vitamins and medicines—of course, were he to get really ill or get hurt in some way, it might be the end ... but that was something he wouldn't think of—something that couldn't possibly happen to him....

For his relaxation he had an antique hand-wound phonograph, together with thousands of old-fashioned records. And then, of course, he had the whole planet, the whole world to amuse him.

He even had provided himself with a heat-ray gun and a substantial supply of ammunition, although he couldn't imagine himself ever killing an animal for food. It was squeamishness that stood in his way rather than any ethical considerations, although he did indeed believe that every creature had the right to live. Nonetheless, there was the possibility that the craving for fresh meat might change his mind for him. Besides, although hostile animals had long been gone from this part of the world—the only animals would be birds and squirrels and, farther up the Hudson, rabbits and chipmunks and deer ... perhaps an occasional bear in the mountains—who knew what harmless life form might become a threat now that its development would be left unchecked?

A cat sitting atop one of the stately stone lions outside the library met his eye with such a steady gaze of understanding, though not of sympathy, that he found himself needing to repeat the by-now almost magic phrase to himself: "Not in my lifetime anyway." Would some intelligent life form develop to supplant man? Or would the planet revert to a primeval state of mindless innocence? He would never know and he didn't really care ... no point in speculating over unanswerable questions.

He settled back luxuriously on the worn cushions of his car. Even so little as twenty years before, it would have been impossible for him—for anyone—to stop his vehicle in the middle of Forty-second Street and Fifth Avenue purely to meditate. But it was his domain now. He could go in the wrong direction on one-way streets, stop wherever he pleased, drive as fast or as slowly as he would (and could, of course). If he wanted to do anything as vulgar as spit in the street, he could (but they were his streets now, not to be sullied) ... cross the roads without waiting for the lights to change (it would be a long, long wait if he did) ... go to sleep when he wanted, eat as many meals as he wanted whenever he chose.... He could go naked in hot weather and there'd be no one to raise an eyebrow, deface public buildings (except that they were private buildings now, his buildings), idle without the guilty feeling that there was always something better he could and should be doing ... even if there were not. There would be no more guilty feelings; without people and their knowledge there was no more guilt.

A flash of movement in the bushes behind the library caught his eye. Surely that couldn't be a fawn in Bryant Park? So soon?... He'd thought it would be another ten years at least before the wild animals came sniffing timidly along the Hudson, venturing a little further each time they saw no sign of their age-old enemy.

But probably the deer was only his imagination. He would investigate further after he had moved into the library.

Perhaps a higher building than the library.... But then he would have to climb too many flights of stairs. The elevators wouldn't be working ... silly of him to forget that. There were a lot of steps outside the library too—it would be a chore to get his bicycles up those steps.

Then he smiled to himself. Robinson Crusoe would have been glad to have had bicycles and steps and such relatively harmless animals as bears to worry about. No, Robinson Crusoe never had it so good as he, Johnson, would have, and what more could he want?

For, whoever before in history had had his dreams—and what was wrong with dreams, after all?–so completely gratified? What child, envisioning a desert island all his own could imagine that his island would be the whole world? Together Johnson and the Earth would grow young again.

No, the stars were for others. Johnson was not the first man in history who had wanted the Earth, but he had been the first man—and probably the last—who had actually been given it. And he was well content with his bargain.

There was plenty of room for the bears too.

THE BLUE TOWER

ORIGINALLY PUBLISHED IN *GALAXY*
FEBRUARY 1958

ILLUSTRATED BY DICK FRANCIS

As the vastly advanced guardians
of mankind, the Belphins knew how
to make a lesson stick—but whom?

THE BLUE TOWER

Ludovick Eversole sat in the golden sunshine outside his house, writing a poem as he watched the street flow gently past him. There were very few people on it, for he lived in a slow part of town, and those who went in for travel generally preferred streets where the pace was quicker.

Moreover, on a sultry spring afternoon like this one, there would be few people wandering abroad. Most would be lying on sun-kissed white beaches or in sun-drenched parks, or, for those who did not fancy being either kissed or drenched by the sun, basking in the comfort of their own air-conditioned villas.

Some would, like Ludovick, be writing poems; others composing symphonies; still others painting pictures. Those who were without creative talent or the inclination to indulge it would be relaxing their well-kept golden bodies in whatever surroundings they had chosen to spend this particular one of the perfect days that stretched in an unbroken line before every member of the human race from the cradle to the crematorium.

Only the Belphins were much in evidence. Only the Belphins had duties to perform. Only the Belphins worked.

Ludovick stretched his own well-kept golden body and rejoiced in the knowing that he was a man and not a Belphin. Immediately afterward, he was sorry for the heartless thought. Didn't the Belphins work only to serve humanity? How ungrateful, then, it was to gloat over them! Besides, he comforted himself, probably, if the truth were known, the Belphins liked to work. He hailed a passing Belphin for assurance on this point.

Courteous, like all members of his species, the creature leaped from the street and listened attentively to the young man's question. "We Belphins have but one like and one dislike," he replied. "We like what is right and we dislike what is wrong."

"But how can you tell what is right and what is wrong?" Ludovick persisted.

"We know," the Belphin said, gazing reverently across the city to the blue spire of the tower where The Belphin of Belphins dwelt, in constant communication with every member of his race at all times, or so they said. "That is why we were placed in charge of humanity. Someday you, too, may advance to the point where you know, and we shall return whence we came."

"But who placed you in charge," Ludovick asked, "and whence did you come?" Fearing he might seem motivated by vulgar curiosity, he explained, "I am doing research for an epic poem."

*   *   *   *   *

A lifetime spent under their gentle guardianship had made Ludovick able to interpret the expression that flitted across this Belphin's frontispiece as a sad, sweet smile.

"We come from beyond the stars," he said. Ludovick already knew that; he had hoped for something a little more specific. "We were placed in power by those who had the right. And the power through which we rule is the power of love! Be happy!"

And with that conventional farewell (which also served as a greeting), he stepped onto the sidewalk and was borne off. Ludovick looked after him pensively for a moment, then shrugged. Why should the Belphins surrender their secrets to gratify the idle curiosity of a poet?

Ludovick packed his portable scriptwriter in its case and went to call on the girl next door, whom he loved with a deep and intermittently requited passion.

As he passed between the tall columns leading into the Flockhart courtyard, he noted with regret that there were quite a number of Corisande's relatives present, lying about sunning themselves and sipping beverages which probably touched the legal limit of intoxicatability.

Much as he hated to think harshly of anyone, he did not like Corisande Flockhart's relatives. He had never known anybody who had as many relatives as she did, and sometimes he suspected they were not all related to her. Then he would dismiss the thought as unworthy of him or any right-thinking human being. He loved Corisande for herself alone and not for her family. Whether they were actually her family or not was none of his business.

"Be happy!" he greeted the assemblage cordially, sitting down beside Corisande on the tessellated pavement.

"Bah!" said old Osmond Flockhart, Corisande's grandfather. Ludovick was sure that, underneath his crustiness, the gnarled patriarch hid a heart of gold. Although he had been mining assiduously, the young man had not yet been able to strike that vein; however, he did not give up hope, for not giving up hope was one of the principles that his wise old Belphin teacher had inculcated in him. Other principles were to lead the good life and keep healthy.

"Now, Grandfather," Corisande said, "no matter what your politics, that does not excuse impoliteness."

Ludovick wished she would not allude so blatantly to politics, because he had a lurking notion that Corisande's "family" was, in fact, a band of conspirators ... such as still dotted the green and pleasant planet and proved by their existence that Man was not advancing anywhere within measurable distance of that totality of knowledge implied by the Belphin.

You could tell malcontents, even if they did not voice their dissatisfactions, by their faces. The vast majority of the human race, living good and happy lives, had smooth and pleasant faces. Malcontents' faces were lined and sometimes, in extreme cases, furrowed. Everyone could easily tell who they were by looking at them, and most people avoided them.

*   *   *   *   *

It was not that griping was illegal, for the Belphins permitted free speech and reasonable conspiracy; it was that such behavior was considered ungenteel. Ludovick would never have dreamed of associating with this set of neighbors, once he had discovered their tendencies, had he not lost his heart to the purple-eyed Corisande at their first meeting.

"Politeness, bah!" old Osmond said. "To see a healthy young man simply—simply accepting the status quo!"

"If the status quo is a good status quo," Ludovick said uneasily, for he did not like to discuss such subjects, "why should I not accept it? We have everything we could possibly want. What do we lack?"

"Our freedom," Osmond retorted.

"But we are free," Ludovick said, perplexed. "We can say what we like, do what we like, so long as it is consonant with the public good."

"Ah, but who determines what is consonant with the public good?"

Ludovick could no longer temporize with truth, even for Corisande's sake. "Look here, old man, I have read books. I know about the old days before the Belphins came from the stars. Men were destroying themselves quickly through wars, or slowly through want. There is none of that any more."

"All lies and exaggeration," old Osmond said. "My grandfather told me that, when the Belphins took over Earth, they rewrote all the textbooks to suit their own purposes. Now nothing but Belphin propaganda is taught in the schools."

"But surely some of what they teach about the past must be true," Ludovick insisted. "And today every one of us has enough to eat and drink, a place to live, beautiful garments to wear, and all the time in the world to utilize as he chooses in all sorts of pleasant activities. What is missing?"

"They've taken away our frontiers!"

Behind his back, Corisande made a little filial face at Ludovick.

Ludovick tried to make the old man see reason. "But I'm happy. And everybody is happy, except—except a few killjoys like you."

"They certainly did a good job of brainwashing you, boy," Osmond sighed. "And of most of the young ones," he added mournfully. "With each succeeding generation, more of our heritage is lost." He patted the girl's hand. "You're a good girl, Corrie. You don't hold with this being cared for like some damn pet poodle."

"Never mind Osmond, Eversole," one of Corisande's alleged uncles grinned. "He talks a lot, but of course he doesn't mean a quarter of what he says. Come, have some wine."

*   *   *   *   *

He handed a glass to Ludovick. Ludovick sipped and coughed. It tasted as if it were well above the legal alcohol limit, but he didn't like to say anything. They were taking an awful risk, though, doing a thing like that. If they got caught, they might receive a public scolding—which was, of course, no more than they deserved—but he could not bear to think of Corisande exposed to such an ordeal.

"It's only reasonable," the uncle went on, "that older people should have a—a thing about being governed by foreigners."

Ludovick smiled and set his nearly full glass down on a plinth. "You could hardly call the Belphins foreigners; they've been on Earth longer than even the oldest of us."

"You seem to be pretty chummy with 'em," the uncle said, looking narrow-eyed at Ludovick.

"No more so than any other loyal citizen," Ludovick replied.

The uncle sat up and wrapped his arms around his thick bare legs. He was a powerful, hairy brute of a creature who had not taken advantage of the numerous cosmetic techniques offered by the benevolent Belphins. "Don't you think it's funny they can breathe our air so easily?"

"Why shouldn't they?" Ludovick bit into an apple that Corisande handed him from one of the dishes of fruit and other delicacies strewn about the courtyard. "It's excellent air," he continued through a full mouth, "especially now that it's all purified. I understand that in the old days—"

"Yes," the uncle said, "but don't you think it's a coincidence they breathe exactly the same kind of air we do, considering they claim to come from another solar system?"

"No coincidence at all," said Ludovick shortly, no longer able to pretend he didn't know what the other was getting at. He had heard the ugly rumor before. Of course sacrilege was not illegal, but it was in bad taste. "Only one combination of elements spawns intelligent life."

"They say," the uncle continued, impervious to Ludovick's unconcealed dislike for the subject, "that there's really only one Belphin, who lives in the Blue Tower–in a tank or something, because he can't breathe our atmosphere–and that the others are a sort of robot he sends out to do his work for him."

"Nonsense!" Ludovick was goaded to irritation at last. "How could a robot have that delicate play of expression, that subtle economy of movement?"

Corisande and the uncle exchanged glances. "But they are absolutely blank," the uncle began hesitantly. "Perhaps, with your rich poetic imagination...."

"See?" old Osmond remarked with satisfaction. "The kid's brain-washed. I told you so."

*   *   *   *   *

"Even if The Belphin is a single entity," Ludovick went on, "that doesn't necessarily make him less benevolent—"

He was again interrupted by the grandfather. "I won't listen to any more of this twaddle. Benevolent, bah! He or she or it or them is or are just plain exploiting us! Taking our mineral resources away—I've seen 'em loading ore on the spaceships—and—"

"—and exchanging it for other resources from the stars," Ludovick said tightly, "without which we could not have the perfectly balanced society we have today. Without which we would be, technologically, back in the dark ages from which they rescued us."

"It's not the stuff they bring in from outside that runs this technology," the uncle said. "It's some power they've got that we can't seem to figure out. Though Lord knows we've tried," he added musingly.

"Of course they have their own source of power," Ludovick informed them, smiling to himself, for his old Belphin teacher had taken great care to instill a sense of humor into him. "A Belphin was explaining that to me only today."

Twenty heads swiveled toward him. He felt uncomfortable, for he was a modest young man and did not like to be the cynosure of all eyes.

"Tell us, dear boy," the uncle said, grabbing Ludovick's glass from the plinth and filling it, "what exactly did he say?"

"He said the Belphins rule through the power of love."

The glass crashed to the tesserae as the uncle uttered a very unworthy word.

"And I suppose it was love that killed Mieczyslaw and George when they tried to storm the Blue Tower—" old Osmond began, then halted at the looks he was getting from everybody.

Ludovick could no longer pretend his neighbors were a group of eccentrics whom he himself was eccentric enough to regard as charming.

"So!" He stood up and wrapped his mantle about him. "I knew you were against the government, and, of course, you have a legal right to disagree with its policies, but I didn't think you were actual–actual–" he dredged a word up out of his schooldays–"anarchists."

He turned to the girl, who was looking thoughtful as she stroked the glittering jewel that always hung at her neck. "Corisande, how can you stay with these–" he found another word–"these subversives?"

She smiled sadly. "Don't forget: they're my family, Ludovick, and I owe them dutiful respect, no matter how pig-headed they are." She pressed his hand. "But don't give up hope."

That rang a bell inside his brain. "I won't," he vowed, giving her hand a return squeeze. "I promise I won't."

*   *   *   *   *

Outside the Flockhart villa, he paused, struggling with his inner self. It was an unworthy thing to inform upon one's neighbors; on the other hand, could he stand idly by and let those neighbors attempt to destroy the social order? Deciding that the greater good was the more important–and that, moreover, it was the only way of taking Corisande away from all this–he went in search of a Belphin. That is, he waited until one glided past and called to him to leave the walk.

"I wish to report a conspiracy at No. 7 Mimosa Lane," he said. "The girl is innocent, but the others are in it to the hilt."

The Belphin appeared to think for a minute. Then he gave off a smile. "Oh, them," he said. "We know. They are harmless."

"Harmless!" Ludovick repeated. "Why, I understand they've already tried to–to attack the Blue Tower by force!"

"Quite. And failed. For we are protected from hostile forces, as you were told earlier, by the power of love."

Ludovick knew, of course, that the Belphin used the word love metaphorically, that the Tower was protected by a series of highly efficient barriers of force to repel attackers–barriers which, he realized now, from the sad fate of Mieczyslaw and George, were potentially lethal. However, he did not blame the Belphin for being so cagy about his race's source of power, not with people like the Flockharts running about subverting and whatnot.

"You certainly do have a wonderful intercommunication system," he murmured.

"Everything about us is wonderful," the Belphin said noncommittally. "That's why we're so good to you people. Be happy!" And he was off.

But Ludovick could not be happy. He wasn't precisely sad yet, but he was thoughtful. Of course the Belphins knew better than he did, but still.... Perhaps they underestimated the seriousness of the Flockhart conspiracy. On the other hand, perhaps it was he who was taking the Flockharts too seriously. Maybe he should investigate further before doing anything rash.

Later that night, he slipped over to the Flockhart villa and nosed about in the courtyard until he found the window behind which the family was conspiring. He peered through a chink in the curtains, so he could both see and hear.

Corisande was saying, "And so I think there is a lot in what Ludovick said...."

Bless her, he thought emotionally. Even in the midst of her plotting, she had time to spare a kind word for him. And then it hit him: she, too, was a plotter.

"You suggest that we try to turn the power of love against the Belphins?" the uncle asked ironically.

Corisande gave a rippling laugh as she twirled her glittering pendant. "In a manner of speaking," she said. "I have an idea for a secret weapon which might do the trick—"

*   *   *   *   *

At that moment, Ludovick stumbled over a jug which some careless relative had apparently left lying about the courtyard. It crashed to the tesserae, spattering Ludovick's legs and sandals with a liquid which later proved to be extremely red wine.

"There's someone outside!" the uncle declared, half-rising.

"Nonsense!" Corisande said, putting her hand on his shoulder. "I didn't hear anything."

The uncle looked dubious, and Ludovick thought it prudent to withdraw at this point. Besides, he had heard enough. Corisande—his Corisande—was an integral part of the conspiracy.

He lay down to sleep that night beset by doubts. If he told the Belphins about the conspiracy, he would be betraying Corisande. As a matter of fact, he now remembered, he had already told them about the conspiracy and they hadn't believed him. But supposing he could convince them, how could he give Corisande up to them? True, it was the right thing to do—but, for the first time in his life, he could not bring himself to do what he knew to be right. He was weak, weak—and weakness was sinful. His old Belphin teacher had taught him that, too.

As Ludovick writhed restlessly upon his bed, he became aware that someone had come into his chamber.

"Ludovick," a soft, beloved voice whispered, "I have come to ask your help...." It was so dark, he could not see her; he knew where she was only by the glitter of the jewel on her neck-chain as it arced through the blackness.

"Corisande...." he breathed.

"Ludovick...." she sighed.

Now that the amenities were over, she resumed, "Against my will, I have been involved in the family plot. My uncle has invented a secret weapon which he believes will counteract the power of the barriers."

"But I thought you devised it!"

"So it was you in the courtyard. Well, what happened was I wanted to gain time, so I said I had a secret weapon of my own invention which I had not perfected, but which would cost considerably less than my uncle's model. We have to watch the budget, you know, because we can hardly expect the Belphins to supply the components for this job. Anyhow, I thought that, while my folks were waiting for me to finish it, you would have a chance to warn the Belphins."

"Corisande," he murmured, "you are as noble and clever as you are beautiful."

*   *   *   *   *

Then he caught the full import of her remarks. "Me! But they won't pay any attention to me!"

"How do you know?" When he remained silent, she said, "I suppose you've already tried to warn them about us."

"I–I said you had nothing to do with the plot."

"That was good of you." She continued in a warmer tone: "How many Belphins did you warn, then?"

"Just one. When you tell one something, you tell them all. You know that. Everyone knows that."

"That's just theory," she said. "It's never been proven. All we do know is that they have some sort of central clearing house of information, presumably The Belphin of Belphins. But we don't know that they are incapable of thinking or acting individually. We don't really know much about them at all; they're very secretive."

"Aloof," he corrected her, "as befits a ruling race. But always affable."

"You must warn as many Belphins as you can."

"And if none listens to me?"

"Then," she said dramatically, "you must approach The Belphin of Belphins himself."

"But no human being has ever come near him!" he said plaintively. "You know that all those who have tried perished. And that can't be a rumor, because your grandfather said—"

"But they came to attack The Belphin. You're coming to warn him! That makes a big difference. Ludovick...." She took his hands in hers; in the darkness, the jewel swung madly on her presumably heaving bosom. "This is bigger than both of us. It's for Earth."

He knew it was his patriotic duty to do as she said; still, he had enjoyed life so much. "Corisande, wouldn't it be much simpler if we just destroyed your uncle's secret weapon?"

"He'd only make another. Don't you see, Ludovick, this is our only chance to save the Belphins, to save humanity.... But, of course, I don't have the right to send you. I'll go myself."

"No, Corisande," he sighed. "I can't let you go. I'll do it."

*   *   *   *   *

Next morning, he set out to warn Belphins. He knew it wasn't much use, but it was all he could do. The first half dozen responded in much the same way the Belphin he had warned the previous day had done, by courteously acknowledging his solicitude and assuring him there was no need for alarm; they knew all about the Flockharts and everything would be all right.

After that, they started to get increasingly huffy—which would, he thought, substantiate the theory that they were all part of one vast coordinate network of identity. Especially since each Belphin behaved as if Ludovick had been repeatedly annoying him.

Finally, they refused to get off the walks when he hailed them—which was unheard of, for no Belphin had ever before failed to respond to an Earthman's call—and when he started running along the walks after them, they ran much faster than he could.

At last he gave up and wandered about the city for hours, speaking to neither human nor Belphin, wondering what to do. That is, he knew what he had to do; he was wondering how to do it. He would never be able to reach The Belphin of Belphins. No human being had ever done it. Mieczyslaw and George had died trying to reach him (or it). Even though their intentions had been hostile and Ludovick's would be helpful, there was little chance he would be allowed to reach The Belphin with all the other Belphins against him. What guarantee was there that The Belphin would not be against him, too?

And yet he knew that he would have to risk his life; there was no help for it. He had never wanted to be a hero, and here he had heroism thrust upon him. He knew he could not succeed; equally well, he knew he could not turn back, for his Belphin teacher had instructed him in the meaning of duty.

It was twilight when he approached the Blue Tower. Commending himself to the Infinite Virtue, he entered. The Belphin at the reception desk did not give off the customary smiling expression. In fact, he seemed to radiate a curiously apprehensive aura.

"Go back, young man," he said. "You're not wanted here."

"I must see The Belphin of Belphins. I must warn him against the Flockharts."

"He has been warned," the receptionist told him. "Go home and be happy!"

"I don't trust you or your brothers. I must see The Belphin himself."

Suddenly this particular Belphin lost his commanding manners. He began to wilt, insofar as so rigidly constructed a creature could go limp. "Please, we've done so much for you. Do this for us."

"The Belphin of Belphins did things for us," Ludovick countered. "You are all only his followers. How do I know you are really following him? How do I know you haven't turned against him?"

Without giving the creature a chance to answer, he strode forward. The Belphin attempted to bar his way. Ludovick knew one Belphin was a myriad times as strong as a human, so it was out of utter futility that he struck.

The Belphin collapsed completely, flying apart in a welter of fragile springs and gears. The fact was of some deeper significance, Ludovick knew, but he was too numbed by his incredible success to be able to think clearly. All he knew was that The Belphin would be able to explain things to him.

*   *   *   *   *

Bells began to clash and clang. That meant the force barriers had gone up. He could see the shimmering insubstance of the first one before him. Squaring his shoulders, he charged it ... and walked right through. He looked himself up and down. He was alive and entire.

Then the whole thing was a fraud; the barriers were not lethal–or perhaps even actual. But what of Mieczyslaw? And George? And countless rumored others? He would not let himself even try to think of them. He would not let himself even try to think of anything save his duty.

A staircase spiraled up ahead of him. A Belphin was at its foot. Behind him, a barrier iridesced.

"Please, young man—" the Belphin began. "You don't understand. Let me explain."

But Ludovick destroyed the thing before it could say anything further, and he passed right through the barrier. He had to get to the top and warn The Belphin of Belphins, whoever or whatever he (or it) was, that the Flockharts had a secret weapon which might be able to annihilate it (or him). Belphin after Belphin Ludovick destroyed, and barrier after barrier he penetrated until he reached the top. At the head of the stairs was a vast golden door.

"Go no further, Ludovick Eversole!" a mighty voice roared from within. "To open that door is to bring disaster upon your race."

But all Ludovick knew was that he had to get to The Belphin within and warn him. He battered down the door; that is, he would have battered down the door if it had not turned out to be unlocked. A stream of noxious vapor rushed out of the opening, causing him to black out.

When he came to, most of the vapor had dissipated. The Belphin of Belphins was already dying of asphyxiation, since it was, in fact, a single alien entity who breathed another combination of elements. The room at the head of the stairs had been its tank.

"You fool...." it gasped. "Through your muddle-headed integrity ... you have destroyed not only me ... but Earth's future. I tried to make ... this planet a better place for humanity ... and this is my reward...."

"But I don't understand!" Ludovick wept. "Why did you let me do it? Why were Mieczyslaw and George and all the others killed? Why was it that I could pass the barriers and they could not?"

"The barriers were triggered ... to respond to hostility.... You meant well ... so our defenses ... could not work." Ludovick had to bend low to hear the creature's last words: "There is ... Earth proverb ... should have warned me ... 'I can protect myself ... against my enemies ... but who will protect me ... from my friends'...?"

The Belphin of Belphins died in Ludovick's arms. He was the last of his race, so far as Earth was concerned, for no more came. If, as they had said themselves, some outside power had sent them to take care of the human race, then that power had given up the race as a bad job. If they were merely exploiting Earth, as the malcontents had kept suggesting, apparently it had proven too dangerous or too costly a venture.

*   *   *   *   *

Shortly after The Belphin's demise, the Flockharts arrived en masse. "We won't need your secret weapons now," Ludovick told them dully. "The Belphin of Belphins is dead."

Corisande gave one of the rippling laughs he was to grow to hate so much. "Darling, you were my secret weapon all along!" She beamed at her "relatives," and it was then he noticed the faint lines of her forehead. "I told

you I could use the power of love to destroy the Belphins!"
And then she added gently: "I think there is no doubt who
is head of 'this family' now."

The uncle gave a strained laugh. "You're going to have
a great little first lady there, boy," he said to Ludovick.

"First lady?" Ludovick repeated, still absorbed in his
grief.

"Yes, I imagine the people will want to make you our
first President by popular acclaim."

Ludovick looked at him through a haze of tears. "But I
killed The Belphin. I didn't mean to, but ... they must
hate me!"

"Nonsense, my boy; they'll adore you. You'll be a
hero!"

Events proved him right. Even those people who had
lived in apparent content under the Belphins, accepting
what they were given and seemingly enjoying their
carefree lives, now declared themselves to have been
suffering in silent resentment all along. They hurled
flowers and adulatory speeches at Ludovick and
composed extremely flattering songs about him.

Shortly after he was universally acclaimed President,
he married Corisande. He couldn't escape.

"Why doesn't she become President herself?" he
wailed, when the relatives came and found him hiding in
the ruins of the Blue Tower. The people had torn the
Tower down as soon as they were sure The Belphin was
dead and the others thereby rendered inoperant. "It
would spare her a lot of bother."

"Because she is not The Belphin-slayer," the uncle
said, dragging him out. "Besides, she loves you. Come on,
Ludovick, be a man." So they hauled him off to the
wedding and, amid much feasting, he was married to
Corisande.

      *   *   *   *   *

He never drew another happy breath. In the first
place, now that The Belphin was dead, all the machinery
that had been operated by him stopped and no one knew

how to fix it. The sidewalks stopped moving, the air conditioners stopped conditioning, the food synthesizers stopped synthesizing, and so on. And, of course, everybody blamed it all on Ludovick—even that year's run of bad weather.

There were famines, riots, plagues, and, after the waves of mob hostility had coalesced into national groupings, wars. It was like the old days again, precisely as described in the textbooks.

In the second place, Ludovick could never forget that, when Corisande had sent him to the Blue Tower, she could not have been sure that her secret weapon would work. Love might not have conquered all—in fact, it was the more likely hypothesis that it wouldn't—and he would have been killed by the first barrier. And no husband likes to think that his wife thinks he's expendable; it makes him feel she doesn't really love him.

So, in thirtieth year of his reign as Dictator of Earth, Ludovick poisoned Corisande—that is, had her poisoned, for by now he had a Minister of Assassination to handle such little matters—and married a very pretty, very young, very affectionate blonde. He wasn't particularly happy with her, either, but at least it was a change.

My Fair Planet
ORIGINALLY PUBLISHED IN *GALAXY SCIENCE FICTION*
MARCH 1958

ILLUSTRATED BY ALICE JULIA CHRISTIE DILLON

*All the world's a stage, so there was room even for this
bad actor ... only he intended to direct it!*

My Fair Planet

As Paul Lambrequin was clambering up the stairs of his rooming house, he met a man whose face was all wrong. "Good evening," Paul said politely and was about to continue on his way when the man stopped him.

"You are the first person I have encountered in this place who has not shuttered at the sight of me," he said in a toneless voice with an accent that was outside the standard repertoire.

"Am I?" Paul asked, bringing himself back from one of the roseate dreams with which he kept himself insulated from a not-too-kind reality. "I daresay that's because I'm a bit near-sighted." He peered vaguely at the stranger. Then he recoiled.

"What is incorrect about me, then?" the stranger demanded. "Do I not have two eyes, one nose and one mouth, the identical as other people?"

Paul studied the other man. "Yes, but somehow they seem to be put together all wrong. Not that you can help it, of course," he added apologetically, for, when he thought of it, he hated to hurt people's feelings.

"Yes, I can, for, of a truth, 'twas I who put myself together. What did I do amiss?"

Paul looked consideringly at him. "I can't quite put my finger on it, but there are certain subtle nuances you just don't seem to have caught. If you want my professional advice, you'll model yourself directly on some real person until you've got the knack of improvisation."

"Like unto this?" The stranger's outline shimmered and blurred into an amorphous cloud, which then coalesced into the shape of a tall, beautiful young man with the face of an ingenuous demon. "Behold, is that superior?"

"Oh, far superior!" Paul reached up to adjust a stray lock of hair, then realized he was not looking into a mirror. "Trouble is—well, I'd rather you chose someone else to model yourself on. You see, in my profession, it's important to look as unique as possible; helps people remember you. I'm an actor, you know. Currently I happen to be at liberty, but the year before last—"

"Well, whom should I appear like? Should I perhaps pick some fine upstanding figure from your public prints to emulate? Like your President, perhaply?"

"I—hardly think so. It wouldn't do to model yourself on someone well known—or even someone obscure whom you might just happen to run into someday." Being a kind-hearted young man, Paul added, "Come up to my room. I have some British film magazines and there are lots of relatively obscure English actors who are very decent-looking chaps."

*   *   *   *   *

So they climbed up to Paul's hot little room under the eaves and, after leafing through several magazines, Paul chose one Ivo Darcy as a likely candidate. Whereupon the stranger deliquesced and reformed into the personable simulacrum of young Mr. Darcy.

"That's quite a trick," Paul observed as it finally got through to him what the other had done. "It would come in handy in the profession—for character parts, you know."

"I fear you would never be able to acquisition it," the stranger said, surveying his new self in the mirror complacently. "It is not a trick but a racial ableness. You see, I feel I can trust you—"

"—Of course I'm not really a character actor; I'm a leading man, but I believe one should be versatile, because there are times when a really good character part comes along–"

"–I am not a human being. I am a native of the fifth planet circulating around the star you call Sirius, and we Sirians have the ableness to change ourselves into the apparition of any other livid form–"

"I thought that might be a near-Eastern accent!" Paul exclaimed, diverted. "Is Lebanese anything like it? Because I understand there's a really juicy part coming up in–"

"I said *Sirian*, not *Syrian*; I do not come from Minor Asia but from outer space, from an other-where solar system. I am an outworlder, an extraterrestrial."

"I hope you had a nice trip," Paul said politely. "From Sirius, did you say? What's the state of the theater there?"

"In its infanticide," the stranger told him, "but–"

"Let's face it," Paul muttered bitterly, "it's in its infancy here, too. No over-all planning. No appreciation of the fact that all the components that go to make up a production should be a continuing totality, instead of a tenuous coalition of separate forces which disintegrate–"

"You, I comprehend, are disemployed at current. I should–"

"You won't find that situation in Russia!" Paul went on, pleased to discover a sympathetic audience in this intelligent foreigner. "Mind you," he added quickly, "I disapprove entirely of their politics. In fact, I disapprove of all politics. But when it comes to the theater, in many respects the Russians–"

"–Like to make a proposal to our mutual advanceage–"

"–You wouldn't find an actor there playing a lead role one season and then not be able to get any parts except summer stock and odd bits for the next two years. All right, so the show I had the lead in folded after two weeks, but the critics all raved about my performance. It was the play that stank!"

"Will you terminate the monologue and hearken unto me!" the alien shouted.

Paul stopped talking. His feelings were hurt. He had thought Ivo liked him; now he saw all the outworlder wanted to do was talk about his own problems.

"I desire to extend to you a position," said Ivo.

"I can't take a regular job," Paul said sulkily. "I have to be available for interviews. Fellow I knew took a job in a store and, when he was called to read for a part, he couldn't get away. The fellow who did get that part became a big star, and maybe the other fellow could have been a star, too, but now all he is is a lousy chairman of the board of some department store chain—"

"This work can be undergone at your convention between readings and interviews, whenever you have the timing. I shall pay you beautifully, being abundant with U.S.A. currency. I want you to teach me how to act."

"Teach you how to act," Paul repeated, rather intrigued. "Well, I'm not a dramatic coach, you know; however, I do happen to have some ideas on the subject. I feel that most acting teachers nowadays fail to give their students a really thorough grounding in all aspects of the dramatic art. All they talk about is method, method, method. But what about technique?"

"I have observed your species with great diligence and I thought I had acquisitioned your habits and speakings to perfectness. But I fear that, like my initial face, I have got them awry. I want you to teach me to act like a human being, to talk like a human being, to think like a human being."

Paul's attention was really caught. "Well, that *is* a challenge! I don't suppose Stanislavsky ever had to teach an extraterrestrial, or even Strasberg—"

"Then we are in accordance," Ivo said. "You will instruction me?" He essayed a smile.

Paul shuddered. "Very well," he said. "We'll start now. And I think the first thing we'd better start with is lessons in smiling."

Ivo proved to be a quick study. He not only learned to smile, but to frown and to express surprise, pleasure, horror–whatever the occasion demanded. He learned the knack of counterfeiting humanity with such skill that, Paul was moved to remark one afternoon when they were leaving Brooks Brothers after a fitting, "Sometimes you seem even more human than I do, Ivo. I wish you'd watch out for that tendency to rant, though. You're supposed to speak, not make speeches."

"I try not to," Ivo said, "but I keep getting carried away by enthusiasm."

"Apparently I have a real flair for teaching," Paul went on as, expertly camouflaged by Brooks, the two young men melted into the dense charcoal-gray underbrush of Madison Avenue. "I seem to be even more versatile than I thought. Perhaps I have been–well, not wasting but limiting my talents."

"That may be because your talents have not been sufficiently appreciated," his star pupil suggested, "or given enough scope."

Ivo was so perceptive! "As a matter of fact," Paul agreed, "it has often seemed to me that if some really gifted individual, equally adept at acting, directing, producing, playwriting, teaching, et al., were to undertake a thorough synthesis of the theater–ah, but that would cost money," he interrupted himself, "and who would underwrite such a project? Certainly not the government of the United States." He gave a bitter laugh.

"Perhaps, under a new regime, conditions might be more favorable for the artist–"

"Shhh!" Paul looked nervously over his shoulder. "There are Senators everywhere. Besides, I never said things were *good* in Russia, just *better*–for the actor, that is. Of course the plays are atrocious propaganda–"

"I was not referring to another human regime. The human being is, at best, save for certain choice spirits, unsympathetic to the arts. We outworlders have a far greater respect for things of the mind."

Paul opened his mouth; Ivo continued without giving him a chance to speak, "No doubt you have often wondered just what I am doing here on Earth?"

The question had never crossed Paul's mind. Feeling vaguely guilty, he murmured, "Some people have funny ideas of where to go for a vacation."

"I am here on business," Ivo told him. "The situation on Sirius is serious."

"You know, that's catchy! 'The situation on Sirius is serious'," Paul repeated, tapping his foot. "I've often thought of trying my hand at a musical com—"

"I mean we have had a ser—grave population problem for the last couple of centuries, hence our government has sent out scouts to look for other planets with similar atmosphere, climate, gravity and so on, where we can ship our excess population. So far, we have found very few."

When Paul's attention was focused, he could be as quick as anybody to put two and two together. "But Earth is already occupied. In fact, when I was in school, I heard something about our having a population problem ourselves."

"The other planets we already—ah—took over were in a similar state," Ivo explained. "We managed to surmount that difficulty."

"How?" Paul asked, though he already suspected the answer.

"Oh, we didn't dispose of *all* of the inhabitants. We merely weeded out the undesirables—who, by fortunate chance, happened to be in the majority—and achieved a happy and peaceful coexistence with the rest."

"But, look," Paul protested. "I mean to say—"

"For instance," Ivo said suavely, "take the vast body of people who watch television and who have never seen a legitimate play in their lives and, indeed, rarely go to the motion pictures. Surely they are expendable."

"Well, yes, of course. But even among them there might be—oh, say, a playwright's mother—"

"One of the first measures our regime would take would be to establish a vast network of community theaters throughout the world. And you, Paul, would receive first choice of starring roles."

"Now wait a minute!" Paul cried hotly. He seldom allowed himself to lose his temper, but when he did ... he got *angry*! "I pride myself that I've gotten this far wholly on my own merits. I don't believe in using influence to—"

"But, my dear fellow, all I meant was that, with an intelligently coordinated theater and an intellectually adult audience, your abilities would be recognized automatically."

"Oh," said Paul.

He was not unaware that he was being flattered, but it was so seldom that anyone bothered to pay him any attention when he was not playing a role that it was difficult not to succumb. "Are—are you figuring on taking over the planet single-handed?" he asked curiously.

"Heavens, no! Talented as I am, there are limits. I don't do the—ah—dirty work myself. I just conduct the preliminary investigation to determine how powerful the local defenses are."

"We have hydrogen bombs," Paul said, trying to remember details of a newspaper article he had once read in a producer's ante-room, "and plutonium bombs and—"

"Oh, I know about all those," Ivo smiled expertly. "My job is checking to make sure you don't have anything really dangerous."

All that night, Paul wrestled with his conscience. He knew he shouldn't just let Ivo go on. Yet what else could he do? Go to the proper authorities? But which authorities were the proper ones? And even if he found them, who would believe an actor offstage, delivering such improbable lines? He would either be laughed at or accused of being part of a subversive plot. It might result in a lot of bad publicity which could ruin his career.

So Paul did nothing about Ivo. He went back to the usual rounds of agents' and producers' offices, and the knowledge of why Ivo was on Earth got pushed farther into the back of his mind as he trudged from interview to reading to interview.

It was an exceptionally hot October–the kind of weather when sometimes he almost lost his faith and began to wonder why he was batting his head against a stone wall, why he didn't get a job in a department store somewhere or teaching school. And then he thought of the applause, the curtain calls, the dream of some day seeing his name in lights above the title of the play–and he knew he would never give up. Quitting the theater would be like committing suicide, for off the stage he was alive only technically. He was good; he knew he was good, so some day, he assured himself, he was bound to get his big break.

Toward the end of that month, it came. After the maximum three readings, between which his hopes alternately waxed and waned, he was cast as the male lead in *The Holiday Tree*. The producers were more interested, they said, in getting someone who fitted the role of Eric Everard than in a big name–especially since the female star preferred to have her luster undimmed by competition.

Rehearsals took up so much of his time that he saw very little of Ivo for the next five weeks–but by then Ivo didn't need him any more. Actually, they were no longer teacher and pupil now but companions, drawn together by the fact that they both belonged to different worlds from the one in which they were living. Insofar as he could like anyone who existed outside of his imagination, Paul had grown rather fond of Ivo. And he rather thought Ivo liked him, too–but, because he couldn't ever be quite sure of ordinary people's reactions toward him, how could he be sure of an outworlder's?

Ivo came around to rehearsals sometimes, but naturally it would be boring for him, since he wasn't in the profession, and, after a while, he didn't come around very often. At first, Paul felt a twinge of guilt; then he remembered that he need not worry. Ivo had his own work.

*   *   *   *   *

The whole *Holiday Tree* troupe went out of town for the tryouts, and Paul didn't see Ivo at all for six weeks. Busy, happy weeks they were, for the play was a smash hit from the start. It played to packed houses in New Haven and Boston, and the box office in New York was sold out for months in advance before they even opened.

"Must be kinda fun–acting," Ivo told Paul the morning after the New York opening, as Paul weltered contentedly on his bed–he had the best room in the house now–amid a pile of rave notices. At long last, he had arrived. Everybody loved him. He was a success.

And now that he had read the reviews and they were all favorable, he could pay attention to the strange things that had happened to his friend. Raising himself up on an elbow, Paul cried, "Ivo, you're *mumbling*! After all I taught you about articulation!"

"I got t'hanging 'round with this here buncha actors while y'were gone," Ivo said. "They say mumbling's the comin' thing. 'Sides, y'kept yapping that I declaimed, so–"

"But you don't have to go to the opposite extreme and–*Ivo*!" Incredulously, Paul took in the full details of the other's appearance. "What happened to your Brooks Brothers' suits?"

"Hung 'em inna closet," Ivo replied, looking abashed. "I did wear one las' night, though," he went on defensively. "Wooden come dressed like this to y'opening. But all the other fellas wear blue jeans 'n leather jackets. I mean, hell, I gotta conform more'n anybody. Y'know that, Paul."

"And–" Paul sat bolt upright; this was the supreme outrage–"you've changed yourself! You've gotten *younger*!"

"This is an age of yout'," Ivo mumbled. "An' I figured I was 'bout ready for improvisation, like you said."

"Look, Ivo, if you really want to go on the stage—"

"Hell, I don' wanna be no actor!" Ivo protested, far too vehemently. "Y'know damn' well I'm a–a spy, scoutin' 'round t'see if y'have any secret defenses before I make m'report."

"I don't feel I'm giving away any government secrets," Paul said, "when I tell you that the bastions of our defenses are not erected at the Actors' Studio."

"Listen, pal, you lemme spy the way I wanna an' I'll letcha act the way you wanna."

Paul was disturbed by this change in Ivo because, although he had always tried to steer clear of social involvement, he could not help feeling that the young alien had become in a measure his responsibility– particularly now that he was a teen-ager. Paul would even have worried about Ivo, if there hadn't been so many other things to occupy his mind. First of all, the producers of *The Holiday Tree* could not resist the pressure of an adoring public; although the original star sulked, three months after the play had opened in New York, Paul's name went up in lights next to hers, *over the title of the play. He was a star.*

That was good. But then there was Gregory. And that was bad. Gregory was Paul's understudy–a handsome, sullen youth who had, on numerous occasions, been heard to utter words to the effect of: "It's the part that's so good, not him. If I had the chance to play Eric Everard just once, they'd give Lambrequin back to the Indians."

Sometimes he had said the words in Paul's hearing; sometimes the remarks had been lovingly passed on by fellow members of the cast who felt that Paul ought to know.

*   *   *   *   *

"I don't like that Gregory," Paul told Ivo one Monday evening as they were enjoying a quiet smoke together, for there was no performance that night. "He used to be a juvenile delinquent, got sent to one of those reform schools where they use acting as therapy and it turned out to be his *metier*. But you never know when that kind'll hear the call of the wild again."

"Aaaah, he's a good kid," Ivo said. "He just never had a chanct."

"Trouble is, I'm afraid he's going to *make* himself a chanct—chance, that is."

"Aaaah," retorted Ivo, with prideful inarticulateness.

However, when at six-thirty that Friday, Paul fell over a wire stretched between the jambs of the doorway leading to his private bathroom and broke a leg, even Ivo was forced to admit that this did not look like an accident.

"Ivo," Paul wailed when the doctor had left, "what am I going to do? I refuse to let Gregory go on in my place tonight!"

"Y'gonna hafta," Ivo said, shifting his gum to the other side of his mouth. "He's y'unnastudy."

"But the doctor said it would be weeks before I can get around again. Either Gregory'll take over the part completely with his interpretation and I'll be left out in the cold, or more likely, he'll louse up the play and it'll fold before I'm on my feet."

"Y'gotta have more confidence in y'self, kid. The public ain't gonna forgetcha in a few weeks."

But Paul knew far better than the idealistic Ivo how fickle the public can be. However, he chose an argument that would appeal to the boy. "Don't forget, he booby-trapped me!"

"Cert'ny looks like it," Ivo was forced to concede. "But watcha gonna do? Y'can't prove it. 'Sides, the curtain's gonna gwup in a li'l over a nour—"

Paul gripped Ivo's sinewy wrist. "Ivo, you've got to go on for me!"

"Y'got rocks in y'head or somepin?" Ivo demanded, trying not to look pleased. "I ain't gotta Nequity card, and even if I did, *he's* y'unnastudy."

"No, you don't understand. I don't want you to go on as Ivo Darcy playing Eric Everard. I want you to go on as Paul Lambrequin playing Eric Everard. *You can do it, Ivo!*"

"Good Lord, so I can!" Ivo whispered, temporarily neglecting to mumble. "I'd almost forgotten."

"You know my lines, too. You've cued me in my part often enough."

Ivo rubbed his hand over his forehead. "Yeah, I guess I do."

"Ivo," Paul beseeched him, "I thought we were—pals. I don't want to ask any favors, but I helped you out when you were in trouble. I always figured I could rely on you. I never thought you'd let me down."

"An' I won't." Ivo gripped Paul's hand. "I'll go on t'night 'n play 'at part like it ain't never been played before! I'll—"

"No! No! Play it the way I played it. You're supposed to be *me*, Ivo! Forget Strasberg; go back to Stanislavsky."

"Okay, pal," Ivo said. "Will do."

"And promise me one thing, Ivo. Promise me *you won't mumble.*"

Ivo winced. "Okay, but you're the on'y one I'd do 'at for."

Slowly, he began to shimmer. Paul held his breath. Maybe Ivo had forgotten how to transmute himself. But technique triumphed over method. Ivo Darcy gradually coalesced into the semblance of Paul Lambrequin. The show would go on!

*   *   *   *   *

"Well, how was everything?" Paul asked anxiously when Ivo came into his room shortly after midnight.

"Pretty good," Ivo said, sitting down on the edge of the bed. "Gregory was extremely surprised to see me—asked me half a dozen times how I was feeling." Ivo was not only articulating, Paul was gratified to notice; he was enunciating.

"But the show—how did that go? Did anyone suspect you were a ringer?"

"No," Ivo said slowly. "No, I don't think so. I got twelve curtain calls," he added, staring straight ahead of him with a dreamy smile. "Twelve."

"Friday nights, the audience is always enthusiastic." Then Paul swallowed hard and said, "Besides, I'm sure you were great in the role."

But Ivo didn't seem to hear him. Ivo was still wrapped in his golden daze. "Just before the curtain went up, I didn't think I was going to be able to do it. I began to feel all quivery inside, the way I do before I—I change."

"Butterflies in the stomach is the professional term." Paul nodded wisely. "A really good actor gets them before every performance. No matter how many times I play a role, there's that minute when the house lights start to dim when I'm in an absolute panic—"

"—And then the curtain went up and I was all right. I was fine. I was Paul Lambrequin. I was Eric Everard. I was—everything."

"Ivo," Paul said, clapping him on the shoulder, "you're a born trouper."

"Yes," Ivo murmured, "I'm beginning to think so myself."

For the next four weeks, Paul Lambrequin lurked in his room while Ivo Darcy played Paul Lambrequin playing Eric Everard.

"It's terrific of you to take all this time away from your duties, old chap," Paul said to Ivo one day between the matinee and the evening performances. "I really do appreciate it. Although I suppose you've managed to squeeze some of them in. I never see you on non-matinee afternoons."

"Duties?" Ivo repeated vacantly. "Yes, of course—my duties."

"Let me give you some professional advice, though. Be more careful when you take off your makeup. There's still some grease paint in the roots of your hair."

"Sloppy of me," Ivo agreed, getting to work with a towel.

"I can't understand why you bother to put on the stuff at all," Paul grinned, "when all you need to do is just change a little more."

"I know." Ivo rubbed his temples vigorously. "I suppose I just like the—smell of the stuff."

"Ivo," Paul laughed, "there's no use trying to kid me; you are stagestruck. I'm sure I have enough pull now to get you a bit part somewhere, when I'm up and around again, and then you can get yourself an Equity card. Maybe," he added amusedly, "I can even have you replace Gregory as my understudy."

*   *   *   *   *

Later, in retrospect, Paul thought perhaps there had been a curious expression in Ivo's eyes, but right then he'd had no inkling that anything untoward was up. He did not find out what had been at the back of Ivo's mind until the Sunday before the Tuesday on which he was planning to resume his role.

"Lord, it's going to be good to feel that stage under my feet again," he said as he went through a series of complicated limbering-up exercises of his own devisement, which he had sometimes thought of publishing as *The Lambrequin Time and Motion Studies*. It seemed unfair to keep them from other actors.

Ivo turned around from the mirror in which he had been contemplating their mutual beauty, "Paul," he said quietly, "you're never going to feel that stage under your feet again."

Paul sat on the floor and stared at him.

"You see, Paul," Ivo said, "I am Paul Lambrequin now. I am more Paul Lambrequin than I was–whoever I was on my native planet. I am more Paul Lambrequin than *you* ever were. You learned the part superficially, Paul, but I really *feel* it."

"It's not a part," Paul said querulously. "It's me. I've always been Paul Lambrequin."

"How can you be sure of that? You've had so many identities, why should this be the true one? No, you only *think* you're Paul Lambrequin. I *know* I am."

"Dammit," Paul said, "that's the identity in which I've taken out Equity membership. And be reasonable, Ivo– there can't be two Paul Lambrequins."

Ivo smiled sadly. "No, Paul, you're right. There can't."

Of course Paul had known all along that Ivo was not a human being. It was only now, however, that full realization came to him of what a ruthless alien monster the other was, existing only to gratify his own purposes, unaware that others had a right to exist.

"Are–are you going to–dispose of me, then?" Paul asked faintly.

"To dispose of you, yes, Paul. But not to kill you. My kind has killed enough, conquered enough. We have no real population problem; that was just an excuse we made to salve our own consciences."

"You have consciences, do you?" Paul's face twisted in a sneer that he himself sensed right away was overly melodramatic and utterly unconvincing. Somehow, he could never be really genuine offstage.

Ivo made a sweeping gesture. "Don't be bitter, Paul. Of course we do. All intelligent life-forms do. It's one of the penalties of sentience!"

For a moment, Paul forgot himself. "Watch it, Ivo. You're beginning to ham up your lines."

"We can institute birth control," Ivo went on, his manner subdued. "We can build taller buildings. Oh, there are many ways we can cope with the population increase. That's not the problem. The problem is how to divert our creative energies from destruction to construction. And I think I have solved it."

"How will your people know you have," Paul asked cunningly, "since you say you're not going back?"

"*I* am not going back to Sirius, Paul—*you* are. It is you who are going to teach my people the art of peace to replace the art of war."

Paul felt himself turn what was probably a very effective white. "But—but I can't even speak the language! I—"

"You will learn the language during the journey. I spent those afternoons I was away making a set of *Sirian-in-a-Jiffy* records for you. Sirian's a beautiful language, Paul, much more expressive than any of your Earth languages. You'll like it."

"I'm sure I shall, but—"

"Paul, you are going to bring my people the outlet for self-expression they have always needed. You see, I lied to you. The theater on Sirius is not in its infancy; it has never been conceived. If it had been, we would never have become what we are today. Can you imagine—a race like mine, so superbly fitted to practice the dramatic art, remaining in blind ignorance that such an art exists!"

"It does seem a terrible waste," Paul had to agree, although he could not be truly sympathetic just then. "But I am hardly equipped—"

"Who is better equipped than you to meet this mighty challenge? Can't you see that at long last you will be able to achieve your great synthesis of the theatrical arts—as producer, teacher, director, actor, playwright, whatever you will, working with a cast of individuals who can assume any shape or form, who have no preconceived notions of what can be done and what cannot. Oh, Paul, what a glorious opportunity awaits you on Sirius V. How I envy you!"

"Then why don't you do it yourself?" Paul asked.

Ivo smiled sadly again. "Unfortunately, I do not have your manifold abilities. All I can do is act. Superbly, of course, but that's all. I don't have the capacity to build a living theater from scratch. You do. I have talent, Paul, but you have genius."

"It *is* a temptation," Paul admitted. "But to leave my own world...."

"Paul, Earth isn't your world. You carry yours along with you wherever you go. Your world exists in the mind and heart, not in reality. In any real situation, you're just as uncomfortable on Earth as you would be on Sirius."

"Yes, but—"

"Think of it this way, Paul. You're not leaving your world. You're just leaving Earth to go on the road. It's a longer road, but look at what's waiting for you at the end of it."

"Yes, look," Paul said, reality very much to the fore in his mind and heart at that moment, "death or vivisection."

"Paul, do you believe I'd do that to you?" There were tears in Ivo's eyes. If he was acting, he was a great performer. *I really am one hell of a good teacher*, Paul thought, *and with lots of raw material like Ivo to work with, I could.... Could he really mean what he's saying?*

"They won't harm you, Paul, because you will come to Sirius bearing a message from me. You will tell my people that Earth has a powerful defensive weapon and you have come to teach them its secret. And it's true, Paul. The theater is your world's most powerful weapon, its best defense against the universal enemy—reality."

"Ivo," Paul said, "you really must check that tendency toward bombast. Especially with a purple speech like that; you've simply got to learn to underplay. You'll watch out for that when I'm gone, won't you?"

"I will!" Ivo's face lighted up. "Oh, I will, Paul. I promise never to chew the scenery again. I won't so much as nibble on a prop!"

*   *   *   *   *

The next day, the two of them went up to Bear Mountain where Ivo's ship had been cached all those months. Ivo explained to Paul how the controls worked and showed him where the clean towels were.

Pausing in the airlock, Paul looked back toward Manhattan. "I'd dreamed so many years of seeing my name up in lights on Broadway," he murmured, "and now, just when I made it—"

"I'll keep it up there," Ivo vowed. "I promise. And, meanwhile, you'll be building a new Broadway up there in the stars!"

"Yes," Paul said dreamily, "that is something to look forward to, isn't it?" Fresh, enthusiastic audiences, performers untrammeled by tradition, a cooperative government, unlimited funds—why, there was a whole wonderful new world opening up before him.

"—In another ten years or so," Ivo was saying, "Sirian actors will be coming to Earth in droves, making the native performers look sick—"

Paul smiled wisely. "Now, Ivo, you know Equity would never stand for *that*."

"Equity won't be able to help itself. Public pressure will surge upward in a mounting wave and—" Ivo stopped. "Sorry. I was ranting again, wasn't I? It's being out in the open air that does it. I need to be bounded by the four walls of a theater."

"That's a fallacy," Paul began. "On the Greek stage—"

"Save that for the stars, fella," Ivo smiled. "You've got to leave before it gets light." Then he wrung Paul's hand. "Good-by, kid," he said. "You'll knock 'em dead on Sirius."

"Good-by, Ivo." Paul returned the grip. Then he got inside and closed the airlock door behind him. He did hope Ivo would correct that tendency toward declamation; on the other hand, it was certainly better than mumbling.

Paul put a *Sirian-in-a-jiffy* record on the turntable, because he might as well start learning the language right away. Of course he'd have no one to talk to but himself for many months, but then, when all was said and done, he was his own favorite audience. He strapped himself into the acceleration couch and prepared for take-off.

"Next week, *East Lynne*," he said to himself.

And Now a Message . . .
By Greg Fowlkes

A short Story from the upcoming Book - *Back Road to the Stars*

And Now A Message . . .

For the third time that night Jack Olsen was about to nod off over the copy of *Statistical Information Theory* that he was attempting to read. Giving it up as a bad effort, he shut the book and looked out the window of the control room at the giant bowl of the Arecibo radio telescope. Theoretically he was running the huge instrument, but in reality all the controlling was being done by the computers in the room around him. For six months he had been working eight hour shifts every night, and his job had consisted of the five minutes a shift that it took to enter the coordinates to be examined on the control console. Other than that, he was on hand only for the off chance that the monitoring programs would recognize some pattern in the radio noise, in which case an alarm would sound. So far, in the six months, it hadn't happened.

He walked over to the coffee machine in the hopes that a cup would revive him enough so that he could continue his studies. He never made it, for as if to prove the lie of his earlier thoughts, the alarm sounded. For a moment Jack was frozen, the alarm beating raucously in his ears, then he pulled himself together and flicked off the switch on the bell. With the room returned to the relative quiet of the whoosh of the cooling fans on the equipment, Jack sat down at the console and keyed in an enquiry. Within seconds the computer had replied that it was receiving a strong periodic signal on the 42 centimeter band. Further questioning showed that it was not a program malfunction but a genuine signal.

Jack picked up the phone and dialed his boss's number. It was three in the morning, but his instructions had been clear. If anything was received that could possibly be an intelligent signal, he was supposed to contact his superior immediately.

Despite the long drive through the mountains in the cool Puerto Rican night, Professor Kraft showed up with his eyes still sleepy. Shuffling over to the coffee pot by the window he poured himself a large mug before he said anything. "You'd better have something good to get me up at this hour."

"I think so," Jack said, aware that his boss's irritation was only feigned. "I've been checking with the computer since I called you. It shows a strong periodic signal with a sharp pulse every fifty milliseconds. It runs on like that for about two and a half minutes before the signal fades below the background."

"Any chance that it might be a pulsar?" Kraft asked, referring to the radio signals of rapidly rotating neutron stars. "That's within the range of periods for them. When the first one was discovered, they thought that they had received intelligent signals."

"I thought of that, so I checked the record of the broad band receiver." Jack brought out a long strip of graph paper and pointed to the evenly spaced patterns of peaks on it. "Where the narrow band shows only a single repetitive pulse, the wide band gives us this fine structure. It's far too regular to be a pulsar and much too detailed. It's more like some sort of timing signal or spacer. And in between the pulses there is another signal. It's not as repetitive as the main pulse. That's why the program doesn't bring it out. But there definitely is some sort of transmission in between. It's weaker, but I think that we can write a processing program to pick it out from the noise."

Kraft looked at the trace in his hand thoughtfully. "I hate to make snap judgements. You can be suckered in too easily that way. But it does look like some kind of artificial signal. We'll get the team working on it in the morning. Have you received any additional signals?"

"No. I've kept the dish tracking the source, but all we get on 42 cm. is background noise. It's like there was a moment of freak atmospheric conditions that opened a window, and then it shut again. Just like you get with shortwave sometimes because of the ionosphere."

"Well, we should be grateful for what we've got. I don't think I can sleep anymore tonight, so I'll keep you company. I'd like to be here if we get any more messages from our friends out there," he said, pointing with his cup towards the star filled sky that loomed over the radio telescope's antenna.

"Frustrating, isn't it?" Prof. Kraft remarked to the team of graduate students and post doctoral fellows that were working under him on the interstellar communications project. And frustrating it had been. For six months they had continuously monitored the sky searching for signs of life finally to be rewarded by a two minute snippet of extraterrestrial conversation.

Now, another six months later, they had still made no sense of the signal, nor had they received any further transmissions from that part of the sky, though they had concentrated their efforts in that direction.

"Rumors have leaked out about our discovery, and I've been getting requests for the data. I'd sure hate to have someone else steal our thunder by deciphering the signal, but if we don't make some progress soon, we're going to have to release it." He looked around the table at the young faces of his assistants. At the moment they didn't look nearly as bright and intelligent as he knew they were.

"Why don't I summarize what we've found so far in hopes that it will give us some new ideas?"

"First, we've got this repetitive pattern of pulses every twentieth of a second as regular as clockwork. So regular, in fact, that we can't decide whether they serve as breaks in the message or were just put there to attract our attention. Remember, it was these pulses that were first recognized by the computer."

"But the pulses aren't the real message. That lays in the spaces in between. We've been able to deduce that the messages are digitized and the computer has been able to enhance them so that we have a fairly error free record of them. There is some repetitive structure to them, and they do vary in some sort of progression, but beyond that, we haven't been able to get the least notion of what they mean. Anyone have something to add?"

Bill Warden, one of the post docs, spoke up. "Well, we've tried mathematical analysis on the signals and have gotten zero results. It has already been assumed that any sort of interstellar communications would be based on sort of easily recognizable mathematical progression. Like one, two three. Something like that to show that they were rational. From there you can always build up more complicated concepts."

"With this message we don't have that, which leads us to one of two assumptions. One, we have only a fragment of a broadcast, and from a very advanced lesson at that. If that's the case, I don't see much hope of our being able to decipher the message until we can receive more signals to give us a broader base to work from."

"The other alternative is that they, whoever they are, just don't think like us. Their minds work in some fashion so that this mess we have makes sense to them. If so, I don't see any hope at all. Their minds may just be too foreign for us to hold a dialog with them."

"Thank you for that optimistic note," Prof. Kraft said wryly. "For the first time mankind has received a message from another species and we can't tell whether it is a cure for cancer, a means of achieving universal peace, or a recipe for sauerbraten. Any comments?"

"If it's sauerbraten, where do we go for a tablespoon of powdered bandersnatch egg?" quipped one of the grad students. They all laughed at the joke more than it deserved. Six months of unrewarded work had left them all a little giddy. After the giggles and comments had died down, Jack Olsen coughed, trying to get their attention.

"You've got something useful to say, Jack?" Kraft asked. "You might as well tell us. I don't think anyone else has anything useful to add," he said, pointedly looking at the wisecracker.

"I've been thinking about the signal, and I remember something that I said to you the night it came in. I don't know if you recall, but I called the pulses timing signals. Now there is one type of common transmission that has the same kind of pulses, and that's television. They use the pulses to synchronize the frames. It's possible that the message in between each pulse is a picture, and the whole transmission is meant to be viewed in sequence."

"How long have you been sitting on this while the rest of us were beating our brains out?" Kraft asked.

"It just came to me," Jack said, his face flushed. "I should have thought of it earlier, but like Bill said, we've all been conditioned to look for something like one plus one equals two."

"I think that we should all have seen it," Kraft said. "It makes as much sense as anything else that's been suggested. Do you think that you can get us a picture?"

"If it's there, I should be able to pick it out using the computer," Jack answered.

"Good. Then, since it was your idea, you're in charge. Dragoon anything or anybody that you need to help you."

Five days later they were all gathered around the conference room table again, but this time there was a TV set and a video recorder on a cart at its end. From the nervous stubbing of cigarette butts and fingers drumming on the table, it was obvious that all the members of the team were in a state of anticipation.

"It took some time to figure out exactly how the signal was put together," Jack began. "After all, we didn't know how many lines there were in each frame or how many bits made up each unit of picture. In the end, I had to have the computer run through all the likely possibilities for one of the frames. It took a lot of computer time, but I've finally got some recognizable pictures."

"It turns out that the original broadcast was in color. That threw us for a while, but we finally psyched it out. The aliens must have eyes structurally different from ours; there are only two colors, not three in the signal. Which colors they are is anybody's guess. They might be ultraviolet and infrared for all we can tell. Arbitrarily, I've assigned them red and bluish green, so keep that in mind. Also, because the video recorder uses thirty frames a second instead of the twenty in the transmission, it was necessary to compress the program a bit. This means that everything you'll be seeing has been speeded up about fifty percent.

"I guess you're all more interested in seeing the tape than in listening to me." A snort from Prof. Kraft indicated agreement. Jack flicked off the lights and started the tape. For a minute the screen showed only snow, then a face became recognizable. It was a sickly chartreuse, and there was no nose between the two large, oval eyes, but it was recognizable as a face. The figures movements were quick and jerky like an old silent movie, the result of the difference in frame speed, and the picture left a lot to be desired in clarity, the product of interstellar noise, but it was a picture, the first of an alien race.

As the tape played, a weird, sings song voice came from the speaker sounding something like a Chinese chipmunk. "I forgot to mention that there was also an audio track along with the signal. Again, it's only a reconstruction and may not bear much resemblance to the original, but then, we'll never know," Jack commented. They had determined that the source of the transmission was at least several dozen light years away. It would take twice that number of years to send a message and receive a reply, by which time they would all be dead.

They continued to watch the tape. The camera had drawn back to show the alien from the waist up revealing rounded shoulders and a pair of six fingered hands. Apparently he was standing behind a low lectern or a table of some sort. The fuzzy picture and camera angle made it hard to tell which. As he, or her, or it, spoke, the alien pointed at a chart or poster suspended on the backdrop. A pattern of red and blue that hurt the eye with violent contrasts seemed to be some sort of text. The voice continued as the picture disappeared in a sea of snow and then it broke into static. The transmission had ended.

"You've done a fine job, Jack," Prof. Kraft said after they had played the tape through a half dozen times. "It's actually far better than I thought it would be, and I think we can accept any of the shortcomings that you mentioned."

"So, we've got a face and body of what certainly is a rational creature. He seemed to be giving us a lesson or lecture of some sort, though I for one don't have the faintest idea of what he was talking about. We have an idea of what they look like which I am sure will give the biologists a lot to speculate on, so I guess that we should be thankful for small favors, but I still don't see how we're going to learn any more about them without receiving further signals."

"I wouldn't hold out much hope of that," Jack interjected. "I think that it's clear now that the signal we picked up was not meant for interstellar communication. Any such signal would have been designed with much greater noise immunity. We were able to receive it only because of an accident of atmospheric conditions. It was actually just a local TV broadcast. As we haven't received anything since, those conditions must be rare."

"So," Kraft said, "we have a message of great potential import, that at the very least could provide us with insights on a totally alien culture, and no way to decipher it."

"I've got an idea," Bill said. "We've all been looking at the problem from the point of view of hardware and computer programs. That's natural because of our backgrounds, but now that we have what amounts to an artifact, maybe we should call in a specialist. We need someone who is trained in resurrecting a culture from its fragments. I suggest that we show the tape to some archeologists and get their opinions."

Convincing an archeologist to look at the tape was harder than it had sounded. Most of them were more interested in ancient rather than alien civilizations. Jack suspected that they felt out of their depth with the computers and electronics. With some pressure and pleading, a group finally agreed to view the tape, but after the showing, only one evinced any interest in following up on it.

A visiting lecturer from Norway, she was reputed to have a good background in languages, though Jack lacked the knowledge to judge her qualifications. However, as she was young, blond, and attractive, he was quite willing to spend the time required to familiarize her with the tape and the equipment they had used to come up with it. Together, they spent hours viewing the tape, studying it frame by frame attempting to pick out the slightest piece of information.

The project team had been assembled in the conference room, and this time it was the archeologist's turn to address them. For three weeks Cristina Peterson had been studying the tape almost constantly, and now she was ready to give her opinion. With the exception of Jack, who had been working closely with her, they were all, even Prof. Kraft, eagerly awaiting the report. There had been a great deal of speculation about what her findings would be.

"First," she began, "before I get your hopes up, I want to say that I have not been able to get a word for word translation of the voice on the tape. The sample of speech is just too brief for that to be possible. If the scene had contained more action, I might have been more successful, but we were not that fortunate. I have, however, been able to form a hypothesis based on the spoken word as well as visual clues such as facial expression, setting, and so on."

"An important point to remember is that the aliens, despite certain differences in appearance, are not too dissimilar from ourselves. They are bipedal, intelligent, and possess opposable thumbs. They have binocular vision and a form of color perception as well. Brain size is about the same in relationship to total body size as in humans, and I would be greatly surprised if they were much larger or smaller than ourselves. That much can be guessed on the basis of physiology from the picture and the nature of the signal. From this information, I think that we can draw the conclusion that their planet is, within limits, earthlike."

"Probably more relevant is their state of culture. They obviously have a technology and one that is recognizable in terms of our own. That we can receive their signals is proof of that. Also, they speak, they wear clothing, we can even guess at the purpose of some of the objects visible in the tape. I might add that this is more than we can do for some of the artifacts of primitive human cultures. In some ways we have more in common with the aliens than we do with the Tasadi or Bushman."

"I want you to bear in mind that these beings are not greatly different from ourselves. If we are to properly analyze the contents of the message, we must remember that they are influenced by the same drives and forces as humans." There was an uneasy shifting in their seats on the part of the team members as they took in the meaning of her statement.

"If we accept this premise, and replace the alien with a human, we can make an educated guess as to what we are seen on the tape. I'll run it again for you so that you can make the substitution." Jack tapped the switch, and for the next minute and a half they watched the now familiar scene replay itself.

"Before I give my own opinion, would anyone else like to make a guess?" Cristina asked.

Kraft looked around the room, but it appeared as though no one had the courage to be the first to put his own views forward. To break the silence he said, "It's only a guess, but to start the discussion, I'd say that the alien might be a lecturer. He's obviously standing at some sort of podium or speaker's table."

"He seems a little too impassioned for a lecturer, at least in the physical sciences," one of the grad students remarked. "I've never seen you that excited before a class." Kraft smiled at the reference to his own low keyed classroom delivery.

"Maybe it's a political science class. They get more aroused."

Bill Warden broke in, "Why a class? It looks to me more like he's a politician trying to persuade the voters. He must be up for reelection. The sign in back could be an election poster." That brought a couple of laughs and a few less than serious comments.

"We've all had a crack at it," Prof. Kraft said. "You obviously have your own interpretation, and I think that we've been kept in suspense long enough. From the look on Jack's face, it must be a good one. Let's hear it now. After all, the communication between two species is one of the most important events in human history."

She smiled at the jibe. "All your suggestions are plausible, but I've spent more time analyzing the tape than you have. I'll play it again for you and point out the features that have led me to my interpretation."

"The first thing that caught my attention was the fact that the word 'gratach' was mentioned fourteen times, an unusually high incidence in such a brief speech. Furthermore, at least four of those times the speaker pointed to the symbols on the chart behind him. I think that we can assume that 'gratach' is a name, and the symbols form the written version."

"Now here's something that I want you to see." She froze the picture on the television. "Note the artifacts on the table, a bowl filled with a substance and a box or container. There appears to be some writing on the box, but the resolution of the picture isn't good enough to allow us to make it out. However," she said as the tape began to roll again, "as the alien points to the box and says 'gratach' it is likely that the symbols again spell out the name in the chart behind the alien. Note, too, the expression on his face. Despite the lack of a nose, the face is surprisingly human, and if that expression was on a human face, it would be one of approval or pleasure."

"I think that if you put all the clues together, you can come to only one conclusion. Dr. Warden was not far off when he suggested a political campaign. The speaker is definitely trying to persuade his audience, but it is the package, not himself, that he is trying to sell."

"Oh, god," Kraft sputtered. "You can't mean it. The first communication from another planet and it's only . . ."

"Yes, I'm afraid so," Cristina said. "The first and only signal received from another world is nothing more than a breakfast food commercial."

Special Preview!

THE LAWS OF MAGIC

BY GREG FOWLKES

Now available from The Fictional Press
www.TheFictionalPress.com

THE LAWS OF MAGIC
WITHOUT LICENSE

☆　☆　☆　☆　☆

As Egil Njalsson climbed the steps of the criminal courts building he wondered if it was really worth it. Eighteen months of practicing law on his own and here he was in his only suit, about to attend the preliminary hearing in a petty case for which with luck he would be able to recover his expenses. It wasn't even a paying client. The state would be picking up the tab for this one, and he'd ended up being the lawyer appointed by the court. At the moment it wasn't clear who would benefit most from the charity, the client or the lawyer. He hadn't had a case in three months and he'd just been eking out a living writing briefs for other lawyers. He could do that well enough. His technical background gave him a depth of knowledge most lawyers lacked when it came to cases involving points of science as well as law. If he hadn't had that he'd be starving.

He'd been thinking about that a lot lately; whether he had made the right decision giving up science and going into the law. At the time, with the aerospace industry in a depression in the early seventies, it had seemed like a good idea. Engineers were pumping gas and PhD's in physics were selling insurance. Being a lawyer had seemed like a good way to make money. A stable income, no ups and downs. He'd put in his time at law school and done well. After the grind at CalThaum, law school had been a snap. So here he was a lawyer barely making ends meet and his school mates, the ones who had stuck with science were all making it rich designing personal calculating engines and disk storage units.

He tried to put all these thoughts out of his mind as he passed through the big brass doors of the court house. After all, he did have a client to defend, and a duty to him. It wasn't easy, though. It wasn't, after all, a very important case. Just a charge of fortune telling and practicing the Art without a license. Minor offenses, probably not even any jail time involved. This wouldn't even be a trial today, just a plea and arranging of bail.

It wouldn't even have amounted to that if his client hadn't instisted on pleading not guilty. He'd met him at the county jail, an old man, one Jake Schmidts. He'd tried to talk him out of pleading not guilty, too. A guilty plea, a small fine, and they both could be done with it. His client, though, had turned out to be something of a character. So here he was.

It took an hour and a half before their case came up. The judge looked at him questioningly when he had pleaded not guilty, but thankfully had released his client on his own recognizance when he indicated he had a permanent address. It was over in five minutes.

They got the release papers and the court date from the bailiff. Egil started to head out when he noticed that his client seemed lost and disoriented by it all. "Do you have car fare home?"

"No," Schmidts said. "I didn't have any money on me when they came and arrested me. Not a cent."

"Which way do you live?"

The old man gave an address on Fair Oaks Street. It wasn't far out of his way. Neither one of them lived in the best part of town.

"I can give you a lift," Egil said.

"That's kind of you, Mr. Njalsson," Schmidts said. The mister was ironic. The arrest report hadn't given an age, just "somewhere around seventy." As far as Egil could tell that might have been off by a decade or two.

The address turned out to be a sort of second hand junk store. The operative word was junk. If the pieces in the dirty window were the best of the lot then Egil could see how Schmidts qualified as indigent.

"Thanks for the ride. I've a beer inside if you'd like."

Njalsson looked at his watch. It wasn't too early to start drinking, at least just a beer. The work at the office would wait. He had to talk to Schmidts anyway to prepare a case. Besides, the old man seemed to want to pay him back for the ride.

If anything, the shop was worse on the inside than it looked from the front. Odd bits of bric-a-brac were strewn around everywhere; most of it looking like it hadn't been moved or even dusted in twenty years. Broken down pieces of furniture were covered with moldering sheets.

The old man led him to the back and up some stairs to an apartment above the shop. The kitchen was cleaner, though still hardly spotless. Of course, Egil's own small apartment wasn't the neatest of place, either.

The refrigerator looked as old as Schmidt's, but the beer was cold. Schmidt's took out two and motioned him to a chair at the kitchen table.

"So what happens now, Mr. Njalsson?"

"The trial will be held on the date on the summons. The district attorney will call his witnesses and make his case. Then I'll make my case. The judge will then decide."

"No jury?" Schmidt's asked disappointedly.

"Not unless we've got a very strong case to present. This is a small matter. It's better left to a judge. A jury would be considered a waste of time, I'm afraid, and would probably result in a higher fine. Maybe even jail."

"So you think I'm guilty?"

"I don't think you have much of a case."

"That's different?"

"To a lawyer it is."

Schmidts snorted in disgust.

"I don't want to disillusion you, Mr. Schmidts, but you've got to face the facts. Do you have a license to practice Magic?"

"No."

"Did you tell the fortune of one Mrs. Einar Johnson?"

"Yes, and an ungrateful woman she is, too. Just because I told her the truth about that shifty salesman she thinks is going to marry her. He's just after her late husband's money."

Egil raised an eyebrow.

"It's the truth. I've been reading the cards longer than you've been alive, Mr. Njalsson, and I know what I'm doing. That salesman is the one that got her to swear out a complaint against me."

"It doesn't matter whether what you said was the truth or not. What matters is that you were practicing the Art without a license. Magic is a potentially dangerous business. It's not something that untrained people should be dealing with. That's what the law is about."

"What would you know about the Art, Mr. Lawyer?" Schmidts asked sharply.

"I know more than most, Mr. Schmidts. I studied applied metaphysics at the California Institute of Thaumaturgy for four years before going into the law. I've got a Bachelor's of Science degree. I've also got my practitioner's license from both the state of California and Wisconsin. I may not be the greatest practitioner of the Art, but I am competent enough to know what I am and am not capable of."

"So maybe you did study at a fancy school out west. Those scientists don't know everything. They think that they've discovered magic, but magic goes back. Way back. Back before Helmholtz and Gauss. Before the Egyptians and Babylonians. Magic is old, Mr. Njalsson, and the doctors and professors haven't learned half of it."

"And you have?" Egil asked sarcastically. He was getting annoyed at the old man's pretensions of knowledge. He was surprised, though, that Schmidts knew that the two physicists Helmholtz and Gauss had been instrumental in proving the scientific basis for magic.

"No. I'm no fool. I've been studying the Art all my life. I know what I know and I have a good idea of what I don't. What I do know is more than a youngster like you learns in four years at college, even if it is a fancy one."

"Look, Mr. Schmidts," Egil said. "This isn't working out. Maybe you should get yourself a different lawyer."

The old man looked at him in surprise, then shook his head. "No. I guess you were just telling me the way it is. I may not like it, but I can't fault you for telling the truth."

"Okay. Is there anything I can use in your defense?"

"Guess not."

"Well, where did you learn to tell fortunes, to read the cards?" Egil asked.

"From an old Romany woman," the old man answered.

"Where? Here in the city?"

"No, it was a long time ago. Bohemia, I think it was."

"Bohemia? You mean Czechoslovakia."

"Yes, that's what they call it now I think. Prague. I was a student there."

"A student? At a university? I thought you didn't believe in learning."

"I was younger then. I thought there were things I might learn. I was wrong."

"Did you get a degree, though? That might carry some weight, especially a foreign one."

"Wait a moment. I think I have one someplace. Let me go look." Schmidts went down to his shop. From below Egil could hear noises as if boxes were being moved around. He didn't quite know what to make of the old man's gypsy tale. Bohemia had become part of Czechoslovakia after the First World War in the breakup of the Austrian Empire. It hadn't been a separate country since the Hapsburgs.

There were footsteps on the stairway and Schmidts showed up with a small picture frame carrying a piece of parchment. It was certainly a degree, but not from the University of Prague. The writing had faded with age and Egil had never learned French, but it appeared to be a doctorate granted by the Sorbonne. It was also made out to one Jacques Krieger.

"This isn't your name."

"It was the name I was using then."

"Can you prove that?"

"Not that I can see."

"Oh well. Maybe we can use it. If you can find anymore old papers like this save them for me. We might have some defense if we can prove you had an education, particularly if it was before the current examination system went into effect."

"I'll do that, Mr. Njalsson."

"Well I've got to get going now. Can I take this with me?" the lawyer asked, holding up the sheepskin.

"Yes, if it will help."

Egil let himself out through the shop. He dumped the diploma on the car seat next to him and started the car. While the engine was warming up he glanced down at it. The date was written in Roman numerals. It took him a moment to figure out the year. It was 1847. Either the old man was lying to him or he might find himself defending him in a commitment hearing.

Also From Resurrected Press

Science Fiction Authors Resurrected

Fyfe Resurrected - The Stories of H. B. Fyfe

Stories from the Golden Age of Science Fiction by the author of D-99. dealing with the interaction of humans and aliens on far off worlds in ways that were as creative as they were imaginative.

Bone Resurrected - The Stories of J. F. Bone

More stories from the Golden Age of Science Fiction. Includes "The Issahar Artifact," "Assassin," "To Choke an Ocean" and more.

Nourse Resurrected - The Stories of Alan E. Nourse

Stories from the Golden Age of Science Fiction. Includes "Contamination Crew." "Coffin Cure," "The Link," and more.

Dick Resurrected - The Early Stories of Philip K. Dick

Early stories from the author of the novels that inspired "Blade Runner," "Total Recall," and through a scanner darkly. Science Fiction Authors Resurrected

OTHER CLASSIC SCIENCE FICTION NOVELS BEING RESURRECTED SOON

TALENTS, INCORPORATED - BY MURRAY LEINSTER
When a Mekinese fleet conquers his home planet, Captain Bors turns to Talents, Incorporated for help using their collection of individuals with unusual abilities to defeat the enemy and save the galaxy.

THE PIRATES OF ERSATZ - BY MURRAY LEINSTER
Bran Hodden just wanted to be an electronic engineer and marry a delightful girl. But when he's framed by the powers on Walden he's forced to turn back to his family's trade, piracy. Also published as The Pirates of Zan.

EMPIRE - BY CLIFFORD SIMAK
Spencer Chambers and Interplanetary Power owned the Solar System because they controlled the source of power. It fell to Russell Page and Harry Wilson to challenge that control if they had to cross the universe to do it.

NIGHT OF THE LONG KNIVES - THE CREATURE FROM THE CLEVELAND DEPTHS - BY FRITZ LEIBER
Two classic novellas set in the not too distant future from a classic master of science fiction.

ARMAGEDDON - 2419 A.D. - THE AIR LORDS OF HAN - BY PHILLIP FRANCIS NOWLAN
The two novels that introduced the world to that intrepid hero of the 25th Century, Buck Rogers. Buck Rogers must save the world from the clutches of the insidious Han.

Other Classic Resurrected Science Fiction
Edited by Greg Fowlkes

RESURRECTED MARTIANS
Classic Stories about Mars and Martians from the Golden Age of Science Fiction

RESURRECTED ALIENS
Classic Stories of Aliens and Alien Encounters from the Golden Age of Science Fiction

RESURRECTED FLYING SAUCERS
Classic Stories of Flying Saucers and Alien Invasions from the Golden Age of Science Fiction

RESURRECTED ROBOTS
Classic Stories of Robots, Cyborgs and Androids from the Golden Age of Science Fiction

RESURRECTED SPACE SHIPS -
Classic Stories of Space Ships from the Golden Age of Science Fiction

RESURRECTED TIME TRAVEL
Classic Stories of Time Travel from the Golden Age of Science Fiction

RESURRECTED DIMENSIONS
Classic Stories of other Dimensions from the Golden Age of Science Fiction

RESURRECTED FUTURES
Classic Stories of the Far Future from the Golden Age of Science Fiction

RESURRECTED MAD SCIENTISTS
Classic Stories of Mad Scientists and their Creations from the Golden Age of Science Fiction

RESURRECTED MONSTERS
Classic Stories of Monsters and Mayhem from the Golden Age of Science Fiction

The Fictional Detective
by Greg Fowlkes

Who killed Ezekial O. Handler?

A beautiful dame, a hard-boiled private eye — and a dead body.

It started like any other case. When a famous writer dies in a mysterious car crash, private detective Frank Slade is called in to find answers, but all he finds is more questions. Who killed Ezekial Handler? Who is Janet Nielsen and why is she so interested in finding out? Who is leaving the neatly typed clues? And as Slade tries to find answers to these questions he starts to wonder if the ultimate answer will threaten his very existence.

Read about it in
The Fictional Detective

Visit www.thefictionaldetective.com

About Resurrected Press

A division of Intrepid Ink, LLC, Resurrected Press is dedicated to bringing high quality, vintage books back into publication. See our entire catalogue and find out more at www.ResurrectedPress.com.

About Intrepid Ink, LLC

Intrepid Ink, LLC provides full publishing services to authors of fiction and non-fiction books, eBooks and websites. From editing to formatting, from publishing to marketing, Intrepid Ink gets your creative works into the hands of the people who want to read them. Find out more at www.IntrepidInk.com.

www.ingramcontent.com/pod-product-compliance
Lightning Source LLC
Chambersburg PA
CBHW070848250626
47159CB00003B/990